From the author of the bestselling *Lucy Crown*
and *The Young Lions*, here is an exciting new
collection of powerfully-wrought short stories,
brilliant vignettes revealing the loves, loneliness,
dreams and rebellion of modern Americans, at
home and in exile:

- A disheartened ex-pilot abroad, sweating
  out a buddy's return from a risky, illicit
  flight he'd lacked the nerve to try himself

- Two college students and a girl touring
  France, fighting unbidden emotions that
  threatened the innocence of their alliance

- An embittered career girl in Paris, ready
  to end her futile affair with a foreign cor-
  respondent for the security of loveless
  marriage

- A little boy accidentally witnessing the hidden passions and hatred of his apartment-
  house neighbors

Ranging in background from New York to the
Riviera, and in mood from tenderness to irony,
these stories display the vigorous narrative style
that has placed Irwin Shaw among the nation's
major writers. The title story has been produced
as a striking motion picture.

THIS BOOK IS A REPRINT OF THE ORIGINAL HARD-
COVER EDITION PUBLISHED BY RANDOM HOUSE

Tip
on a Dead Jockey

AND OTHER STORIES

by

IRWIN SHAW

A SIGNET BOOK

Published by THE NEW AMERICAN LIBRARY

to Gus Lobrano
1902-1956

"Tip on a Dead Jockey," "A Wicked Story," "In the
French Style," "Peter Two," "Age of Reason," "The
Sunny Banks of the River Lethe," "Voyage Out,
Voyage Home," appeared originally in *The New
Yorker.*

"The Kiss at Croton Falls," appeared originally in
Collier's

"Then We Were Three," appeared originally in
McCall's.

*Published as a SIGNET BOOK
By Arrangement with Random House, Inc.*

*SIGNET BOOKS are published by
The New American Library of World Literature, Inc.
501 Madison Avenue, New York 22, New York*

PRINTED IN THE UNITED STATES OF AMERICA

Contents

Tip on a Dead Jockey

LLOYD BARBER WAS LYING ON HIS BED READING *France-Soir* when the phone rang. It was only two o'clock in the afternoon, but it was raining for the fifth consecutive day and he had no place to go anyway. He was reading about the relative standing of the teams in the Rugby leagues. He never went to Rugby games and he had no interest in the relative standings of Lille and Pau and Bordeaux, but he had finished everything else in the paper. It was cold in the small, dark room, because there was no heat provided between ten in the morning and six in the evening, and he lay on the lumpy double bed, his shoes off, covered with his overcoat.

He picked up the phone, and the man at the desk downstairs said, "There is a lady waiting for you here, M. Barber."

Barber squinted at himself in the mirror above the bureau across from the bed. He wished he was better-looking. "Did she give her name?" he asked.

"No, Monsieur. Should I demand it?"

"Never mind," Barber said. "I'll be right down."

He hung up the phone and put on his shoes. He always put the left one on first, for luck. He buttoned his collar and pulled his tie into place, noticing that it was frayed at the knot. He got into his jacket and patted his pockets to see if he had cigarettes. He had no cigarettes. He shrugged, and left the light on vindictively, because the manager was being unpleasant about the bill, and went downstairs.

Maureen Richardson was sitting in the little room off the lobby, in one of those age-colored plush chairs that fourth-rate Parisian hotels furnish their clientele to discourage excessive conviviality on the ground floor. None of the lamps was lit, and a dark, dead, greenish light filtered in through the dusty curtains from the rainy street outside. Maureen had been a young, pretty girl with bright, credulous blue eyes when Barber first met her,

7

during the war, just before she married Jimmy Richardson. But she had had two children since then and
Richardson hadn't done so well, and now she was
wearing a worn cloth coat that was soaked, and her complexion had gone, and in the greenish lobby light she
seemed bone-colored and her eyes were pale.

"Hello, Beauty," Barber said. Richardson always
called her that, and while it had amused his friends in the
squadron, he had loyally stuck to it, and finally everyone
had picked it up.

Maureen turned around quickly, almost as though he
had frightened her. "Lloyd," she said. "I'm so glad I
found you in."

They shook hands, and Barber asked if she wanted to
go someplace for a coffee.

"I'd rather not," Maureen said. "I left the kids with a
friend for lunch and I promised I'd collect them at two-
thirty and I don't have much time."

"Sure," Barber said. "How's Jimmy?"

"Oh, Lloyd . . ." Maureen pulled at her fingers, and
Barber noticed that they were reddened and the nails
were uneven. "Have you seen him?"

"What?" Barber peered through the gloom at her, puzzled. "What do you mean?"

"Have you seen him?" Maureen persisted. Her voice
was thin and frightened.

"Not for a month or so," Barber said. "Why?" He
asked it, but he almost knew why.

"He's gone, Lloyd," Maureen said. "He's been gone
thirty-two days. I don't know what I'm going to do."

"Where did he go?" Barber asked.

"I don't know." Maureen took out a pack of cigarettes
and lit one. She was too distracted to offer the pack to
Barber. "He didn't tell me." She smoked the cigarette
avidly but absently. "I'm so worried. I thought maybe he'd
said something to you—or that you'd bumped into him."

"No," Barber said carefully. "He didn't say anything."

"It's the queerest thing. We've been married over ten
years and he never did anything like this before," Maureen
said, trying to control her voice. "He just came to me one
night and he said he'd got leave of absence from his job
for a month and that he'd be back inside of thirty days
and he'd tell me all about it when he got back, and he
begged me not to ask any questions."

"And you didn't ask any questions?"

"He was acting so strangely," Maureen said. "I'd never seen him like that before. All hopped up. Excited. You might even say happy, except that he kept going in all night to look at the kids. And he's never given me anything to worry about in the—the girl department," Maureen said primly. "Not like some of the other boys we know. And if there was one thing about Jimmy, it was that you could trust him. So I helped him pack."

"What did he take?"

"Just one Valpak," Maureen said. "With light clothes. As though he was going off on a summer vacation. He even took a tennis racket."

"A tennis racket," Barber nodded, as though it were the most natural thing in the world for husbands to take tennis rackets along when disappearing. "Did you hear from him at all?'

"No," Maureen said. "He told me he wouldn't write. Did you ever hear of anything like that?" Even in her anguish, she permitted herself a tone of wifely grievance. "I knew we shouldn't have come to Europe. It's different for you. You're not married and you were always kind of wild anyway, not like Jimmy—"

"Did you call his office?" Barber asked, interrupting. He didn't want to hear how wild people thought he was, or how unmarried.

"I had a friend call," Maureen said. "It would look too fishy—his wife calling to ask where he was."

"What did they say?"

"They said that they had expected him two days ago but he hadn't come in yet."

Barber took one of Maureen's cigarettes and lit it. It was the first one in four hours and it tasted wonderful. He had a little selfish twinge of gratitude that Maureen had come to his hotel.

"Lloyd, do you know anything?" Maureen asked, worn and shabby in her damp, thin coat in the foggy green light.

Barber hesitated. "No," he said. "But I'll put in a couple of calls and I'll telephone you tomorrow."

They both stood up. Maureen pulled on gloves over her reddened hands. The gloves were worn and greenish black. Looking at them, Barber suddenly remembered how neat and shining Maureen had been when they first met, in Louisiana, so many years before, and how healthy and well-dressed he and Jimmy and the others had been in their lieutenants' uniforms with the new wings on their breasts.

"Listen, Beauty," Barber said. "How are you fixed for dough?"

"I didn't come over for that," Maureen said firmly.

Barber took out his wallet and peered judiciously into it. It wasn't necessary. He knew exactly what was there. He took out a five-thousand-franc note. "Here," he said, handing it to her. "Try this on for size."

Maureen made a motion as though to give it back to him. "I really don't think I should . . ." she began.

"Sh-h-h, Beauty," Barber said. "There isn't an American girl in Paris who couldn't use five *mille* on a day like this."

Maureen sighed and put the bill in her pocketbook. "I feel terrible about taking your money, Lloyd."

Barber kissed her forehead. "In memory of the wild blue yonder," he said, pocketing the wallet, with its remaining fifteen thousand francs, which, as far as he knew, would have to last him for the rest of his life. "Jimmy'll give it back to me."

"Do you think he's all right?" Maureen asked, standing close to him.

"Of course," Lloyd said lightly and falsely. "There's nothing to worry about. I'll call you tomorrow. He'll probably be there, answering the phone, getting sore at me for sucking around his wife when he's out of town."

"I bet," Maureen smiled miserably. She went through the cavelike murk of the lobby, out into the rainy street, on her way to pick up the two children, who had been sent out to lunch at the home of a friend.

Barber went to his room and picked up the phone and waited for the old man downstairs to plug in. There were two suitcases standing open on the floor, with shirts piled in them, because there wasn't enough drawer space in the tiny bureau supplied by the hotel. On top of the bureau there were: a bill, marked overdue, from a tailor; a letter from his ex-wife, in New York, saying she had found an Army pistol of his in the bottom of a trunk and asking him what he wanted her to do with it, because she was afraid of the Sullivan Law; a letter from his mother, telling him to stop being a damn fool and come home and get a regular job; a letter from a woman in whom he was not interested, inviting him to come and stay with her in her villa near Eze, where it was beautiful and warm, she said, and where she needed a man around the house; a letter from a boy who had flown as his waist-gunner during the war and who insisted that Barber had saved his life when he was hit in the stomach over Palermo, and who, surprisingly, had written a book since then. Now he sent long, rather literary letters at least once a month to Barber. He was an odd, intense boy, who had been an excitable gunner, and he was constantly examining himself to find out whether he and the people he loved, among whom he rather embarrassingly included Barber, mostly because of the eight minutes over Palermo, were living up to their promise. "Our generation is in danger," the boy had typed in the letter on the bureau, "the danger of diminution. We have had our adventures too early. Our love has turned to affection, our hate to distaste, our despair to melancholy, our passion to preference. We have settled for the life of obedient dwarfs in a small but fatal sideshow."

The letter had depressed Barber and he hadn't answered it. You got enough of that sort of thing from the French. He wished the ex-waist-gunner would stop writing him, or at least write on different subjects. Barber hadn't answered his ex-wife, either, because he had come to Europe to try to forget her. He hadn't answered his mother, because he was afraid she was right. And he hadn't gone down to Eze, because no matter how broke he was, he wasn't selling that particular commodity yet.

Stuck into the mirror above the bureau was a photograph of himself and Jimmy Richardson, taken on the beach at Deauville the summer before. The Richardsons had taken a cottage there, and Barber had spent a couple of weekends with them. Jimmy Richardson was another one who had attached himself to Barber during the war. Somehow, Barber was always being presented with the devotion of people whose devotion he didn't want. "People hang on to you," a girl who was angry at him once told him, "because you're an automatic hypocrite. As soon as somebody comes into the room, you become gay and confident."

Jimmy and he had been in bathing trunks when the picture was snapped, and Barber was tall and blessed with a blond, California kind of good looks next to Jimmy, who seemed like a fat, incompetent infant, standing there with the sunny sea behind him.

Barber peered at the photograph. Jimmy didn't look

like the sort of man who would ever be missing from anywhere for thirty-two days. As for himself, Barber thought wryly, he looked automatically gay and confident.

He leaned over and took the picture down and threw it into a drawer. Then, holding the phone loosely, he stared around him with distaste. In the glare of the un-shaded lamp, the dark woodwork looked gloomy and termite-ridden, and the bed, with its mottled velours spread, the color of spoiled pears, looked as though it had been wallowed on by countless hundreds of obscenely shaped men and women who had rented the room for an hour at a time. For a second, he was piercingly home-sick for all the rooms of all the Hotel Statlers he had slept in and all the roomettes on trains between New York and Chicago, and St. Louis and Los Angeles.

There was a whistling, static-like sound in the phone, and he shook himself and gave the number of the George V. When he got the George V, he asked for M. Smith, M. Bert Smith. After a while, the girl said M. Smith was no longer at the hotel. Barber asked hurriedly, before the girl could cut him off, whether M. Smith was ex-pected to return shortly or if he had left a forwarding address. No, the girl said after a long wait, he was not expected to return and there was no forwarding address.

Barber hung up. He was not surprised about Bert Smith. He was a man who wandered mysteriously from hotel to hotel, and he might have used a half-dozen names besides Smith since Barber had spoken to him last.

With a conscious effort, Barber tried not to think about Jimmy Richardson or his wife, who was called, as a friendly squadron joke, Beauty, or about Jimmy Richard-son's two small sons.

Scowling, Barber went over to the window. The winter rain of Paris was seeping down into the narrow street, blurring it with the unproductive malice of city rain, chipping colorlessly at the buildings opposite, making it impossible to imagine what they had looked like when they were new. A workman was unloading cases of wine from a truck, looking persecuted by the weather, the Paris sound of clinking bottles muted and made hollow and mournful by the flow of gray water from the skies and from window ledges and signs and rolled awnings. It was not a day for a husband to be missing, for a friend to be missing. It was not a day to be alone or to have only fifteen thousand francs in your pocket or to be in a narrow hotel room where the heat was off from ten in the morning till six at night. It was not a day to be without a job or cigarettes or lunch. It was not a day on which to examine yourself and realize that no matter how many excuses you gave yourself, you were going to wind up knowing that, finally, you were responsible.

Barber shook himself again. There was no sense in just staying in the room all day. If he was going to do any good, he would have to find Bert Smith. He looked at his watch. It was nearly two-thirty. He tried to remember all the places he had ever seen Bert Smith at two-thirty in the afternoon. The fancy restaurant near the Rond-Point, where the movie people and the French newspaper owners and the rich tourists ate; the bistro on the Boulevard Latour-Maubourg, on the Left Bank; the restaurants at Auteuil and Longchamps and St. Cloud. Barber looked at the newspaper. They were running at Auteuil today.

If he was not at the races and if he was still in Paris, Bert Smith was likely to be in one art gallery or another in the middle of the afternoon. Bert Smith was an art lover, or at least he bought pictures, shrewdly and knowingly. Since Smith lived in hotel rooms, which were unlikely places for a collection, it was probable that he bought paintings on speculation or as an agent or, when they were important ones that the government did not wish to have leave the country, to be smuggled out of France.

Barber had also seen Smith late in the afternoons in the steam room at Claridge's, a small, round man with surprisingly well-shaped legs, sitting in the vapor, wrapped in a sheet, growing pinker and pinker, smiling luxuriously in the steam, sweating off the fat that he had accumulated in many years of eating in the best restaurants in Europe.

He had also seen Smith several times around six o'clock in the evening in the barbershop at the George V getting shaved, and after that in the bar upstairs, and in the bar at the Relais Plaza and the English bar downstairs at the Plaza-Athénée. And late at night he had seen him at various night clubs—L'Eléphant Blanc, Carroll's, La Rose Rouge . . .

Barber thought unhappily of the last fifteen thousand francs in his wallet. It was going to be a long, wet, hard, expensive day. He put on his hat and coat and went out. It was still raining, and he hailed a taxi and gave the driver the address of the restaurant near the Rond-Point.

It had started about two months before, in the stand at Auteuil just before the sixth race. The day was misty and there weren't many spectators, and Barber had not been doing very well, but he had got a tip on the sixth race, on an eight-to-one shot. He put five thousand down on the nose and climbed high up in the stand to get a good view of the race.

There was only one other spectator near him in the stand, a small, round man wearing an expensive-looking velours hat, and carrying a pair of binoculars and a rolled umbrella, like an Englishman. He smiled at Barber and nodded. As Barber smiled back politely, he realized that he had seen the man many times before, or his brother, or a half-dozen other men who looked like him, in restaurants and in bars and on the street, usually with tall girls who might have been lower-class mannequins or upper-class tarts.

The man with the umbrella moved over to him along the damp concrete row of seats. He had little, dapper feet and a bright necktie, and he had a well-cared-for, international kind of face, with large, pretty dark eyes, fringed by thick black lashes. He had what Barber had come to call an import-export face. It was a face that was at the same time bland, cynical, self-assured, sensual, hopeless, and daring, and its owner might be Turkish or Hungarian or Greek or he might have been born in Basra. It was a face you might see in Paris or Rome or Brussels or Tangier, always in the best places, always doing business. It was a face, you felt somehow, that was occasionally of interest to the police.

"Good afternoon," the man said, in English, tipping his hat. "Are you having a lucky day?" He had an accent, but it was difficult to place it. It was as though as a child he had gone to school everywhere and had had ten nurses of ten different nationalities.

"Not bad," Barber said carefully.

"Which do you like in this one?" The man pointed with his umbrella at the track, where the horses were gingerly going up to the distant starting line on the muddied grass.

"Number Three," Barber said.

"Number Three." The man shrugged, as though he pitied Barber but was restrained by his good breeding from saying so. "How is the movie business these days?" the man asked.

"The movie business went home a month ago," Barber said, slightly surprised that the man knew anything about it. An American company had been making a picture about the war, and Barber had had four lucky, well-paid months as a technical expert, buckling leading men into parachutes and explaining the difference between a P-47 and a B-25 to the director.

"And the blond star?" the man asked, taking his glasses from his eyes. "With the exquisite behind?"

"Also home."

The man moved his eyebrows and shook his head gently, indicating his regret that his new acquaintance and the city of Paris were now deprived of the exquisite behind. "Well," he said, "at least it leaves you free in the afternoon to come to the races." He peered out across the track through the glasses. "There they go."

No. 3 led all the way until the stretch. In the stretch, he was passed rapidly by four other horses.

"Every race in this country," Barber said as the horses crossed the finish line, "is a hundred metres too long." He took out his tickets and tore them once and dropped them on the wet concrete.

He watched with surprise as the man with the umbrella took out some tickets and tore them up, too. They were on No. 3, and Barber could see that they were big ones. The man with the umbrella dropped the tickets with a resigned, half-amused expression on his face, as though all his life he had been used to tearing up things that had suddenly become of no value.

"Are you staying for the last race?" the man with the umbrella asked as they started to descend through the empty stands.

"I don't think so," Barber said. "This day has been glorious enough already."

"Why don't you stay?" the man said. "I may have something."

Barber thought for a moment, listening to their footsteps on the concrete.

"I have a car," the man said. "I could give you a lift into town, Mr. Barber."

"Oh," Barber said, surprised, "you know my name."

"Of course," the man said, smiling. "Why don't you wait for me at the bar? I have to go and cash some tickets."

"I thought you lost," Barber said suspiciously.

"On Number Three," the man said. From another pocket he took out some more tickets and waved them gently. "But there is always the insurance. One must always think of the insurance," he said. "Will I see you at the bar?"

"O.K.," Barber said, not because he hoped for anything in the way of information on the next race from the man with the umbrella but because of the ride home. "I'll be there. Oh—by the way, what's your name?"

"Smith," the man said. "Bert Smith."

Barber went to the bar and ordered a coffee, then changed it to a brandy, because coffee wasn't enough after a race like that. He stood there, hunched over the bar, reflecting sourly that he was one of the category of people who never think of the insurance. Smith, he thought, Bert Smith. More insurance. On how many other names, Barber wondered, had the man lost before he picked that one?

Smith came to the bar softly, on his dapper feet, smiling, and laid a hand lightly on Barber's arm. "Mr. Barber," he said, "there is a rumor for the seventh race. Number Six."

"I never win on Number Six," Barber said.

"It is a lovely little rumor," Smith said. "At present, a twenty-two-to-one rumor."

Barber looked at the man doubtfully. He wondered briefly what there was in it for Smith. "What the hell," he said, moving toward the seller's window. "What have I got to lose?"

He put five thousand francs on No. 6 and superstitiously remained at the bar during the race, drinking brandy. No. 6 won, all out, by half a length, and, although the odds had dropped somewhat, paid eighteen to one.

Barber walked through the damp twilight, across the discarded newspapers and the scarred grass, with its farm-like smell, patting his inside pocket with the ninety thousand francs in a comforting bulge there, pleased with the little man trotting beside him.

Bert Smith had a Citroën, and he drove swiftly and well and objectionably, cutting in on other cars and swinging wide into the outside lane to gain advantage at lights.

"Do you bet often on the races, Mr. Barber?" he was saying as they passed a traffic policeman, forlorn in his white cape on the gleaming street.

"Too often," Barber said, enjoying the warmth of the car and the effects of the last brandy and the bulge in his pocket.

"You like to gamble?"

"Who doesn't?"

"There are many who do not like to gamble," Smith said, nearly scraping a truck. "I pity them."

"Pity them?" Barber looked over at Smith, a little surprised at the word. "Why?"

"Because," Smith said softly, smiling, "in this age there comes a time when every one finds that he is forced to gamble—and not only for money, and not only at the seller's window. And when that time comes, and you are not in the habit, and it does not amuse you, you are most likely to lose."

They rode in silence for a while. From time to time, Barber peered across at the soft, self-assured face above the wheel, lit by the dashboard glow. I would like to get a look at his passport, Barber thought—at all the passports he's carried for the last twenty years.

"For example," Smith said, "during the war . . ."

"Yes?"

"When you were in your plane," Smith said, "on a mission. Weren't there times when you had to decide suddenly to try something, to depend on your luck for one split second, and if you hesitated, if you balked at the act of gambling—sssszt!" Smith took one hand from the wheel and made a gliding, falling motion, with his thumb down. He smiled across at Barber. "I suppose you are one of the young men who were nearly killed a dozen times," he said.

"I suppose so," Barber said.

"I prefer that in Americans," Smith said. "It makes them more like Europeans."

"How did you know I was in the war?" Barber said. For the first time, he began to wonder if it was only a coincidence that Smith had been near him in the stand before the sixth race.

Smith chuckled. "You have been in Paris how long?" he said. "A year and a half?"

"Sixteen months," Barber said, wondering how the man knew *that*.

"Nothing very mysterious about it," Smith said. "People talk at bars, at dinner parties. One girl tells another girl. Paris is a small city. Where shall I drop you?"

Barber looked out the window to see where they were. "Not far from here," he said. "My hotel is just off the Avenue Victor Hugo. You can't get in there with a car."

"Oh, yes," Smith said, as though he knew about all hotels. "If it doesn't seem too inquisitive," he said, "do you intend to stay long in Europe?"

"It depends."

"On what?"

"On luck." Barber grinned.

"Did you have a good job in America?" Smith asked, keeping his eyes on the traffic ahead of him.

"In thirty years, working ten hours a day, I would have been the third biggest man in the company," Barber said.

Smith smiled. "Calamitous," he said. "Have you found more interesting things to do here?"

"Occasionally," Barber said, beginning to be conscious that he was being quizzed.

"After a war it is difficult to remain interested," Smith said. "While it is on, a war is absolutely boring. But then when it is over, you discover peace is even more boring. It is the worst result of wars. Do you still fly?"

"Once in a while."

Smith nodded. "Do you maintain your license?"

"Yes."

"Yes, that's wise," Smith said.

He pulled the car sharply in to the curb and stopped, and Barber got out.

"Here you are," Smith said. He put out his hand, smiling, and Barber shook it. Smith's hand was softly fleshed, but there was a feeling of stone beneath it.

"Thanks for everything," Barber said.

"Thank you, Mr. Barber, for your company," Smith said. He held Barber's hand for a moment, looking across the seat at him. "This has been very pleasant," he said. "I hope we can see each other again soon. Maybe we are lucky for each other."

"Sure," Barber said, grinning. "I'm always at home to people who can pick eighteen-to-one shots."

Smith smiled, relinquishing Barber's hand. "Maybe one of these days we'll have something even better than an eighteen-to-one shot," he said.

He waved a little and Barber closed the car door. Smith spurted out into the traffic, nearly causing two *quatre chevaux* to pile up behind him.

It had taken two weeks for Smith to declare himself. From the beginning, Barber had known that something was coming, but he had waited patiently, curious and amused, lunching with Smith in the fine restaurants Smith patronized, going to galleries with him and listening to Smith on the subject of the Impressionists, going out to the race tracks with him and winning more often than not on the information Smith picked up from tight-lipped men around the paddocks. Barber pretended to enjoy the little clever man more than he actually did, and Smith, on his part, Barber knew, was pretending to like *him* more than he actually did. It was a kind of veiled and cynical wooing, in which neither party had yet committed himself. Only, unlike more ordinary wooings, Barber for the first two weeks was not sure in just which direction his desirability, as far as Smith was concerned, might lie.

Then, late one night, after a large dinner and a desultory tour of the night clubs, during which Smith had seemed unusually silent and abstracted, they were standing in front of Smith's hotel and he made his move. It was a cold night, and the street was deserted except for a prostitute with a dog, who looked at them without hope as she passed them on the way to the Champs-Élysées.

"Are you going to be in your hotel tomorrow morning, Lloyd?" Smith asked.

"Yes," Barber said. "Why?"

"Why?" Smith repeated absently, staring after the chilled-looking girl and her poodle walking despairingly down the empty, dark street. "Why?" He chuckled irrelevantly. "I have something I would like to show you," he said.

"I'll be in all morning," Barber said.

"Tell me, my friend," Smith said, touching Barber's sleeve lightly with his gloved hand. "Don't you have any idea why I have been calling you so often for the last two weeks, and buying you so many good meals and so much good whiskey?"

"Because I am charming and interesting and full of fun," Barber said, grinning. "And because you want something from me."

Smith chuckled, louder this time, and caressed Barber's sleeve. "You are not absolutely stupid, my friend, are you?"

"Not absolutely," said Barber.

"Tell me, my friend," Smith said, almost in a whisper. "How would you like to make twenty-five thousand dollars?"

"What?" Barber asked, certain that he had not heard correctly.

"Sh-h-h," Smith said. He smiled, suddenly gay. "Think about it. I'll see you in the morning. Thank you for walking me home." He dropped Barber's arm and started into the hotel.

"Smith!" Barber called.

"Sh-h-h." Smith put his finger playfully to his mouth. "Sleep well. See you in the morning."

Barber watched him go through the glass revolving doors into the huge, brightly lit, empty lobby of the hotel. Barber took a step toward the doors to follow him in, then stopped and shrugged and put his collar up, and walked slowly in the direction of his own hotel. I've waited this long, he thought, I can wait till morning.

Barber was still in bed the next mornnig when the door opened and Smith came in. The room was dark, with the curtains drawn, and Barber was lying there, half asleep, thinking drowsily, Twenty-five thousand, twenty-five thousand. He opened his eyes when he heard the door open. There was a short, bulky silhouette framed in the doorway against the pallid light of the corridor.

"Who's that?" Barber asked, without sitting up.

"Lloyd. I'm sorry," Smith said. "Go back to sleep. I'll see you later."

Barber sat up abruptly. "Smith," he said. "Come in."

"I don't want to disturb—"

"Come in, come in." Barber got out of bed and, barefooted, went over to the window and threw back the curtains. He looked out at the street. "By God, what do you know?" he said, shivering and closing the window. "The sun is shining. Shut the door."

Smith closed the door. He was wearing a loose gray tweed overcoat, very British, and a soft Italian felt hat, and he was carrying a large manila envelope. He looked newly bathed and shaved, and wide awake.

Barber, blinking in the sudden sunshine, put on a robe and a pair of moccasins and lit a cigarette. "Excuse me," he said. "I want to wash." He went behind the screen that separated the washbasin and the *bidet* from the rest

of the room. As he washed, scrubbing his face and soaking his hair with cold water, he heard Smith go over to
the window. Smith was humming, in a soft, true, melodious tenor voice, a passage from an opera that Barber
knew he had heard but could not remember. Aside from
everything else, Barber thought, combing his hair roughly,
I bet the bastard knows fifty operas.

Feeling fresher and less at a disadvantage with his teeth
washed and his hair combed, Barber stepped out from
behind the screen.

"Paris," Smith said, at the window, looking out. "What
a satisfactory city. What a farce." He turned around,
smiling. "Ah," he said, "how lucky you are. You can
afford to put water on your head." He touch his thin,
well-brushed hair sadly. "Every time I wash my hair, it
falls like the leaves. How old did you say you are?"

"Thirty," Barber said, knowing that Smith remembered it.

"What an age." Smith sighed. "The wonderful moment
of balance. Old enough to know what you want, still
young enough to be ready for anything." He came back
and sat down and propped the manila envelope on the
floor next to the chair. "Anything." He looked up at
Barber, almost coquettishly. "You recall our conversation,
I trust," he said.

"I recall a man said something about twenty-five
thousand dollars," Barber said.

"Ah—you do remember," Smith said gaily. "Well?"

"Well what?"

"Well, do you want to make it?"

"I'm listening," Barber said.

Smith rubbed his soft hands together gently in front of
his face, his fingers rigid, making a slight, dry, sliding
sound. "A little proposition has come up," he said. "An
interesting little proposition."

"What do I have to do for my twenty-five thousand
dollars?" Barber asked.

"What do you have to do for your twenty-five thousand
dollars?" Smith repeated softly. "You have to do a little
flying. You have flown for considerably less, from time to
time, haven't you?" he chuckled.

"I sure have," Barber said. "What else do I have to
do?"

"Nothing else," Smith said, sounding surprised. "Just
fly. Are you still interested?"

"Go on," said Barber.

"A friend of mine has just bought a brand-new single-engine plane. A Beechcraft, single engine. A perfect, pleasant, comfortable, one-hundred-per-cent dependable aircraft," Smith said, describing the perfect little plane with pleasure in its newness and its dependability. "He himself does not fly, of course. He needs a private pilot, who will be on tap at all times."

"For how long?" Barber asked, watching Smith closely.

"For thirty days. Not more." Smith smiled up at him. "The pay is not bad, is it?"

"I can't tell yet," Barber said. "Go on. Where does he want to fly to?"

"He happens to be an Egyptian," Smith said, a little deprecatingly, as though being an Egyptian were a slight private misfortune, which one did not mention except among friends, and then in lowered tones. "He is a wealthy Egyptian who likes to travel. Especially back and forth to France. To the South of France. He is in love with the South of France. He goes there at every opportunity."

"Yes?"

"He would like to make two round trips from Egypt to the vicinity of Cannes within the next month," Smith said, peering steadily at Barber, "in his private new plane. Then on the third trip, he will find that he is in a hurry and he will take the commercial plane and his pilot will follow two days later, alone."

"Alone?" Barber asked, trying to keep all the facts straight.

"Alone, that is," Smith said, "except for a small box."

"Ah," Barber said, grinning. "Finally the small box."

"Finally." Smith smiled up at him delightedly. "It has already been calculated. The small box will weigh two hundred and fifty pounds. A comfortable margin of safety for this particular aircraft for each leg of the journey."

"And what will there be in the small two-hundred-and-fifty-pound box?" Barber asked, cool and relieved now that he saw what was being offered to him.

"Is it absolutely necessary to know?"

"What do I tell the customs people when they ask me what's in the box?" Barber said. " 'Go ask Bert Smith'?"

"You have nothing to do with customs people," Smith said. "I assure you. When you take off from the airport in Cairo, the box is not on board. And when you land at the airport at Cannes, the box is not on board. Isn't that enough?"

Barber took a last pull at his cigarette and doused it. He peered thoughtfully at Smith, sitting easily on the straight-backed chair in the rumpled room, looking too neat and too well dressed for such a place at such an hour. Drugs, Barber thought, and he can stuff them . . .

"No, Bertie boy," Barber said roughly. "It is not enough. Come on. Tell."

Smith sighed. "Are you interested up to now?"

"I am interested up to now," Barber said.

"All right," Smith said regretfully. "This is how it will be done. You will have established a pattern. You will have been in and out of the Cairo airport several times. Your papers always impeccable. They will know you. You will have become a part of the legitimate routine of the field. Then, on the trip when you will be taking off alone, everything will be perfectly legitimate. You will have only a small bag with you of your personal effects. Your flight plan will show that your destination is Cannes and that you will come down at Malta and Rome for refuelling only. You will take off from Cairo. You will go off course by only a few miles. Some distance from the coast, you will be over the desert. You will come down on an old R.A.F. landing strip that hasn't been used since 1943. There will be several men there. . . . Are you listening?"

"I'm listening." Barber had walked to the window and was standing there, looking out at the sunny street below, his back to Smith.

"They will put the box on board. The whole thing will not take more than ten minutes," Smith said. "At Malta, nobody will ask you anything, because you will be in transit and you will not leave the plane and you will stay only long enough to refuel. The same thing at Rome. You will arrive over the south coast of France in the evening, before the moon is up. Once more," Smith said, speaking as though he was savoring his words, "you will be just a little off course. You will fly low over the hills between Cannes and Grasse. At a certain point, you will see an arrangement of lights. You will throttle down, open the door, and push the box out, from a height of a hundred feet. Then you will close the door and turn toward the sea and land at the Cannes airport. Your papers will be perfectly in order. There will have been no deviations from your flight plan. You will have nothing to declare. You will walk away from the airplane once and for all, and we will pay you the twenty-five thousand dollars I have spoken of. Isn't it lovely?"

"Lovely," Barber said. "It's just a delicious little old plan, Bertie boy." He turned away from the window. "Now tell me what will be in the box."

Smith chuckled delightedly, as though what he was going to say was too funny to keep to himself. "Money," he said. "Just money."

"How much money?"

"Two hundred and fifty pounds of money," Smith said, his eyes crinkled with amusement. "Two hundred and fifty pounds of tightly packed English notes in a nice, strong, lightweight metal box. Five-pound notes."

At that moment, it occurred to Barber that he was speaking to a lunatic. But Smith was sitting there, matter-of-fact and healthy, obviously a man who has never for a minute in all his life had a single doubt about his sanity.

"When would I get paid?" Barber asked.

"When the box was delivered," Smith said.

"Bertie boy . . ." Barber shook his head reprovingly.

Smith chuckled. "I have warned myself that you were not stupid," he said. "All right. We will deposit twelve thousand five hundred dollars in your name in a Swiss bank before you start for the first time to Egypt."

"You trust me for that?"

Fleetingly the smile left Smith's face. "We'll trust you for that," he said. Then the smile reappeared. "And immediately after the delivery is made, we will deposit the rest. A lovely deal. Hard currency. No income tax. You will be a rich man. Semi-rich." He chuckled at his joke. "Just for a little plane ride. Just to help an Egyptian who is fond of the South of France and who is naturally a little disturbed by the insecurity of his own country."

"When will I meet this Egyptian?" Barber asked.

"When you go to the airfield to take off for your first flight," Smith said. "He'll be there. Don't you worry. He'll be there. Do you hesitate?" he asked anxiously.

"I'm thinking," Barber said.

"It's not as though you were involved in your own country," Smith said piously. "I wouldn't ask a man to do that, a man who had fought for his country in the war. It isn't even as though it had anything to do with the English, for whom it is possible you have a certain affection. But the Egyptians . . ." He shrugged and bent over and picked up the manila envelope and opened it. "I have all the maps here," he said, "if you would like to study them. The route is all marked out, but, of course, it would be finally in your hands, since it would be you who was doing the flying."

Barber took the thick packet of maps. He opened one at random. All it showed was the sea approaches to Malta and the location of the landing strips there. Barber thought of twenty-five thousand dollars and the map shook a little in his hands.

"It is ridiculously easy," Smith said, watching Barber intently. "Foolproof."

Barber put the map down. "If it's so easy, what are you paying twenty-five thousand bucks for?" he said.

Smith laughed. "I admit," he said, "there may be certain little risks. It is improbable, but one never knows. We pay you for the improbability, if you want to put it that way." He shrugged. "After all, after a whole war you must be somewhat hardened to risks."

"When do you have to know?" Barber asked.

"Tonight," Smith said. "If you say no, naturally we have to make other plans. And my Egyptian friend is impatient."

"Who is we?" Barber asked.

"Naturally," Smith said, "I have certain colleagues."

"Who are they?"

Smith made a small regretful gesture. "I am terribly sorry," he said, "but I cannot tell you."

"I'll call you tonight," said Barber.

"Good." Smith stood up and buttoned his coat and carefully put the soft Italian felt hat on his head, at a conservative angle. He played gently and appreciatively with the brim. "This afternoon, I will be at the track. Maybe you would like to join me there."

"Where're they running today?"

"Auteuil," Smith said. "Jumping today."

"Have you heard anything?"

"Perhaps," Smith said. "There is a mare who is doing the jumps for the first time. I have spoken to the jockey and I have been told the mare has responded in training, but I'll hear more at three o'clock."

"I'll be there."

"Good," Smith said enthusiastically. "Although it is

against my interests, of course, to make you too rich in
advance." He chuckled. "However, for the sake of friend-
ship . . . Should I leave the maps?"

"Yes," said Barber.

"Until three o'clock," Smith said as Barber opened the
door. They shook hands, and Smith went out into the
corridor, a rich, tweedy, perfumed figure in the impov-
erished light of the pallid hotel lamps.

Barber locked the door behind him and picked up the
packet of maps and spread them on the bed, over the
rumpled sheets and blankets. He hadn't looked at aerial
maps for a long time. Northern Egypt. The Mediterranean.
The island of Malta. Sicily and the Italian coast. The
Gulf of Genoa. The Alpes-Maritimes. He stared at the
maps. The Mediterranean looked very wide. He didn't
like to fly over open water in a single-engined plane. In
fact, he didn't like to fly. Since the war, he had flown
as little as possible. He hadn't made any explanations
to himself, but when he had had to travel, he had gone
by car or train or boat whenever he could.

Twenty-five thousand dollars, he thought.

He folded the maps neatly and put them back into
the envelope. At this point, the maps weren't going to
help.

He lay down on the bed again, propped against the
pillows, with his hands clasped behind his head. Open
water, he thought. Five times. Even that wouldn't be too
bad. But what about the Egyptians? He had been in
Cairo briefly during the war. He remembered that at
night the policemen walked in pairs, carrying carbines.
He didn't like places where the policemen carried carbines. And Egyptian prisons . . .

He moved uneasily on the bed.

Who knew how many people were in on a scheme like
this? And it would only take one to cook you. One dissatisfied servant or accomplice, one greedy or timid part-
ner . . . He closed his eyes and almost saw the fat, dark
uniformed men with their carbines walking up to the
shiny, new little plane.

Or suppose you blew a tire or crumpled a wheel on
the landing strip? Who knew what the strip was like,
abandoned in the desert since 1943?

Twenty-five thousand dollars.

Or you would think you were making it. The box
would be on the seat beside you and the coast of Egypt

would be falling off behind you and the sea stretching blue below and ahead and the engine running like a watch—and then the first sign of the patrol. The shimmering dot growing into . . . What did the Egyptian Air Force fly? Spitfires, left over from the war, he supposed. Coming up swiftly, going twice as fast as you, signalling you to turn around . . . He lit a cigarette. Two hundred and fifty pounds. Say the box alone—it would have to be really solid—weighed a hundred and fifty pounds. How much did a five-pound note weigh? Would there be a thousand to a pound? Five thousand multiplied by a hundred, with the pound at two-eighty. Close to a million and a half dollars.

His mouth felt dry, and he got up and drank two glasses of water. Then he made himself sit down on the chair, keeping his hands still. If there was an accident, if for any reason you failed to come through with it . . . If the money was lost, but you were saved. Smith didn't look like a murderer, although who knew what murderers looked like these days? And who knew what other people he was involved with? My colleagues, as Smith called them, who would then be your colleagues. The wealthy Egyptian, the several men at the old R.A.F. landing strip in the desert, the people who were to set out the lights in the certain arrangements in the hills behind Cannes— How many others, sliding across frontiers, going secretly and illegally from one country to another with guns and gold in their suitcases, the survivors of war, prison, denunciation—How many others whom you didn't know, whom you would see briefly in the glare of the African sun, as a running figure on a dark French hillside, whom you couldn't judge or assess and on whom your life depended, who were risking prison, deportation, police bullets for their share of a box full of money . . .

He jumped up and put on his clothes and went out, locking the door. He didn't want to sit in the cold, disordered room, staring at the maps.

He walked around the city aimlessly for the rest of the morning, looking blindly into shopwindows and thinking of the things he would buy if he had money. Turning away from a window, he saw a policeman watching him incuriously. Barber looked speculatively at the policeman, who was small, with a mean face and a thin mustache. Looking at the policeman, Barber remembered some of the stories about what they did to suspects when they

questioned them in the back rooms of the local pre-
fectures. An American passport wouldn't do much good if
they picked you up with five hundred thousand English
pounds under your arm.

This is the first time in my life, Barber thought curiously, walking slowly on the crowded street, that I have
contemplated moving over to the other side of the law.
He was surprised that he was considering it so calmly. He
wondered why that was. Perhaps the movies and the
newspapers, he thought. You get so familiar with crime it
becomes humanized and accessible. You don't think about
it, but then, suddenly, when it enters your life, you realize
that subconsciously you have been accepting the idea of
crime as an almost normal accompaniment of everyday
life. Policemen must know that, he thought, all at once
seeing things from the other side. They must look at all
the shut, ordinary faces going past them and they must
know how close to theft, murder, and defaulting everyone
is, and it must drive them crazy. They must want to
arrest everybody.

While Barber was watching the horses move in their
stiff-legged, trembling walk around the paddock before
the sixth race, he felt a light tap on his shoulder.

"Bertie boy," he said, without turning around.

"I'm sorry I'm late," Smith said, coming up to the
paddock rail beside Barber. "Were you afraid I wouldn't
come?"

"What's the word from the jock?" Barber asked.

Smith looked around him suspiciously. Then he smiled.
"The jockey is confident," Smith said. "He is betting himself."

"Which one is it?"

"Number Five."

Barber looked at No. 5. It was a light-boned chestnut
mare with a delicate, gentle head. Her tail and mane were
braided, and she walked alertly but not too nervously,
well-mannered and with a glistening coat. Her jockey was
a man of about forty, with a long, scooped French nose.
He was an ugly man, and when he opened his mouth, you
saw that most of his front teeth were missing. He wore a
maroon cap, with his ears tucked in, and a white silk shirt
dotted with maroon stars.

Barber, looking at him, thought, It's too bad such ugly
men get to ride such beautiful animals.

"O.K., Bertie boy," he said. "Lead me to the window."

Barber bet ten thousand francs on the nose. The odds were a comfortable seven to one. Smith bet twenty-five thousand francs. They walked side by side to the stands and climbed up together as the horses came out on the track. The crowd was small and there were only a few other spectators that high up.

"Well, Lloyd?" Smith said. "Did you look at the maps?"

"I looked at the maps," Barber said.

'What did you think?"

"They're very nice maps."

Smith looked at him sharply. Then he decided to chuckle. "You want to make me fish, eh?" he said. "You know what I mean. Did you decide?"

"I . . ." Barber began, staring down at the cantering horses. He took a deep breath. "I'll tell you after the race," he said.

"Lloyd!" The voice came from below, to the right, and Barber turned in that direction. Toiling up the steps was Jimmy Richardson. He had always been rather round and baby-plump, and Parisian food had done nothing to slim him down, and he was panting, his coat flapping open, disclosing a checkered vest, as he hurried toward Barber.

"How are you?" he said breathlessly as he reached their level. He clapped Barber on the back. "I saw you up here and I thought maybe you had something for this race. I can't figure this one and they've been murdering me all day. I'm lousy on the jumps."

"Hello, Jimmy," Barber said. "Mr. Richardson. Mr. Smith."

"Pleased to meet you," Richardson said. "How do you spell it?" He laughed loudly at his joke. "Say, really, Lloyd, do you know anything? Maureen'll murder me if I go home and tell her I went into the hole for the afternoon."

Barber looked across at Smith, who was watching Richardson benignly. "Well," he said, "Bertie boy, here, thinks he heard something."

"Bertie boy," Richardson said, "please . . ."

Smith smiled thinly. "Number Five looks very good," he said. "But you'd better hurry. They're going to start in a minute."

"Number Five," Richardson said. "Roger. I'll be right back." He went galloping down the steps, his coat flying behind him.

"He's a trusting soul, isn't he?" Smith said.

"He was an only child," Barber said, "and he never got over it."

Smith smiled politely. "Where do you know him from?"

"He was in my squadron."

"In your squadron." Smith nodded, looking after Richardson's hurrying, diminishing figure on the way to the seller's window. "Pilot?"

"Uh-huh."

"Good?"

Barber shrugged. "Better ones got killed and worse ones won every medal in the collection."

"What is he doing in Paris?"

"He works for a drug company," Barber said.

The bell rang and the horses raced toward the first jump.

"Your friend was too late, I'm afraid," Smith said, putting his binoculars to his eyes.

"Yep," Barber said, watching the bunched horses.

No. 5 fell on the fourth jump. She went over with two other horses, and suddenly she was down and rolling. The pack passed around her. The fourth jump was far off down the track, and it was hard to see what, exactly, was happening until, a moment later, the mare struggled to her feet and cantered after the pack, her reins broken and trailing. Then Barber saw that the jockey was lying there motionless, crumpled up clumsily on his face, with his head turned in under his shoulder.

"We've lost our money," Smith said calmly. He took his binoculars from his eyes and pulled out his tickets and tore them and dropped them.

"May I have those, please?" Barber reached over for the binoculars. Smith lifted the strap over his head, and Barber trained the glasses on the distant jump where the jockey was lying. Two men were running out to him and turning him over.

Barber adjusted the binoculars, and the figures of the two men working on the motionless figure in the maroon-starred shirt came out of the blur into focus. Even in the glasses, there was something terribly urgent and despairing in the movements of the distant men. They picked the jockey up between them and started running clumsily off with him.

"Damn it!" It was Richardson, who had climbed up beside them again. "The window closed just as I—"

"Do not complain, Mr. Richardson," Smith said. "We fell at the fourth jump."

Richardson grinned. "That's the first bit of luck I had all day."

Down below, in front of the stands, the riderless mare was swerving and trotting off down the track to avoid a groom who was trying to grab the torn reins.

Barber kept the glasses on the two men who were carrying the jockey. Suddenly, they put him down on the grass, and one of the men bent down and put his ear against the white silk racing shirt. After a while, he stood up. Then the two men started to carry the jockey again, only now they walked slowly, as though there was no sense in hurrying.

Barber gave the glasses back to Smith. "I'm going home," he said. "I've had enough of the sport for one day."

Smith glanced at him sharply. He put the glasses to his eyes and stared at the men carrying the jockey. Then he put the glasses into their case and hung the case by its strap over his shoulder. "They kill at least one a year," he said in a low voice. "It is to be expected in a sport like this. I'll take you home."

"Say," Richardson said. "Is that fellow dead?"

"He was getting too old," Smith said. "He kept at it too long."

"Holy man!" Richardson said, staring down the track. "And I was sore because I came too late to bet on him. That was some tip." He made a babyish grimace. "A tip on a dead jock."

Barber started down toward the exit.

"I'll come with you," Richardson said. "This isn't my lucky day."

The three men went down under the stands without speaking. People were standing in little groups, and there was a queer rising, hissing sound of whispering all over the place, now that the news was spreading.

When they reached the car, Barber got into the back, allowing Richardson to sit next to Smith, on the front seat. He wanted to be at least that much alone for the time being.

Smith drove slowly and in silence. Even Richardson spoke only once. "What a way to get it," he said as they drove between the bare, high trees. "In a lousy, three-hundred-thousand-franc claiming race."

Barber sat in the corner, his eyes half closed, not looking out. He kept remembering the second time the two men had picked up the jockey. Smith's selection for the afternoon, Barber thought. He closed his eyes altogether and saw the maps spread out on the bed in his room. The Mediterranean. The wide reaches of open water. He remembered the smell of burning. The worst smell. The smell of your dreams during the war. The smell of hot metal, smoldering rubber. Smith's tip.

"Here we are," Smith was saying.

Barber opened his eyes. They were stopped at the corner of the dead-end street down which was the entrance to his hotel. He got out.

"Wait a minute, Bertie boy," Barber said. "I have something I want to give you."

Smith looked at him inquiringly. "Can't it wait, Lloyd?" he asked.

"No. I'll just be a minute." Barber went into his hotel and up to his room. The maps were folded in a pile on the bureau, except for one, which was lying open beside the others. The approaches to Malta. He folded it quickly and put all the maps into the manila envelope and went back to the car. Smith was standing beside the car, smoking, nervously holding on to his hat, because a wind had come up and dead leaves were skittering along the pavement.

"Here you are, Bertie boy," Barber said, holding out the envelope.

Smith didn't take it. "You're sure you know what you're doing?" he said.

"I'm sure."

Smith still didn't take the maps. "I'm in no hurry," he said softly. "Why don't you hold on to them another day?"

"Thanks, no."

Smith looked at him silently for a moment. The fluorescent street lamps had just gone on, hard white-blue light, and Smith's smooth face looked powdery in the shadows under his expensive hat, and his pretty eyes were dark and flat under the curled lashes.

"Just because a jockey falls at a jump—" Smith began.

"Take them," Barber said, "or I'll throw them in the gutter."

Smith shrugged. He put out his hand and took the envelope. "You'll never have a chance like this again," he said, running his finger caressingly over the envelope edge.

"Good night, Jimmy." Barber leaned over the car and

spoke to Richardson, who was sitting there watching them, puzzled. "Give my love to Maureen."

"Say, Lloyd," Richardson said, starting to get out. "I thought maybe we could have a couple of drinks. Maureen doesn't expect me home for another hour yet and I thought maybe we could cut up some old touches and—"

"Sorry," Barber said, because he wanted, more than anything else, to be alone. "I have a date. Some other time."

Smith turned and looked thoughtfully at Richardson. "He always has a date, your friend," Smith said. "He's a very popular boy, I feel like a drink myself, Mr. Richardson. I would be honored if you'd join me."

"Well," Richardson said uncertainly, "I live way down near the Hôtel de Ville and—"

"It's on my way," Smith said, smiling warmly.

Richardson settled back in his seat, and Smith started to get into the car. He stopped and looked up at Barber. "I made a mistake about you, didn't I, Lloyd?" he said contemptuously.

"Yes," Barber said. "I'm getting too old. I don't want to keep at it too long."

Smith chuckled and got into the car. They didn't shake hands. He slammed the door, and Barber watched him pull sharply away from the curb, making a taxi-driver behind him jam on his brakes to avoid hitting him.

Barber watched the big black car weave swiftly down the street, under the hard white-blue lights. Then he went back to the hotel and up to his room and lay down, because an afternoon at the races always exhausted him.

An hour later, he got up. He splashed cold water on his face to wake himself, but even so he felt listless and empty. He wasn't hungry and he wasn't thirsty and he kept thinking about the dead jockey in his soiled silks. There was no one he wanted to see. He put on his coat and went out, hating the room as he closed the door behind him.

He walked slowly toward the Etoile. It was a raw night and a fog was moving in from the river, and the streets were almost empty, because everybody was inside eating dinner. He didn't look at any of the lighted windows, because he wasn't going to buy anything for a long time. He passed several movie houses, neon in the drifting fog. In the movies, he thought, the hero would have been on his way to Africa by now. He would nearly be caught several times in Egypt, and he would fight his way out of a trap on the desert, killing several dark men just in time on the airstrip. And he would develop engine trouble over the Mediterranean and just pull out, with the water lapping at the wing tips, and he would undoubtedly crash, without doing too much damage to himself, probably just a photogenic cut on the forehead, and would drag the box out just in time. And he would turn out to be a Treasury agent or a member of British Intelligence and he would never doubt his luck and his nerve would never fail him and he would not end the picture with only a few thousand francs in his pocket. Or, if it was an artistic picture, there would be a heavy ground mist over the hills and the plane would drone on and on, desperate and lost, and then, finally, with the fuel tanks empty, the hero would crash in flames. Battered and staggering as he was, he would try to get the box out, but he wouldn't be able to move it, and finally the flames would drive him back and he would stand against a tree, laughing crazily, his face blackened with smoke, watching the plane and the money burn, to show the vanity of human aspiration and greed.

Barber grinned bleakly, rehearsing the scenarios in front of the giant posters outside the theatres. The movies do it better, he thought. They have their adventures happen to adventurers. He turned off the Champs-Élysées, walking slowly and aimlessly, trying to decide whether to eat now or have a drink first. Almost automatically, he walked toward the Plaza-Athénée. In the two weeks that he had been wooed by Smith, they had met in the English bar of the Plaza-Athénée almost every evening.

He went into the hotel and downstairs to the English bar. As he came into the room, he saw, in the corner, Smith and Jimmy Richardson.

Barber smiled. Bertie boy, he thought, are you whatever wasting your time. He stood at the bar and ordered a whiskey.

". . . fifty missions," he heard Richardson say. Richardson had a loud, empty voice that carried anywhere. "Africa, Sicily, Italy, Yugo—"

Then Smith saw him. He nodded coolly, with no hint of invitation. Richardson swivelled in his chair then, too. He smiled uncomfortably at Barber, getting red in the face, like a man who has been caught by a friend with his friend's girl.

Barber waved to them. For a moment, he wondered if he ought to go over and sit down and try to get Richardson out of there. He watched the two men, trying to figure out what they thought of each other. Or, more accurately, what Smith thought of Richardson. You didn't have to speculate about Jimmy. If you bought Jimmy a drink, he was your friend for life. For all that he had been through —war and marriage and being a father and living in a foreign country—it had still never occurred to Jimmy that people might not like him or might try to do him harm. When you were enjoying Jimmy, you called it trustfulness. When he was boring you, you called it stupidity.

Barber watched Smith's face carefully. By now, he knew Smith well enough to be able to tell a great deal of what was going on behind the pretty eyes and the pale, powdered face. Right now, Barber could tell that Smith was bored and that he wanted to get away from Jimmy Richardson.

Barber turned back to his drink, smiling to himself. It took Bertie boy just about an hour, he thought, an hour of looking at that good-natured empty face, an hour of listening to that booming, vacant voice, to decide that this was no man to fly a small box of five-pound notes from Cairo to Cannes.

Barber finished his drink quickly and went out of the bar before Smith and Richardson got up from the table. He had nothing to do for the evening, but he didn't want to get stuck with Jimmy and Maureen Richardson for dinner.

And now it was almost two months later and nobody had heard from Jimmy Richardson for thirty-two days.

In the whole afternoon of searching, Barber had not come upon any trace of Bert Smith. He had not been at the restaurants or the track or the art galleries, the barbershop, the steam bath, the bars. And no one had seen him for weeks.

It was nearly eight o'clock when Barber arrived at the English bar of the Plaza-Athénée. He was wet from walking in the day's rain, and tired, and his shoes were soggy and he felt a cold coming on. He looked around the room, but it was almost empty. Indulging himself, thinking unhappily of all the taxi fares he had paid that day, he ordered a whiskey.

Barber sipped his whiskey in the quiet room, thinking circularly, I should have said something. But what could I have said? And Jimmy wouldn't have listened. But I should have said something. *The omens are bad, Jimmy, go on home. . . . : I saw a plane crashing at the fourth jump, I saw a corpse being carried across dead grass by Egyptians, Jimmy, I saw silks and maps stained by blood.*

I had to be so damned superior, Barber thought bitterly. I had to be so damned sure that Jimmy Richardson was too stupid to be offered that much money. I had to be so damned sure that Bert Smith was too clever to hire him.

He hadn't said any of the things he should have said, and it had all wound up with a frantic, husbandless, penniless girl pleading for help that could only be too late now. Penniless. Jimmy Richardson had been too stupid even to get any of the money in advance.

He remembered what Jimmy and Maureen had looked like, smiling and embarrassed and youthfully important, standing next to Colonel Sumners, the Group Commander, at their wedding in Shreveport. He remembered Jimmy's plane just off his wing over Sicily; he remembered Jimmy's face when he landed at Foggia with an engine on fire; he remembered Jimmy's voice singing drunkenly in a bar in Naples; he remembered Jimmy the day after he arrived in Paris, saying, "Kid, this is the town for me, I got Europe in my blood."

He finished his drink and paid and went upstairs slowly. He went into a phone booth and called his hotel to see if there were any messages for him.

"Mme. Richardson has been calling you all day," the old man at the switchboard said. "Ever since four o'clock. She wanted you to call her back."

"All right," Barber said. "Thank you." He started to hang up.

"Wait a minute, wait a minute," the old man said irritably. "She called an hour ago to say she was going out. She said that if you came in before nine o'clock, she would like you to join her at the bar of the Hotel Bellman."

"Thanks, Henri," Barber said. "If she happens to call again, tell her I'm on my way." He went out of the hotel. The Bellman was nearby, and he walked toward it slowly, even though it was still raining. He was in no hurry to see Maureen Richardson.

When he reached the Bellman, he hesitated before going in, feeling too tired for this, wishing Maureen could be put off at least until the next day. He sighed, and pushed the door open.

The bar was a small one, but it was crowded with large,

well-dressed men who were taking their time over drinks before going out to dinner. Then he saw Maureen. She was sitting in a corner, half turned away from the room, her shabby, thin coat thrown back over her chair. She was sitting alone and there was a bottle of champagne in a bucket in a stand beside her.

Barber went over to her, irritated by the sight of the champagne. Is that what she's doing with my five thousand francs, he thought, annoyed. Women are going crazy, too, these days.

He leaned over and kissed the top of her head. She jumped nervously, then smiled when she saw who it was. "Oh, Lloyd," she said, in a funny kind of whisper. She jumped up and kissed him, holding him hard against her. There was a big smell of champagne on her breath and he wondered if she was drunk. "Lloyd Lloyd . . ." she said. She pushed him away a little, holding on to both his hands. Her eyes were smeary with tears and her mouth kept trembling.

"I came as soon as I got your message," Lloyd said, trying to sound practical, afraid Maureen was going to break down in front of all the people in the bar. She kept standing there, her mouth working, her hands gripping his avidly. He looked down, embarrassed, at her hands. They were still reddened and the nails were still uneven, but there was an enormous ring glittering, white and blue, on her finger. It hadn't been there when she came to his hotel, and he knew he had never seen her with a ring like that before. He looked up, almost frightened, thinking, What the hell has she started? What has she got herself into?

Then he saw Jimmy. Jimmy was making his way among the tables toward him. He was smiling broadly and he had lost some weight and he was dark brown and he looked as though he had just come from a month's vacation on a southern beach.

"Hi, kid," Jimmy said, his voice booming across the tables, across the barroom murmur of conversation. "I was just calling you again."

"He came home," Maureen said. "He came home at four o'clock this afternoon, Lloyd." She sank suddenly into her chair. Whatever else had happened that afternoon, it was plain that she had had access to a bottle. She sat in her chair, still holding on to one of Barber's hands, looking up, with a shimmering, half-dazed expression on her face, at her husband.

Jimmy clapped Barber on the back and shook hands fiercely. "Lloyd," he said. "Good old Lloyd. *Garçon!*" he shouted, his voice reverberating through the whole room. "Another glass. Take your coat off. Sit down. Sit down."

Lloyd took his coat off and sat down slowly.

"Welcome home," he said quietly. He blew his nose. The cold had arrived.

"First," Jimmy said, "I have something for you." Ceremoniously he dug his hand into his pocket and brought out a roll of ten-thousand-franc notes. The roll was three inches thick. He took off one of the notes. "Maureen told me," he said seriously. "You were a damn good friend, Lloyd. Have you got change of ten?"

"I don't think so," Barber said. "No."

"*Garçon,*" Jimmy said to the waiter, who was putting down a third glass, "get me two fives for this, please." When he spoke French, Jimmy had an accent that made even Americans wince.

Jimmy filled the three glasses carefully. He lifted his glass and clinked it first against Barber's and then against Maureen's. Maureen kept looking at him as though she had just seen him for the first time and never hoped to see anything as wonderful again in her whole life.

"To crime," Jimmy said. He winked. He made a complicated face when he winked, like a baby who has trouble with a movement of such subtlety and has to use the whole side of its face and its forehead to effect it.

Maureen giggled.

They drank. It was very good champagne.

"You're having dinner with us," Jimmy said. "Just the three of us. The victory dinner. Just Beauty and me and you, because if it hadn't been for you . . ." Suddenly solemn, he put his hand on Barber's shoulder.

"Yes," said Barber. His feet were icy and his trousers hung soddenly around his wet socks and he had to blow his nose again.

"Did Beauty show you her ring?" Jimmy asked.

"Yes," Barber said.

"She's only had it since six o'clock," Jimmy said.

Maureen held her hand up and stared at her ring. She giggled again.

"I know a place," Jimmy said, "where you can get pheasant and the best bottle of wine in Paris and . . ."

The waiter came back and gave Jimmy the two five-

thousand-franc notes. Dimly, Barber wondered how much
they weighed.

"If ever you're in a hole," Jimmy said, giving him one
of the notes, "you know where to come, don't you?"

"Yes," Barber said. He put the note in his pocket.

He started to sneeze then, and ten minutes later he said
he was sorry but he didn't think he could last the evening
with a cold like that. Both Jimmy and Maureen tried to
get him to stay, but he could tell that they were going to
be happier without him.

He finished a second glass of champagne, and said he'd
keep in touch, and went out of the bar, feeling his toes
squish in his wet shoes. He was hungry and he was very
fond of pheasant and actually the cold wasn't so bad, even
if his nose kept running all the time. But he knew he
couldn't bear to sit between Maureen and Jimmy Richardson all night and watch the way they kept looking at
each other.

He walked back to his hotel, because he was through
with taxis, and went up and sat on the edge of his bed
in his room, in the dark, without taking his coat off. I better get out of here, he thought, rubbing the wet off the
end of his nose with the back of his hand. This continent
is not for me.

A Wicked Story

THE CURTAIN CAME DOWN AND THE APPLAUSE BEGAN. THE
theatre was warm now, after the three long acts, and
Robert Harvey applauded lightly, only from the wrists,
because he didn't want to sweat. He was a big, heavy
man, and he had found that when he permitted himself
enthusiasm in the overheated midtown auditoriums, he
came away soaking wet. He had once caught a bad cold
that way, going out into a rainstorm after *A Streetcar
Named Desire*, and he had learned to temper his gratitude,
moving his hands politely but making very little noise.
The curtain went up again and the cast took their bows,
smiling widely because the play had been running three
months and was going to run at least a year and they were
all eating. Robert regarded them coolly, thinking, Well,
they certainly aren't worth four-eighty a seat. What has

happened, he thought, to the plays I used to see when I was a younger man?

Virginia, in the next seat, was applauding briskly. Her eyes were shining, as they did when she was enjoying herself. Robert decided not to say anything about the four-eighty a seat when he talked to her later about the play. The actors were taking individual curtain calls now, and when the girl who played the cynical friend of the heroine came on, Robert clapped his hands quite powerfully, risking perspiration, because he had met her once at a party. Besides, she was not a bad-looking girl, with longish black hair, cut in an unusual way, and large blue eyes. She was a bit too big and eventually she was going to be fat and you had the feeling she never was going to get very far as an actress, but none of these things would be crucial for several more years. Robert felt the beads of perspiration coming out on his forehead, and he was glad when the girl, after a bosomy curtsy, went off into the wings.

The lights came on and the Harveys moved slowly up the aisle in the newly disturbed waves of perfume and fur. Virginia said "That was a very nice little play, wasn't it?" and Robert nodded, hoping that there were no relatives of the playwright within earshot. In the lobby, as he put on his coat, he saw a young man with a yellow muffler who was leaning against the box-office window staring at Virginia. In a more realistic society, he thought, taking Virginia's arm and moving her toward the street, you would be permitted to walk over and punch the nose of any man who looked at your wife that way.

They spurted across the street among the taxis, Virginia fleet on her high heels, and went through the alley, between the stage doors and the gay posters for musical comedies. There were three hits playing on the next street, and the people flowing from the theatres sounded good-natured and jubilant, and you knew that they would remain that way for at least another half hour, and it was pleasant to be among them in the windless, cold night air. The lights of the restaurant across the street were warm among the dark buildings, and the doorman, while not effusive, was agreeably polite as he swung the door open for them. The headwaiter was a little chillier than the doorman and seated them at the rear of the restaurant, although there were several empty tables closer to the entrance. Robert humbly accepted the table, thinking philosophically, Well, this is a theatrical restaurant, there are dozens of places where they'd put me near the front of the room and actors'd be lucky to get through the door.

Virginia settled herself on the banquette with a hundred small subsiding movements, then took out her glasses and carefully surveyed the room. After a minute, she put the glasses down on the table and turned toward Robert. "What're you smiling at?" she asked.

"Because you're so pleased," said Robert.

"Who says I'm pleased?"

"You examined the terrain and you said to yourself, 'Isn't this nice? I'm prettier than any of them,' and now you can enjoy your supper."

"Oh, you're so sharp," Virginia said. She smiled, "You're such a sharp man."

The waiter came, and they ordered spaghetti and half a bottle of Chianti, and watched the restaurant fill up with people who had been to the theatre and actors who still had traces of greasepaint around their collars and tall, astonishing-looking girls in mink coats from the musicals across the street. Robert ate hungrily and drank his wine slowly, nursing it.

"That play tonight," Virginia was saying, delicately winding spaghetti on her fork against a spoon, "was all right and I enjoyed it while I was there, but I'm getting tired of how awful all the female characters are in plays these days. All the women always are drunks or nympho-maniacs or they drive their sons crazy or they ruin the lives of two or three people an act. If I were a play-wright, I'd write a nice, old-fashioned play in which the heroine is pure and beautiful and makes a man out of her husband, even though he's weak and drinks too much and occasionally robs his boss to bet on the horses."

"If you were a playwright, you'd be in Hollywood," Robert said.

"Anyway, I bet it'd be a big success," Virginia insisted. "I bet people are just dying to go to see a play that they can come out of and say, 'Yes, that's just how Mother was the time Dad had his trouble down at the bank and those two men in plainclothes came to see him from New York.'"

"If anything like that comes up," Robert said comfort-ably, "you go to see it some matinée. By yourself."

"And all the actresses these days. They try to act so ordinary. Just like anybody you'd meet in the street. Sometimes you wonder how they dare charge you admission to watch them. When I was a little girl, actresses used to be so affected you'd *know* you had to pay to see them, because you'd never meet anybody like that in real life in a million years."

"How did you like Duse?" Robert asked. "What did you think of Bernhardt when you were ten?"

"Don't be so witty. You know what I mean. That girl you liked so much tonight, for example . . ."

"Which girl I liked so much?" Robert asked, puzzled.

"The big one. The one that played the friend."

"Oh, that one," Robert said. "I didn't like her so much."

"You certainly sounded as though you did. I thought your hands'd be a bloody pulp by the time she got off the stage."

"I was just being neighborly," Robert said. "I met her once at a party."

"Whose party?" Virginia stopped eating.

"The Lawtons'. She went to school with Anne Lawton," Robert said. "Didn't you meet her?"

"I didn't go to that party. I had the flu that week." Virginia sipped her wine. "What's her name?"

"Carol Something. Look at the program."

"I left the program in the theatre. Was she nice?"

Robert shrugged. "I only talked to her for five minutes. She told me she came from California and she hates working for television and she was divorced last year but they're still good friends. The usual kind of talk you get at the Lawtons'."

"She looks as though she came from California," Virginia said, making it sound like a criticism.

"Oakland," Robert said. "It's not exactly the same thing."

"There she is now," said Virginia. "Near the door."

Robert looked up. The girl was alone and was making her way down the center of the room. She wasn't wearing a hat, and her hair looked careless, and she had on a shapeless polo coat and flat shoes, and Robert decided, looking at her, that actresses were getting plainer every year. She stopped briefly once or twice to greet friends at other tables, then headed for a table in the corner, where a group of three men and two women were waiting for her. Robert realized that she was going to pass their table, and wondered if he ought to greet her. The party at which they'd met had been almost two months before, and he had a modest theory that people like actresses and book publishers and movie directors never remembered anyone they met who wasn't in a related profession. He doubted whether the girl would recognize him, but he arranged a slight impersonal smile on his face, so that if she did happen to remember, he would seem to be saluting her. If she just passed by, Robert hoped that it would merely look as though he were responding with polite amusement to one of Virginia's remarks.

But the girl stopped in front of the table, smiling widely. She put out her hand and said, "Why, Mr. Harvey, isn't it nice seeing you agian!"

She wasn't any prettier close up, Robert decided, but when she smiled, she seemed friendly and simple, and her voice sounded as though she really was glad to see him again after the five minutes in the noisy corner at the Lawtons' two months ago. Robert stood up and took her hand. "Hello," he said. "May I present my wife. Miss Byrne."

"How do you do, Miss Byrne," Virginia said. "We were just talking about you."

"We saw your show tonight," Robert said. "We thought you were very good indeed."

"Aren't you dear to say that," the girl said. "I love to hear it, even if you don't mean it at all."

"What about the man who wrote the play?" Virginia asked. "He must be rather strange."

"Mother trouble." Miss Byrne glanced significantly up at the ceiling. "All the young writers coming into the theatre these days seem to have the same thing. You'd think it'd be the war that would be haunting them, but it isn't at all. It's only Mama."

Virginia smiled. "Not only young writers," she said. "Is this your first play, Miss Byrne?"

"Heavens, no," the girl said. "I've been in three others. *Regret, The Six-Week Vacation.* . . . I don't even remember the name of the third one. Turkeys. Here today and closed by Saturday."

Virginia turned to Robert. "Did you happen to see any of them, dear?" she asked.

"No," Robert said, surprised. He never went to the theatre without Virginia.

"Three other plays," Virginia went on pleasantly, sounding genuinely interested. "You must have been in New York quite a long time."

"Two years," Miss Byrne said. "A single blink of the eye of a drama critic."

"Two years," Virginia said, politely. She turned to Robert again. "Where did you say Miss Byrne came from? Hollywood?"

"Oakland," Robert said.

"New York must be quite exciting," Virginia said. "After Oakland."

"I love it," Miss Byrne said, sounding young and enthusiastic. "Even with the flops."

"I'm so sorry," Virginia said. "Keeping you standing there like that, talking on and on about the theatre. Wouldn't you like to sit down and join us for a drink?"

"Thanks," the girl said, "I really can't. They're waiting for me over in the corner."

"Some other time, perhaps," Virginia said.

"I'd love it," said Miss Byrne. "It's been fun meeting you, Mrs. Harvey. Mr. Harvey told me about you. I do hope we see each other again. Good night." She waved and smiled widely again and strode over toward her waiting friends.

Robert sat down slowly. There was silence at the table for a moment.

"It's a hard life," Virginia said after a while, "for actresses, isn't it?"

"Yes."

"The Six-Week Vacation," Virginia said. "No wonder it failed, with a title like that. Did she play the lead in it, that girl?"

"I don't know," Robert said, waiting. "I told you I didn't see it."

"That's right," Virginia said. "You told me."

They were silent again. Virginia began to twist the stem of her wineglass with little, jerky movements. "You told me," she repeated. "It's too bad she couldn't have a drink with us. We might have learned a great deal about the theatre tonight. I find people in the theatre so fascinating. Don't you?"

"What's the matter with you?" Robert asked.

"Nothing," Virginia said flatly. "There's nothing the matter with me at all. Are you finished with your food?"

"Yes."

"Let's pay the check and get out of here."

"Virginia . . ." Robert said, drawling the name out complainingly.

"Rah-ahbert . . ." Virginia said, mimicking him.

"All right," said Robert. "What is it?"

"I said nothing."

"I know what you said. What is it?"

Virginia lifted her eyes and looked at him closely. "Miss Byrne," she said. "I thought you didn't know her name."

"Oh," Robert said. "Now it's turning into one of those evenings."

"It's not turning into any kind of evening. Get the check," Virginia said. "I want to go home."

"Waiter!" Robert called. "The check, please." He stared at Virginia. She was beginning to look martyred. "Listen," Robert said. "I didn't know her name."

"Carol Something," said Virginia.

"It came to me just as she got to the table. While I was standing up. Hasn't that ever happened to you?"

"No," said Virginia.

"Well, it's a common phenomenon."

Virginia nodded. "Very common,"she said, "I'm sure."

"Don't you believe me?"

"You haven't forgotten a girl's name since you were six years old," Virginia said. "You remember the name of the girl you danced with once the night of the Yale game in 1935."

"Gladys," Robert said. "Gladys McCreary. She played field hockey for Bryn Mawr."

"No wonder you were so eager to get to the Lawtons' that night."

"I wasn't eager to get to the Lawtons' that night," Robert said, his voice beginning to rise. "And anyway I didn't even know she existed. At least be logical."

"I had a hundred and three fever," Virginia said, pitying herself all over again for the damp eyes, the hot forehead, the painful cough of two months earlier. "I was just lying there all alone, day after day . . ."

"Don't make it sound as though you were on the point of death for the whole winter," Robert said loudly. "You were in bed three days, and on Saturday you went to lunch in a snowstorm."

"Oh," Virginia said, "you can remember that it snowed one Saturday two months ago, but you can't remember the name of a girl you talked to for hours at a party, that you exchanged the most intimate confidences with."

"Virginia," Robert said, "I'm going to get up on this seat and scream at the top of my voice."

"Divorced, she said, but they're still good friends. I'll bet they are. I'll bet that girl is good friends with a lot of people. How about you and *your* ex-wife?" Virginia demanded. "Are you good friends with her, too?"

"You know as well as I do," Robert said, "that the only time I see my ex-wife is when she wants the alimony adjusted."

"If you keep talking in that tone of voice, they'll never let you in this restaurant again," Virginia whispered.

"Let's get out of here," Robert said bluntly. "Waiter, where's that check?"

"She's thick." Virginia stared at Miss Byrne, who was sitting with her back to them twenty feet away, talking brightly and waving a cigarette. "Through the middle. Grotesquely thick."

"Grotesquely," Robert agreed.

"You don't fool me," Virginia said, "I know your tastes."

"Oh, God," Robert murmured.

"Always pretending to be such a connoisseur of beautiful women," Virginia said, "and secretly what you really like are old-fashioned, disgusting brood mares."

"Oh, God," Robert said again.

"Like that Elise Cross," Virginia rolled on, "two summers ago on the Cape. She always looked as though she had to be packed into her girdle under pressure. And whenever I looked around for you at a party, you both were gone, out on the dunes."

"I thought we had agreed never to discuss that subject again," Robert said with dignity.

"What subject am I permitted to discuss?" Virginia demanded. "The United Nations?"

"There never was anything between me and Elise Cross. Not anything. And you know it," Robert said firmly and convincingly. It was true that there had been something, but that had been two years ago, and he hadn't seen Elise Cross since then, or anyone else, for that matter. And anyway it had been summertime then, and he had been drunk a good deal of the time for a reason he could no longer recall, and the people around them had been of that peculiar, handsome, neurotic, wife-changing type that appears at places like that in August and infects the atmosphere. He had been ashamed of himself by Labor Day and had resolved to change his ways once and for all. Now he felt blameless and aggrieved at being called upon to defend himself after all that abstinence.

"You spent more time on the beach than the Coast Guard," Virginia said.

"If the waiter doesn't come with the check," Robert said, "I'm going to walk out of here and they can follow me in a taxi if they want their money."

"I should have known," Virginia said, and there was a remote throb in her voice. "People told me about you before we were married. I knew your reputation."

"Look, that was more than five years ago," Robert said doggedly. "I was younger then and more energetic and I was married to a woman I didn't like and who didn't like me. I was unhappy and lonely and restless—"

"And now?"

"And now," Robert said, thinking how wonderful it would be to get up and walk away from his wife for six or seven months, "and now I am married to a woman I love and I am settled and profoundly happy. I haven't had lunch or a drink with anyone for years. I barely tip my hat to women I know when I pass them in the street."

"And what about that fat actress over there?"

"Look," Robert said, feeling hoarse, as though he had been shouting into the wind for hours. "Let's get it straight. I met her at a party. I spoke to her for five minutes. I don't think she's very pretty. I don't think she's much as an actress. I was surprised when she recognized me. I forgot her name. Then I remembered her name when she came to the table."

"I suppose you expect me to believe that." Virginia smiled coldly.

"I certainly do. Because it's an exact statement of fact."

"I saw that smile," Virginia said. "Don't think I didn't."

"What smile?" Robert asked, honestly puzzled.

"Why, Mr. Harvey," Virginia said, cooing, "isn't it nice seeing you again? And then the teeth and the girlish crinkling of the nose and the long, direct stare . . ."

"Finally," Robert said to the waiter, who was leaning over the table, putting the check down. "Don't go away." Robert counted out some bills, feeling his hands shaking minutely with rage. He watched the waiter going toward the cashier's desk, near the kitchen, for change. Then he spoke, trying to keep his voice under control. "Now," he said, turning back to Virginia, "what, exactly, did you mean by that?"

"I may not be very smart," Virginia said, "but if there's one thing I have, it's intuition. Especially where you're concerned. And anyway that smile was unmistakable."

"Now, wait a minute." Robert felt his fists opening and closing spasmodically. "It's charming of you to think, even after being married to me for five years, that women just drop at my feet after speaking to me for five minutes, but I have to disillusion you. It has never happened to me. Never," he said slowly and distinctly and with some disappointment.

"If there's one thing I can't stand, it's fake modesty," Virginia said. "I've seen you looking at yourself in the mirror, approving of yourself by the hour, pretending you were shaving or looking for gray hairs. And," she added bitterly, "I've talked to your mother. I know how she brought you up. Drilling it into your head that the whole panting female sex was after you because you were a Harvey and you were so dazzling—"

"Good God," Robert said. "Now we have my mother, too."

"She has a lot to answer for," Virginia said, "your mother. Don't think she hasn't."

"All right," Robert said. "My mother is a low, terrible woman and everybody agrees on that. But what has that got to do with the fact that a woman I met at a party happened to smile at me?"

"Happened," Virginia said.

"I still don't see how it could be my fault," Robert said, trying to sound patient. "I can't control the way people smile in restaurants."

"It's always your fault," Virginia said. "Even if you don't say a word. It's just the way you come into the room and stand there and decide to look . . . male."

Robert jumped up, pushing the table back. "I can't stand it," he said. "I can't stand it any more. The hell with the change."

Virginia stood up, too, her face rigid. "I have an idea," Robert said as he helped her on with her coat. "Let's you and I not talk to each other for a week."

"Fine," said Virginia crazily. "That's perfectly fine with me." She walked swiftly toward the door, through the middle of the restaurant, without looking back.

Robert watched her striding down the narrow aisle between the tables, her black coat floating behind her. He wished that he had a worse temper. He wished that he had a temper so bad that he could stay out all night and get drunk.

The waiter came with the change, and Robert fumbled with the tip. Over the waiter's shoulder he saw Miss Byrne swing her head slowly toward him. Everybody else at her table was talking animatedly. For the first time, Robert looked at her carefully. It *is* true, he thought numbly. Most women these days *are* too damn thin.

Then Miss Byrne smiled at him. Her nose crinkled and her teeth showed and she seemed to be looking at him for a long time. He felt flattered and considerably younger and very curious. And as he dropped his eyes and left a large tip for the waiter, he knew, helplessly, that he was going to call her next day and he knew what her voice was going to sound like on the telephone.

Then he got his coat and hurried out of the restaurant after his wife.

In the French Style

BEDDOES GOT IN FROM EGYPT IN THE MIDDLE OF THE morning. He went to his hotel and shook hands with the concierge and told him that the trip had been fine but that Egyptians were impossible. From the concierge he found out that the city was crowded, as usual, and that the price of the room had gone up once more, as usual.

"The tourist season now lasts twelve months a year," the concierge said, giving Beddoes his key. "Nobody stays home any more. It is exhausting."

Beddoes went upstairs and told the porter to put his typewriter in the closet, because he didn't want to see it for a while. He opened the window and looked out with pleasure at the Seine flowing past. Then he took a bath and put on fresh clothes and gave Christina's number over the telephone to the woman at the switchboard. The woman at the switchboard had an insulting habit of repeating numbers in English, and Beddoes noticed, with a smile, that that had not changed. There was the familiar hysteria on the wires as the woman on the switchboard got Christina's number. The telephone in Christina's hotel was

down the hall from her room, and Beddoes had to spell
the name slowly—Mlle. "T" for Théodore, "A" for
André, "T" for Théodore, "E" for Edouard—before the
man on the other end understood and went away to tell
Christina an American gentleman demanded her on the
telephone.

Beddoes heard Christina's footsteps coming down the
hall toward the telephone and he thought he could tell
from the sound that she was wearing high heels.

"Hello," Christina said. There was a sudden crackle
on the wire as Christina spoke, but even so Beddoes
could recognize the breathless, excited tone of her voice.
Christina answered the phone as though she expected
each call to be an invitation to a party.

"Hi, Chris," Beddoes said.

"Who's this?"

"The voice of Egypt," said Beddoes.

"Walter!" Christina said happily. "When did you get
in?"

"This minute," Beddoes said, lying by an hour to
please her. "Are you wearing high heels?"

"What?"

"You're wearing high heels, aren't you?"

"Wait a minute while I look," Christina said. Then,
after a pause, "Did you turn psychic in Cairo?"

Beddoes chuckled. "Semi-Oriental fakery," he said. "I
brought back a supply. Where're we going for lunch?"

"Walter!" Christina said. "I'm in despair."

"You have a date."

"Yes. When are you going to learn to cable?"

"That's O.K.," Beddoes said carelessly. He made a
point of never sounding disappointed. He had a feeling
that if he asked Christina to break the date she would,
but he also made a point of never pleading for anything.
"We'll make it later."

"How about a drink this afternoon?"

"We can start with that," Beddoes said. "Five?"

"Make it five-thirty," Christina said.

"Where're you going to be?" Beddoes asked, minutely
annoyed at the postponement.

"Near the Etoile," Christina said.

"Alexandre's?"

"Fine," Christina said. "Will you be on time for once?"

"Be more polite," Beddoes said, "the first day the man
comes to town."

"*A tout à l'heure,*" Christina said.

"What did you say, Ma'am?"

"All the kids are speaking French this year." Christina laughed. "Isn't it nice to have you back in town."

There was a click as she hung up. Beddoes put the phone down slowly and went over to the window. He stared at the river, thinking that this was the first time in a long while that Christina hadn't come over immediately when he arrived in Paris. The river appeared cold and the trees were bare and the sky looked as though it had been gray for months. But with all that, the city looked promising. Even the sunless, snowless winter weather couldn't prevent Paris from looking promising.

He had lunch with a man from the A.P. who had just come back from America. The man from the A.P. said that things were in unholy shape in America and that even if you ate in drugstores it cost at least a dollar and a half for lunch and Beddoes ought to be damned glad he wasn't there.

Beddoes got to the café a little late, but Christina hadn't arrived. He sat on the glass-enclosed terrace, next to the huge window, feeling it cold from the winter afternoon against his sleeve. The terrace was crowded with women drinking tea and men reading the evening newspapers. Outside, under the trees, a little parade was forming, the veterans of some World War I unit, huddling, middle-aged, and chilled in their overcoats, with their flags and decorations, preparing to walk behind an Army band up to the Arch and put a wreath on the tomb in memory of comrades who had fallen in battles that no one any longer remembered. The French, Beddoes thought sourly, because Christina was late and the afternoon had failed its promise, are always finding occasions to block traffic. They have an endless supply of dead to celebrate.

He ordered a beer, because he had drunk too much at lunch. He had also eaten too much, in the first wave of gluttony after Egyptian food. His stomach felt uncomfortable, and he was suddenly very tired from all the miles he had traveled in the past twenty-four hours. After the age of thirty-five, he thought, in evening melancholy, no matter how swift the plane, how calm the air, how soft the cushion, the bones record the miles inexorably. He had turned thirty-five three months before and he had begun to reflect uneasily upon age. He stared at his face in mirrors, noticing wrinkles under his eyes and gray in

his beard when he shaved. He remembered hearing that
aging ballplayers shaved two and three times a day to
keep managers and sportswriters from seeing the telltale
flecks in beard stubble. Maybe, he thought, career men
in the foreign service ought to do the same thing. Seventy
minus thirty-five leaves thirty-five, he thought. It was an
equation that came ominously to mind, especially late in
the afternoon, more and more often after the midway
anniversary. He stared out through the cold glass at the
shuffling veterans, ranked shabbily behind their flags,
their breath, mingled with cigarette smoke, rising in little
clouds above their heads. He wished they'd start marching
and get away from there. "Veteran" was a word that
suddenly fell on his ear with an unpleasant sound.

He also wished that Christina would arrive. It wasn't
like her to be late. She was one of those rare girls who
always got to places exactly on the appointed hour. Irrelevantly, he remembered that she also dressed with great
speed and took only a minute or two to comb her hair.
She had blond hair, cut in the short Parisian manner,
which left the back of her neck bare. Beddoes thought
about the back of Christina's neck and felt better.

They would give themselves a gay evening, he thought.
One should not permit himself to feel tired or old in Paris.
If the feeling ever gets chronic, he told himself, I'll
move away for good.

He thought about the evening ahead of him. They'd
wander around to a couple of bars, avoiding their friends
and not drinking too much, and go to a *bistro* in the
markets where there were thick steaks and a heavy red
wine, and after that maybe they'd go to the night club
where there was a queer, original puppet show and three
young men who sang funny songs that, unlike so many
night-club songs, really did turn out to be funny. When
you came out into the street after their act you were
charmed and amused and you had the sense that this
was the way a man should feel in Paris at two o'clock
in the morning.

The night before he left for Cairo, he had taken Christina there. The prospect of going back on this first night
home gave him an unexplained but pleasant feeling of
satisfactory design. Christina had looked very pretty, the
prettiest girl in the room full of handsome women, he'd
thought, and he had even danced, for the first time in
months. The music was supplied by a pianist and a man

who got quivering, rich sounds from an electric guitar, and they played those popular French songs that always made you feel how sweet was love in the city, how full of sorrow and tempered regret.

The music had made Christina a little moony, he remembered, which was strange for her, and she had held his hand during the show, and kissed him when the lights went out between numbers. Her eyes had filled with tears for a moment and she had said, "What am I going to do without you for two months?" when he spoke of his departure the next morning. He had felt, a little warily, because he was affected, too, that it was lucky he was leaving, if she was moving into that phase. That was the pre-yearning-for-marriage phase, and you had to be on guard against it, especially late at night, in Paris, in darkened rooms where pianists and electric guitars played songs about dead leaves and dead loves and lovers who were separated by wars.

Beddoes had been married once, and he felt, for the time being, that that was enough. Wives had a tendency to produce children, and sulk and take to drink or other men when their husbands were called away to the other side of the earth for three or four months at a time on jobs.

He had been a little surprised at Christina. Yearning was not in her line. He had known her, although until recently not very well, almost from the time she arrived from the States four years before. She did some modelling for photographers and was pretty enough to have done very well at it, except that, as she said, she felt too silly making the fashionable languorous, sexy grimaces that were demanded of her. She knew how to type and take dictation and she found odd jobs with American businessmen who had worked for a month or two at a time in Paris. She had picked up French immediately, and drove a car, and from time to time she got curious little jobs as a companion for old American ladies who wanted to tour through the château country or into Switzerland. She never seemed to need any sleep (even now she was only about twenty-six) and she would stay up all night with anybody and she went to all the parties and had had, to Beddoes' knowledge, affairs with two friends of his— a free-lance photographer and an Air Transport Command pilot who had been killed in a crash outside Frankfurt. You could telephone her at any hour of the day or

night without making her angry and you could introduce
her into any group and be pleased with the way she behaved. She always knew which bistro was having a rage
at the moment and who was singing at which night club
and which new painter was worth seeing and who was in
town and who was going to arrive next week and which
little hotels outside Paris were pleasant for lunch or a
weekend. She obviously didn't have much money, but
she dressed charmingly, French enough to amuse her
French friends and not so French that she made Americans feel she was trying to pretend she was European.
All in all, while she was not a girl of whom your grand-
mother was likely to approve, she was, as Beddoes had
once told her, an ornament to the wandering and troubled
years of the second half of the twentieth century.

The veterans started to move off, the banners flapping
a little in the dusk as the small parade turned past the
TWA office and up the Champs-Élysées. Beddoes watched
them, thinking vaguely of other parades, other banners.
Then he saw Christina striding diagonally across the street,
swift and sure of herself in the traffic. She could live in
Europe the rest of her life, Beddoes thought, smiling as
he watched her, and all she'd have to do would be to
walk ten steps and everybody would know she had been
born on the other side of the ocean.

He stood when she opened the door into the terrace.
She was hatless, and Beddoes noticed that her hair was
much darker than he remembered and she was wearing
it longer. He kissed her on both cheeks as she came up
to the table. "Welcome," he said. "In the French style."

She hugged him momentarily. "Well, now," she said,
"here's the man again."

She sat down, opening her coat, and smiled across the
table at him. Her cheeks were flushed from the cold and
her eyes were shining and she looked glitteringly young.

"The spirit of Paris," Beddoes said, touching her hand
on the table. "American division. What'll it be to drink?"

"Tea, please. I'm so glad to see you."

"Tea?" Beddoes made a face. "Anything wrong?"

"No." Christina shook her head. "I just want tea."

"That's a hell of a drink to welcome a traveler home
on," Beddoes said.

"With lemon, please," Christina said.

Beddoes shrugged, and ordered one tea from the waiter.

"How was Egypt?" Christina asked.

"Was I in Egypt?" Beddoes stared at Christina, enjoying her face.

"That's what it said in the papers."

"Oh, yes," Beddoes said. "A new world struggling to be born," he said, his voice deep and expert. "Too late for feudalism, too early for democracy . . ."

Christina made a face. "Lovely phrases for the State Department archives," she said. "I mean over a drink how is Egypt."

"Sunny and sad," Beddoes said. "After two weeks in Cairo you feel sorry for everybody. How is Paris?"

"Too late for democracy," Christina said, "too early for feudalism."

Beddoes grinned and leaned across the little table and kissed her gently. "I mean over a kiss," he said, "how is Paris?"

"The same," Christina said. She hesitated. "Almost the same."

"Who's around?"

"The group," Christina said carelessly. "The usual happy exiles. Charles, Boris, Anne, Teddy . . ."

Teddy was the free-lance photographer. "You see much of him?" Beddoes asked, very lightly.

"Uh?" Christina smiled, just a little, at him.

"Merely checking." Beddoes grinned.

"No, I haven't," Christina said. "His Greek's in town."

"Still the Greek?"

"Still the Greek," Christina said.

The waiter came and placed the tea in front of her. She poured it into the cup and squeezed the lemon. She had long, competent fingers, and Beddoes noticed that she no longer used bright nail polish.

"Your hair," he said. "What happened?"

Christina touched her hair absently. "Oh," she said. "You noticed?"

"Where're the blondes of yesteryear?"

"I decided to go natural." Christina stirred her tea. "See what that was like for a change. Like it?"

"I haven't decided yet. It's longer, too."

"Uh-huh. For the winter. The back of my neck was cold. People say it makes me look younger."

"They're absolutely right," Beddoes said. "You now look exactly eleven."

Christina smiled and lifted her cup to him. "To those who return," she said.

"I don't accept toasts in tea," Beddoes said.

"You're a finicky, liquor-loving man," Christina said, and placidly sipped at her tea.

"Now," Beddoes said, "the evening. I thought we might skip our dear friends and go to that place in the markets for dinner, because I'm dying for a steak, and after that—" He stopped. "What's the matter? Can't we have dinner together?"

"It's not that, exactly." Christina kept her head down and stirred her tea slowly. "I have a date—"

"Cancel him," Beddoes said promptly. "Cancel the swine."

"I can't really." Christina looked soberly up at him. "He's coming to meet me here any minute now."

"Oh." Beddoes nodded. "That makes it different, doesn't it."

"Yes."

"Can't we shake him?"

"No," Christina said. "We can't shake him."

"The man doesn't live who can't be shaken," said Beddoes. "Old friend, you say, who just arrived from the horrors of the desert, just escaped dysentery and religious wars by the skin of his teeth, needs soothing, you say, and tender attention for his shattered nerves, et cetera."

Christina was smiling, but shaking her head. "Sorry," she said. "It can't be done."

"Want me to do it?" Beddoes said. "Man to man. See here, old fellow, we're all grown-up, civilized human beings—That sort of thing?"

"No," Christina said.

"Why not?" Beddoes asked, conscious that he was breaking a long-standing and until now jealously adhered-to rule about not pleading for anything. "Why can't we?"

"Because I don't want to," Christina said.

"Oh," said Beddoes. "The wind is in that direction."

"Variably," Christina said softly, "in that direction. We could all have dinner together. The three of us. He's a very nice man. You'd like him."

"I never like any man the first night I'm in Paris," Beddoes said.

They sat in silence for a moment while Beddoes remembered all the times that Christina had said over the phone, "O.K., it's sinful, but I'll brush him. Meet you at eight." It was hard to believe, sitting across from her, noticing that there was no obvious change in the way she looked at him, in the way she touched his hand, that she wouldn't say it in the next minute or so.

"Two months is a long time, isn't it?" Beddoes said. "In Paris?"

"No," Christina said. "It's not a long time. In Paris or anywhere else."

"Hello, Christina." It was a tall, rather heavyset young man, smiling and blond, who was standing, holding a hat, next to the table. "I found the place all right." He leaned over and kissed her forehead.

Beddoes stood up.

"Jack," Christina said, "this is Walter Beddoes. John Haislip. Dr. Haislip."

The two men shook hands.

"He's a surgeon," Christina said as Haislip gave his hat and coat to the attendant and sat down beside her. "He nearly had his picture in *Life* last year for something he did with kidneys. In thirty years he's going to be enormously famous."

Haislip chuckled. He was a big, placid, self-confident-looking man, with the air of an athlete, who was probably older than he looked. And just with one glance Beddoes could tell how the man felt about Christina. Haislip wasn't hiding anything in that department.

"What'll you drink, Doctor?" Beddoes asked.

"Lemonade, please."

"Un citron pressé," Beddoes said to the waiter. He peered curiously at Christina, but she was keeping her face straight.

"Jack doesn't drink," Christina said. "He says it isn't fair for people who make a living out of cutting other people up."

"When I retire," Haislip said cheerfully, "I'm going to soak it up and let my hands shake like leaves in the wind." He turned to Beddoes. You could tell that it took a conscious wrench for him to stop looking at Christina. "Did you have a good time in Egypt?" he asked.

"Oh," Beddoes said, surprised. "You know about my being in Egypt?"

"Christina's told me all about you," Haislip said.

"I swore a solemn oath that I was going to forget Egypt for a month once I got here," Beddoes said.

Haislip chuckled. He had a low, unforced laugh and
his face was friendly and unself-conscious. "I know how
you feel," he said. "The same way I feel about the hospital sometimes."

"Where is the hospital?" Beddoes asked.

"Seattle," Christina said quickly.

"How long have you been here?" Beddoes saw Christina glance at him obliquely as he spoke.

"Three weeks," said Haislip. He turned back toward
Christina, as though he could find comfort in no other
position. "The changes that can take place in three weeks.
My Lord!" He patted Christina's arm and chuckled again.
"One more week and back to the hospital."

"You here for fun or for business?" Beddoes asked,
falling helplessly into the pattern of conversation of all
Americans who meet each other abroad for the first time.

"A little of both," Haislip said. "There was a con-
ference of surgeons I was asked to attend, and I moseyed
around a few hospitals on the side."

"What do you think of French medicine now you've
had a chance to see some of it?" Beddoes asked, the
investigator within operating automatically.

"Well"— Haislip managed to look away from Christina for a moment— "they function differently from us
over here. Intuitively. They don't have the equipment
we have, or the money for research, and they have to
make up for it with insight and intuition." He grinned.
"If you're feeling poorly, Mr. Beddoes," he said, "don't
hesitate to put yourself in their hands. You'll do just about
as well here as anyplace else."

"I feel all right," Beddoes said, then felt that it had
been an idiotic thing to say. The conversation was beginning to make him uncomfortable, not because of anything
that had been said but because of the way the man kept
looking, so openly and confessingly and completely, at
Christina. There was a little pause and Beddoes had the
feeling that unless he jumped in, they would sit in silence
forever. "Do any sightseeing?" he asked lamely.

"Not as much as I'd like," Haislip said. "Just around
Paris. I'd've loved to go down south this time of the
year. That place Christina keeps talking about. St. Paul
de Vence. I guess that's about as different from Seattle
as a man could wish for and still get running water
and Christian nourishment. You've been there, haven't
you, Mr. Beddoes?"

"Yes," Beddoes said.

"Christina told me," said Haislip. "Oh, thank you," he said to the waiter who put the lemonade down in front of him.

Beddoes stared at Christina. They had spent a week together there early in the autumn. He wondered what, exactly, she had told the Doctor.

"We'll make it the next trip," Haislip said.

"Oh," said Beddoes, noting the "we" and wondering whom it included. "You planning to come over again soon?"

"In three years." Haislip carefully extracted the ice from his lemonade and put it on the saucer. "I figure I can get away for six weeks in the summer every three years. People don't get so sick in the summertime." He stood up. "Pardon me," he said, "but I have to make a couple of telephone calls."

"Downstairs and to the right," Christina said. "The woman'll put the calls through for you. She speaks English."

Haislip laughed. "Christina doesn't trust my French," he said. "She says it's the only recognizable Puget Sound accent that has ever been imposed upon the language." He started away from the table, then stopped. "I sincerely hope you'll be able to join us for dinner, Mr. Beddoes."

"Well," Beddoes said, "I made a tentative promise I'd meet some people. But I'll see what I can do."

"Good." Haislip touched Christina's shoulder lightly, as though for some obscure reassurance, and walked away between the tables.

Beddoes watched him, thinking unpleasantly, Well, one thing, I'm better-looking, anyway. Then he turned to Christina. She was stirring the tea leaves at the bottom of her cup absently with her spoon. "That's why the hair is long and natural," Beddoes said. "Isn't it?"

"That's why." Christina kept stirring the tea leaves.

"And the nail polish."

"And the nail polish."

"And the tea."

"And the tea."

"What did you tell him about St. Paul de Vence?"

"Everything."

"Look up from that damned cup."

Slowly Christina put down the spoon and raised her

head. Her eyes were glistening, but not enough to make anything of it, and her mouth was set, as with an effort.

"What do you mean by everything?" Beddoes demanded.

"Everything."

"Why?"

"Because I don't have to hide anything from him."

"How long have you known him?"

"You heard," Christina said. "Three weeks. A friend of mine in New York asked him to look me up."

"What are you going to do with him?"

Christina looked directly into his eyes. "I'm going to marry him next week and I'm going back to Seattle with him."

"And you'll come back here three years from now for six weeks in the summertime, because people don't get so sick in the summertime," Beddoes said.

"Exactly."

"And that's O.K.?"

"Yes."

"You said that too defiantly," Beddoes said.

"Don't be clever with me," Christina said harshly. "I'm through with all that."

"Waiter!" Beddoes called. "Bring me a whiskey, please." He said it in English, because for the moment he had forgotten where he was. "And you," he said to Christina. "For the love of God, have a drink."

"Another tea," Christina said.

"Yes, Madame," said the waiter, and went off.

"Will you answer some questions?" Beddoes asked.

"Yes."

"Do I rate straight answers?"

"Yes."

Beddoes took a deep breath and looked through the window. A man in a raincoat was walking past, reading a newspaper and shaking his head.

"All right," Beddoes said. "What's so great about him?"

"What can I be expected to say to that?" Christina asked. "He's a gentle, good, useful man. And now what do you know?"

"What else?"

"And he loves me." She said it in a low voice. In all the time they'd been together, Beddoes hadn't heard her use the word before. "He loves me," Christina repeated flatly.

"I saw," said Beddoes. "Immoderately."

"Immoderately," Christina said.

"Now let me ask another question," Beddoes said. "Would you like to get up from this table and go off with me tonight?"

Christina pushed her cup away, turning it thoughtfully. "Yes," she said.

"But you won't," said Beddoes.

"No."

"Why not?"

"Let's talk about something else," said Christina. "Where're you going on your next trip? Kenya? Bonn? Tokyo?

"Why not"

"Because I'm tired of people like you," Christina said clearly. "I'm tired of correspondents and pilots and promising junior statesmen. I'm tired of all the brilliant young men who are constantly going someplace to report a revolution or negotiate a treaty or die in a war. I'm tired of airports and I'm tired of seeing people off. I'm tired of not being allowed to cry until the plane gets off the ground. I'm tired of being so damned prompt. I'm tired of answering the telephone. I'm tired of all the spoiled, hung-over international darlings. I'm tired of sitting down to dinner with people I used to love and being polite to their Greeks. I'm tired of being handed around the group. I'm tired of being more in love with people than they are with me. That answer your question?"

"More or less," Beddoes said. He was surprised that no one at any of the other tables seemed to be paying any special attention to them.

"When you left for Egypt," Christina went on, her voice level, "I decided. I leaned against that wire fence watching them refuelling all those monstrous planes, with the lights on, and I dried the tears and I decided. The next time, it was going to be someone who would be shattered when *I* took off."

"And you found him."

"I found him," Christina said flatly. "And I'm not going to shatter him."

Beddoes put out his hands and took hers. They lay limp in his grasp. "Chris . . ." he said. She was looking

out the window. She sat there, outlined against the shining
dusk beyond the plate glass, scrubbed and youthful and
implacable, making him remember, confusedly, the first
time he had met her, and all the best girls he had ever
known, and what she had looked like next to him in the
early-morning autumnal sunlight that streamed, only three
months before, into the hotel room in the south, which
overlooked the brown minor Alps and the distant sea.
Holding her hands, with the familiar touch of the girlish
fingers against his, he felt that if he could get her to
turn her head everything would be different.

"Chris . . ." he whispered.

But she didn't turn her head. "Write me in Seattle,"
she said, staring out the window, which was streaked with
moisture and in which the lights from within the café and
the lights from the restaurant across the street were
reflected and magnified and distorted.

Beddoes let her hands go. She didn't bother to move
them. They lay before her, with their pale nail polish
glistening dully, on the stained wood table. Beddoes
stood up. "I'd better go." It was difficult to talk, and his
voice sounded strange to him inside his head, and he
thought, God, I'm getting senile, I'm tempted to cry in
restaurants. "I don't want to wait for the check," he said.
"Tell your friend I'm sorry I couldn't join you for dinner
and that I apologize for leaving him with the check."

"That's all right," Christina said evenly. "He'll be
happy to pay."

Beddoes leaned over and kissed her, first on one cheek,
then on the other. "Goodbye," he said, thinking he was
smiling. "In the French style."

He got his coat quickly and went out. He went past the
TWA office to the great boulevard and turned the corner,
where the veterans had marched a half hour before. He
walked blindly toward the Arch, where the laurel leaves
of the wreath were already glistening in the evening mist
before the tomb and the flame.

He knew that it was a bad night to be alone and that
he ought to go in somewhere and telephone and ask
someone to have dinner with him. He passed two or
three places with telephones, and although he hesitated
before each one, he didn't go in. Because there was no
one in the whole city he wanted to see that night.

Peter Two

IT WAS SATURDAY NIGHT AND PEOPLE WERE KILLING EACH other by the hour on the small screen. Policemen were shot in the line of duty, gangsters were thrown off roofs, and an elderly lady was slowly poisoned for her pearls, and her murderer brought to justice by a cigarette company after a long series of discussions in the office of a private detective. Brave, unarmed actors leaped at villains holding forty-fives, and ingénues were saved from death by the knife by the quick thinking of various handsome and intrepid young men.

Peter sat in the big chair in front of the screen, his feet up over the arm, eating grapes. His mother wasn't home, so he ate the seeds and all as he stared critically at the violence before him. When his mother was around, the fear of appendicitis hung in the air and she watched carefully to see that each seed was neatly extracted and placed in an ashtray. Too, if she were home, there would be irritated little lectures on the quality of television entertainment for the young, and quick-tempered fiddling with the dials to find something that was vaguely defined as educational. Alone, daringly awake at eleven o'clock, Peter ground the seeds between his teeth, enjoying the impolite noise and the solitude and freedom of the empty house. During the television commercials Peter closed his eyes and imagined himself hurling bottles at large unshaven men with pistols and walking slowly up dark stairways toward the door behind which everyone knew the Boss was waiting, the bulge of his shoulder holster unmistakable under the cloth of his pencil-striped flannel jacket.

Peter was thirteen years old. In his class there were three other boys with the same name, and the history teacher, who thought he was a funny man, called them Peter One, Peter Two (now eating grapes, seeds and all), Peter Three, and Peter the Great. Peter the Great was, of course, the smallest boy in the class. He weighed only sixty-two pounds, and he wore glasses, and in games he was always the last one to be chosen. The class always laughed when the history teacher called out "Peter the

Great," and Peter Two laughed with them, but he didn't
think it was so awfully funny.

He had done something pretty good for Peter the
Great two weeks ago, and now they were what you might
call friends. All the Peters were what you might call
friends, on account of that comedian of a history teacher.
They weren't *real* friends, but they had something together, something the other boys didn't have. They didn't
like it, but they had it, and it made them responsible for
each other. So two weeks ago, when Charley Blaisdell,
who weighed a hundred and twenty, took Peter the Great's
cap at recess and started horsing around with it, and
Peter the Great looked as if he was going to cry, he, Peter
Two, grabbed the cap and gave it back and faced Blaisdell. Of course, there was a fight, and Peter thought it
was going to be his third defeat of the term, but a wonderful thing happened. In the middle of the fight, just
when Peter was hoping one of the teachers would show
up (they sure showed up plenty of times when you didn't
need them), Blaisdell let a hard one go. Peter ducked and
Blaisdell hit him on the top of the head and broke his
arm. You could tell right off he broke his arm, because
he fell to the ground yelling, and his arm just hung like
a piece of string. Walters, the gym teacher, finally showed
up and carried Blaisdell off, yelling all the time, and
Peter the Great came up and said admiringly, "Boy,
one thing you have to admit, you sure have a hard head."

Blaisdell was out of class two days, and he still had
his arm in the sling, and every time he was excused from
writing on the blackboard because he had a broken arm,
Peter got a nice warm feeling all over. Peter the Great
hung around him all the time, doing things for him and
buying him sodas, because Peter the Great's parents were
divorced and gave him all the money he wanted, to make
up to him. And that was O.K.

But the best thing was the feeling he'd had since the
fight. It was like what the people on the television must
feel after they'd gone into a room full of enemies and
come out with the girl or with the papers or with the
suspect, leaving corpses and desolation behind them.
Blaisdell weighed a hundred and twenty pounds but that
hadn't stopped Peter any more than the fact that the
spies all had two guns apiece ever stopped the F.B.I.
men on the screen. They saw what they had to do and
they went in and did it, that was all. Peter couldn't phrase

it for himself, but for the first time in his life he had a conscious feeling of confidence and pride in himself.

"Let them come," he muttered obscurely, munching grape seeds and watching the television set through narrowed eyes, "just let them come."

He was going to be a dangerous man, he felt, when he grew up, but one to whom the weak and the unjustly hunted could safely turn. He was sure he was going to be six feet tall, because his father was six feet tall, and all his uncles, and that would help. But he would have to develop his arms. They were just too thin. After all, you couldn't depend on people breaking their bones on your head every time. He had been doing pushups each morning and night for the past month. He could only do five and a half at a time so far, but he was going to keep at it until he had arms like steel bars. Arms like that really could mean the difference between life and death later on, when you had to dive under the gun and disarm somebody. You had to have quick reflexes, too, of course, and be able to feint to one side with your eyes before the crucial moment. And, most important of all, no matter what the odds, you had to be fearless. One moment of hesitation and it was a case for the morgue. But now, after the battle of Peter the Great's cap, he didn't worry about that part of it, the fearless part. From now on, it would just be a question of technique.

Comedians began to appear all over the dial, laughing with a lot of teeth, and Peter went into the kitchen and got another bunch of grapes and two tangerines from the refrigerator. He didn't put on the light in the kitchen and it was funny how mysterious a kitchen could be near midnight when nobody else was home, and there was only the beam of the light from the open refrigerator, casting shadows from the milk bottles onto the linoleum. Until recently he hadn't liked the dark too much and he always turned on lights wherever he went, but you had to practice being fearless, just like anything else.

He ate the two tangerines standing in the dark in the kitchen, just for practice. He ate the seeds, too, to show his mother. Then he went back into the living room, carrying the grapes.

The comedians were still on and still laughing. He fiddled with the dial, but they were wearing funny hats and laughing and telling jokes about the income tax on

all the channels. If his mother hadn't made him promise
to go to sleep by ten o'clock, he'd have turned off the
set and gone to bed. He decided not to waste his time
and got down on the floor and began to do pushups,
trying to be sure to keep his knees straight. He was up
to four and slowing down when he heard the scream.
He stopped in the middle of a pushup and waited, just
to make sure. The scream came again. It was a woman
and it was real loud. He looked up at the television set.
There was a man there talking about floor wax, a man
with a mustache and a lot of teeth, and it was a cinch
he wasn't doing any screaming.

The next time the scream came there was moaning
and talking at the end of it, and the sound of fists beating
on the front door. Peter got up and turned off the television, just to be sure the sounds he was hearing weren't
somehow being broadcast.

The beating on the door began again and a woman's
voice cried "Please, please, *please* . . ." and there was no
doubt about it any more.

Peter looked around him at the empty room. Three
lamps were lit and the room was nice and bright and the
light was reflected off the grapes and off the glass of the
picture of the boats on Cape Cod that his Aunt Martha
painted the year she was up there. The television set
stood in the corner, like a big blind eye now that the
light was out. The cushions of the soft chair he had been
sitting in to watch the programs were pushed in and he
knew his mother would come and plump them out before
she went to sleep, and the whole room looked like a
place in which it was impossible to hear a woman screaming at midnight and beating on the door with her fists
and yelling, "Please, please, *please* . . ."

The woman at the door yelled "Murder, murder, he's
killing me!" and for the first time Peter was sorry his
parents had gone out that night.

"Open the door!" the woman yelled. "Please, *please*
open the door!" You could tell she wasn't saying please
just to be polite by now.

Peter looked nervously around him. The room, with
all its lights, seemed strange, and there were shadows
behind everything. Then the woman yelled again, just
noise this time. Either a person is fearless, Peter thought
coldly, or he isn't fearless. He started walking slowly
toward the front door. There was a long mirror in the

foyer and he got a good look at himself. His arms looked very thin.

The woman began hammering once more on the front door and Peter looked at it closely. It was a big steel door, but it was shaking minutely, as though somebody with a machine was working on it. For the first time he heard another voice. It was a man's voice, only it didn't sound quite like a man's voice. It sounded like an animal in a cave, growling and deciding to do something unreasonable. In all the scenes of threat and violence on the television set, Peter had never heard anything at all like it. He moved slowly toward the door, feeling the way he had felt when he had the flu, remembering how thin his arms looked in the mirror, regretting that he had decided to be fearless.

"Oh, God!" the woman yelled, "Oh, God, don't do it!"

Then there was some more hammering and the low, animal sound of the beast in the cave that you never heard over the air, and he threw the door open.

Mrs. Chalmers was there in the vestibule, on her knees, facing him, and behind her Mr. Chalmers was standing, leaning against the wall, with the door to his own apartment open behind him. Mr. Chalmers was making that funny sound and he had a gun in his hand and he was pointing it at Mrs. Chalmers.

The vestibule was small and it had what Peter's mother called Early American wallpaper and a brass light fixture. There were only the two doors opening on the vestibule, and the Chalmers had a mat in front of theirs with "Welcome" written on it. The Chalmers were in their midthirties, and Peter's mother always said about them, "One thing about our neighbors, they *are* quiet." She also said that Mrs. Chalmers put a lot of money on her back.

Mrs. Chalmers was kind of fat and her hair was pretty blond and her complexion was soft and pink and she always looked as though she had been in the beauty parlor all afternoon. She always said "My, you're getting to be a big boy" to Peter when she met him in the elevator, in a soft voice, as though she was just about to laugh. She must have said that fifty times by now. She had a good, strong smell of perfume on her all the time, too.

Mr. Chalmers wore pince-nez glasses most of the time and he was getting bald and he worked late at his office a good many evenings of the week. When he met Peter in the elevator he would say, "It's getting colder," or "It's getting warmer," and that was all, so Peter had no opinion about him, except that he looked like the principal of a school.

But now Mrs. Chalmers was on her knees in the vestibule and her dress was torn and she was crying and there were black streaks on her cheeks and she didn't look as though she'd just come from the beauty parlor. And Mr. Chalmers wasn't wearing a jacket and he didn't have his glasses on and what hair he had was mussed all over his head and he was leaning against the Early American wallpaper making this animal noise, and he had a big, heavy pistol in his hand and he was pointing it right at Mrs. Chalmers.

"Let me in!" Mrs. Chalmers yelled, still on her knees. "You've got to let me in. He's going to kill me. *Please!*"

"Mrs. Chalmers . . ." Peter began. His voice sounded as though he were trying to talk under water, and it was very hard to say the "s" at the end of her name. He put out his hands uncertainly in front of him, as though he expected somebody to throw him something.

"Get inside, you," Mr. Chalmers said.

Peter looked at Mr. Chalmers. He was only five feet away and without his glasses he was squinting. Peter feinted with his eyes, or at least later in his life he thought he had feinted with his eyes. Mr. Chalmers didn't do anything. He just stood there, with the pistol pointed, somehow, it seemed to Peter, at both Mrs. Chalmers and himself at the same time. Five feet was a long distance, a long, long distance."

"Good night," Peter said, and he closed the door.

There was a single sob on the other side of the door and that was all.

Peter went in and put the uneaten grapes back in the refrigerator, flicking on the light as he went into the kitchen and leaving it on when he went out. Then he went back to the living room and got the stems from the first bunch of grapes and threw them into the fireplace, because otherwise his mother would notice and look for the seeds and not see them and give him four tablespoons of milk of magnesia the next day.

Then, leaving the lights on in the living room, although he knew what his mother would say about that when she got home, he went into his room and quickly got into bed. He waited for the sound of shots. There were two or three noises that might have been shots, but in the city it was hard to tell.

He was still awake when his parents came home. He heard his mother's voice, and he knew from the sound she was complaining about the lights in the living room and kitchen, but he pretended to be sleeping when she came into his room to look at him. He didn't want to start in with his mother about the Chalmers, because then she'd ask when it had happened and she'd want to know what he was doing up at twelve o'clock.

He kept listening for shots for a long time, and he got hot and damp under the covers and then freezing cold. He heard several sharp, ambiguous noises in the quiet night, but nothing that you could be sure about, and after a while he fell asleep.

In the morning, Peter got out of bed early, dressed quickly, and went silently out of the apartment without waking his parents. The vestibule looked just the way it always did, with the brass lamp and the flowered wallpaper and the Chalmers' doormat with "Welcome" on it. There were no bodies and no blood. Sometimes when Mrs. Chalmers had been standing there waiting for the elevator, you could smell her perfume for a long time after. But now there was no smell of perfume, just the dusty, apartment-house usual smell. Peter stared at the Chalmers' door nervously while waiting for the elevator to come up, but it didn't open and no sound came from within.

Sam, the man who ran the elevator and who didn't like him, anyway, only grunted when Peter got into the elevator, and Peter decided not to ask him any questions. He went out into the chilly, bright Sunday-morning street, half expecting to see the morgue wagon in front of the door, or at least two or three prowl cars. But there was only a sleepy woman in slacks airing a boxer and a man with his collar turned up hurrying up from the corner with the newspapers under his arm.

Peter went across the street and looked up to the sixth floor, at the windows of the Chalmers' apartment. The Venetian blinds were pulled shut in every room and all the windows were closed.

A policeman walked down the other side of the street, heavy, blue and purposeful, and for a moment Peter felt close to arrest. But the policeman continued on toward the avenue and turned the corner and disappeared and Peter said to himself, They never know anything.

He walked up and down the street, first on one side, then on the other, waiting, although it was hard to know what he was waiting for. He saw a hand come out through the blinds in his parents' room and slam the window shut, and he knew he ought to get upstairs quickly with a good excuse for being out, but he couldn't face them this morning, and he would invent an excuse later. Maybe he would even say he had gone to the museum, although he doubted that his mother would swallow that. Some excuse. Later.

Then, after he had been patrolling the street for almost two hours, and just as he was coming up to the entrance of his building, the door opened and Mr. and Mrs. Chalmers came out. He had on his pince-nez and a dark-gray hat, and Mrs. Chalmers had on her fur coat and a red hat with feathers on it. Mr. Chalmers was holding the door open politely for his wife, and she looked, as she came out the door, as though she had just come from the beauty parlor.

It was too late to turn back or avoid them, and Peter just stood still, five feet from the entrance.

"Good morning," Mr. Chalmers said as he took his wife's arm and they started walking past Peter.

"Good morning, Peter," said Mrs. Chalmers in her soft voice, smiling at him. "Isn't it a nice day today?"

"Good morning," Peter said, and he was surprised that it came out and sounded like good morning.

The Chalmers walked down the street toward Madison Avenue, two married people, arm in arm, going to church or to a big hotel for Sunday breakfast. Peter watched them, ashamed. He was ashamed of Mrs. Chalmers for looking the way she did the night before, down on her knees, and yelling like that and being so afraid. He was ashamed of Mr. Chalmers for making the noise that was not like the noise of a human being, and for threatening to shoot Mrs. Chalmers and not doing it. And he was ashamed of himself because he had been fearless when he opened the door, but had not been fearless ten seconds later, with Mr. Chalmers five feet away with the gun. He was ashamed of himself for not taking Mrs. Chalmers into the apartment, ashamed because he was not lying now with a bullet in his heart. But most of all he was ashamed because they had all said good morning to each other and the Chalmers were walking quietly together, arm in arm, in the windy sunlight, toward Madison Avenue.

It was nearly eleven o'clock when Peter got back to the apartment, but his parents had gone back to sleep. There was a pretty good program on at eleven, about counterspies in Asia, and he turned it on automatically, while eating an orange. It was pretty exciting, but then there was a part in which an Oriental held a ticking bomb in his hand in a roomful of Americans, and Peter could tell what was coming. The hero, who was fearless and who came from California, was beginning to feint with his eyes, and Peter reached over and turned the set off. It closed down with a shivering, collapsing pattern. Blinking a little, Peter watched the blind screen for a moment.

Ah, he thought in sudden, permanent disbelief, after the night in which he had faced the incomprehensible, shameless, weaponed grownup world and had failed to disarm it, ah, they can have that, that's for kids.

Age of Reason

HE HAD THE DREAM ONLY ONCE—IN DECEMBER. HE thought about it for a few moments the next morning, and forgot about it until one evening in April, ten minutes before his plane was scheduled to take off. Then, suddenly, it returned to him. Always, when he was about to board a plane, there was a slight tremor, an awareness of risk, however small and controlled; a slight, subconscious realization that each flight might end with death; a hidden knowledge that there was a small, lurking fatality in winds and clouds and valves and wings, and that no amount of airline skill and care and advertising could ever absolutely dispel it. It was that usual minute, buried twinge of disaster that made him remember the dream as he stood at the gate with his wife and sister, looking out at the dark field and the huge, substantial plane and the flickering lights that marked the runways.

The dream had been a simple one. In it, somehow, his sister Elizabeth had died, and he had, in a resigned and hopeless way, followed the coffin to the cemetery and watched with dry eyes as it was lowered into the ground, and then he had returned home. And somehow, in the dream, it had all happened on May 14th. The date had been absolutely clear and definite and had given the dream a real, tragic sense that it might not otherwise have had. When he woke, he tried to figure out why May 14th, an obscure day five months in the future, had been chosen so relentlessly and specifically by his dreaming mind, but it was no use. There were no birthdays in his family in May, no anniversaries, and nothing in particular had ever happened to him or anyone he knew on that day. He had laughed a little, sleepily, to himself, gently touched Alice's bare shoulder in the bed beside him, and had risen and gone to work, in the sensible, everyday atmosphere of drafting boards and blueprints, without saying a word then or later to her or anyone else about the dream.

And then—laughing at the way his five-year-old daughter had sleepily and carelessly said goodbye when he had left the apartment, standing there with the noise of engines filling the fresh April evening air, kissing his sister Elizabeth goodbye—the dream came back. Elizabeth was as rosy and sturdy as ever, a cheerful, pretty girl who looked as though she had just come triumphantly off a tennis court or from a swimming meet, and if there was any touch of doom hanging over her, it was very well hidden.

"Bring me back Cary Grant," Elizabeth said as she brushed his cheek.

"Of course," Roy said.

"I now leave you two to say a fond farewell," Elizabeth said. "Alice, give him his last-minute instructions. Tell him to behave himself."

"I've already briefed him for this mission," Alice said. "No girls. No more than three Martinis before dinner. Telephone me and report twice weekly. Get on the plane and get home the minute the job is done."

"Two weeks," Roy said. "I swear I'll be back in two weeks."

"Don't have too good a time." Alice was smiling but on the verge of tears, as she always was every time he went anyplace without her, even overnight to Washington.

"I won't," Roy said. "I promise to be miserable."

"Good enough." Alice laughed.

"No old telephone numbers secreted on your person?" Elizabeth asked.

"No." There had been a period in Roy's life, just before he married Alice, when he had been quite lively, and during the war some of his friends had come back from Europe with lurid and highly fictionized tales of wild times in Paris and London, and to the women of his family he seemed more dashing and unstable than was the fact.

"God," he said, "it'll be a relief getting away from this female board of directors for a few days."

He and Alice went up to the gate.

"Take care of yourself, darling," Alice said softly.

"Don't worry." He kissed her.

"I hate this," Alice said, holding onto him. "We're always saying goodbye. This is the last time. From now on, no matter where you go, I'm going with you."

"All right." Roy smiled down at her.

"Even if you only go to Yankee Stadium."

"Couldn't be more pleased." He held her tightly for a moment, dear and familiar and forlorn, left behind this way. Then he walked out to the plane. He turned as he started to climb into it, and waved. Alice and Elizabeth waved back, and he noticed again how much alike they looked, standing together, like two sisters in a pretty family, both of them blond and fair, trim, with little tricks of movement and holding themselves that were almost identical.

He turned and went into the plane, and a moment later the door was shut behind him and the plane started rolling toward the end of the runway.

Ten days later, over the phone between Los Angeles and New York, Roy told Alice she would have to come West. "Munson says it's going to take six months," Roy said, "and he's promised me a place to live, and you are hereby invited."

"Thanks," Alice said. "Tell Munson I would like to kick him in the teeth."

"Can't be helped, baby," Roy said. "Commerce above all. You know."

"Why couldn't he have told you before you went out? Then you could've helped me close up the apartment and we could've gone out together."

"He didn't know before I came out," Roy said patiently. "The world is very confused these days."

"I would like to kick him in the teeth."

"O.K." Roy grinned. "You come out and tell him yourself. When do you arrive? Tomorrow?"

"There's one thing you've got to learn, Roy," Alice said. "I am not a troop movement. You can't say, 'Civilian Alice Gaynor will report three thousand miles from here at 4 P.M. tomorrow,' and expect it to happen."

"O.K., you're not a troop movement. When?"

Alice chuckled. "You sound nice and anxious."

"I *am* nice and anxious."

"That's good."

"When?"

"Well"—Alice hesitated thoughtfully—"I have to get Sally out of school, I have to send some things to storage, I have to rent the apartment, I have to get plane reservations—"

"When?"

"Two weeks," Alice said, "if I can get the reservations all right. Can you wait?"

"No," Roy said.

"Neither can I." They both laughed. "Have you been very gay out there?"

Roy recognized the tentative, inquiring tone and sighed to himself. "Dull as mud," he said. "I stay in in the evenings and read. I've read six books and I'm halfway through General Marshall's report on the conduct of the war."

"There was one evening you didn't read." Alice's voice was careful and purposely light.

"All right," Roy said flatly. "Let's hear it."

"Monica came in from the Coast Tuesday and she called me. She said she saw you with a beautiful girl at a fancy restaurant."

"If there was any justice," Roy said, "they would drop Monica on Bikini Atoll."

"She had long black hair, Monica said."

"She was absolutely right," Roy said. "The girl had long black hair."

"Don't shout. I can hear perfectly well."

"What Monica neglected to say was that it was Charlie Lewis's wife—"

"She said you were alone."

"—and Charlie Lewis was twenty feet away, in the men's room."

"Are you sure?"

"No. Maybe he was in the ladies' room."

"It may be funny to you, but with your history—"

"I will match my history with any husband's," Roy said.

"I hate your sense of humor on this subject." Alice's voice began to tremble a little, and Roy relented.

"Listen, baby," he said softly. "Get out here quick. Quick as you can. Then we can stop this nonsense."

"I'm sorry." Alice's voice was soft and repentant. "It's just that we've been away from each other for so long in these last few years. I'm foolish and jittery. Who's paying for this call?"

"The company."

"That's good." Alice chuckled. "I'd hate to fight on our own money. Do you love me?"

"Get out here quick."

"Do you consider that an answer to my question?"

"Yes."

"O.K.," Alice said. "So do I. Goodbye, darling. See you soon."

"Kiss Sally for me," said Roy.

"I will. Goodbye."

Roy hung up. First he shook his head a little wearily, remembering the argument; then he smiled, remembering the end of the conversation. He got up from his chair and went over to the calendar on the desk, to try to figure what day he could expect his wife and child.

The telegram came three days later: "RESERVATIONS ON 2 O'CLOCK FLIGHT MAY 14. WILL ARRIVE BURBANK AT 10 P.M. YOUR TIME. PLEASE SHAVE. LOVE, ALICE."

Roy grinned as he reread the telegram, then became conscious of a sensation of uneasiness that refused to be crystallized or pinned down. He walked around all that day with that undefined sense of trouble, and it wasn't until he was dozing off to sleep that night that it suddenly became clear to him. He woke and got out of bed and read the telegram again. May 14th. He kept the lamp on and lit a cigarette and sat up in the narrow bed in the impersonal hotel room and slowly allowed the thing to take control.

He had never been a superstitious man, or even a religious man, and he had always laughed at his mother, who had a fund of dreams and predictions and omens of good and evil at her command. Alice had one or two superstitious habits—like not talking about anything that she wanted to have happen, because she was sure it wouldn't happen if it were mentioned or hoped for too much—but he had always scorned them, too. During the war, when every magazine assured the world that there were no atheists in foxholes, he had never prayed, even in the most gloomy and dangerous times. He had never, in all his adult life, done anything as a result of superstition or premonition. He looked around him at his efficiently furnished, bright, twentieth-century room and felt foolish to be awake now in the heel of the night, chasing phantoms and echoing warnings and scraps of old dreams through the sensible channels of his engineer's mind.

The dream, of course, had been explicit. His sister was to die on May 14th. But dreams never were what they seemed to be, and Elizabeth and Alice looked so much alike, and they were always together and such good friends. . . . He knew enough about dreams to understand that it would be a simple transference in that shadowy, whimsical world—a wife for a sister, a sister for a wife. And now, of all the days in the year, his wife and child had picked May 14th to fly the three thousand miles over the rivers and mountains of the continent from New York to California.

He put out the light much later, with nothing decided, and tried to sleep. He stared up at the dark ceiling, listening to the occasional swift swhoosh of a car on the street outside, hurrying home through the waning night. For a man who didn't believe in Fate, he thought, who saw the world in terms of simple cause and effect; who felt that no act was inevitable, that what was going to happen tomorrow or the next second was in no place determined and was everlastingly variable; who felt that no man's death or burial place was fixed, that no event was recorded in any future book, that the human race got hints or warnings from no supernatural source—this was a ludicrous and profitless way to spend a night. For a man who walked under ladders, cheerfully broke mirrors, never had his palm read or his fortune told from cards, he felt that he was behaving idiotically, and yet he couldn't sleep.

In the morning he called New York.

"Alice," he said, "I want you to come by train."

"What's the matter?" she said.

"I'm afraid of the plane." He heard her laugh incredulously over the phone. "I'm afraid of the plane," he repeated stubbornly.

"Don't be silly," Alice said. "They haven't had an accident with that plane yet, and they won't start now."

"Even so——"

"And I'm not going to try to keep Sally amused for three days in a roomette," Alice said. "It would take me the whole summer to recover."

"Please," Roy said.

"And I couldn't get train reservations for weeks," Alice said, "and the apartment's rented and everything. What's come over you?" Her voice sounded suspicious and wary.

"Nothing," Roy said. "It's just that I'm worried about flying."

"Good God!" Alice said. "You've flown two hundred thousand miles in all sorts of contraptions."

"I know," Roy said. "That's why I'm worried."

"Are you drunk?" Alice asked.

"Alice, darling," Roy sighed. "It's eight o'clock in the morning out here."

"Well, you sound queer."

"I've been up all night, worrying."

"Well, stop worrying. I'll see you on the fourteenth. Are you sure you're all right?"

"Yes."

"This is a very strange telephone call, I must say."

"I'm sorry."

They talked for a moment more, but quite coldly, and Roy hung up feeling dissatisfied and defeated.

He called again two days later and tried once more.

"Don't ask any questions," he said. "Just do this for me, and I'll explain when you get out here. If you want to come on the plane, that's all right, but don't come on the fourteenth. Come on the fifteenth or sixteenth or seventeenth. Any other day. But not on the fourteenth."

"Roy," Alice said, "you've got me terribly worried. What's come over you? I've asked Elizabeth and she says that this doesn't sound like you at all."

"How is she?" Roy asked.

"Elizabeth is fine. She tells me to ignore you and come out as scheduled."

"Tell her to mind her own damned business." Roy had been working hard and sleeping badly and his voice was raw and nervous, and Alice reacted to it.

"I think I know what's going on," she said coldly. "Monica told me there's a big party at the Condons' on the fourteenth, and you've probably promised to take someone else, and a wife would be a big handicap——"

"Oh, God, will you stop that!" Roy shouted into the phone.

"I haven't been married to you for seven years for nothing," Alice said. "I'm not blind."

"Come out today!" Roy shouted. "Come out tomorrow! Come out the thirteenth! Only not the fourteenth!"

"You know as well as I do that if I give up my reservations, I won't get another until June. If you don't want to see me any more, tell me. You don't have to go through all this rigmarole."

"Alice, darling," Roy pleaded, "I assure you I want to see you."

"Well, then, stop this nonsense or tell me what it's all about."

"Alice, it's this way," he began, resolved to tell her, no matter how much of an idiot it made him feel, but there was a click on the wire and then three thousand miles of whispering silence. By the time he got Alice back on the phone, ten minutes later, he felt too ridiculous, felt that he could not live with himself or his wife if he at this late date exposed himself as a silly, undependable man with a brain gone soft and nervous and irresponsible after all the sane, dependable years.

"I haven't anything else to say," he told Alice when the operator finally made the connection, "except that I love you very much and I couldn't bear it if anything ever happened to you."

He heard Alice crying softly at the other end of the wire. "We have to be together soon," she said. "This is awful. And please don't call me any more, Roy, darling. You're acting so strangely, and after I talk to you, the most miserable ideas grab hold of me. Will it be all right when I get out there?"

"It'll be wonderful, darling," Roy said.

"And you'll never go away without me again? Never?"

"Never." He could close his eyes and see her crouched like a little girl over the phone in the bedroom of their quiet, pleasant home, both her hands on the instrument, her pretty, clever face screwed up with grief and longing, and it was hard to say anything more. "Good night," he said. "Be careful."

He hung up and stared wildly at the blank wall on the other side of the room, knowing he wouldn't sleep again that night.

There was an early fog on the morning of May 14th,
and Roy stared at it, hot-eyed and lightheaded from lack
of sleep, and went out and walked along the quiet, gray
streets, with only police cars and milk-delivery carts disturbing the soft, thick dawn.

California, he thought; it's always foggy in the morning, fog is general in California before eight, and it's a
different time and a different weather on the coast of the
Atlantic, and her plane isn't due to leave for hours yet.

It must be the war, he thought. This would never have
happened to me before the war. I thought I came out all
right, but maybe I was overconfident. All the cemeteries,
with the young men tucked away in the sand and spring
grass, and the old ladies in black lace dresses dying on
the next street in London in the air raids. A man's ima-
gination was bound to take a morbid turn, finally. I must
take hold of myself, he told himself reasonably. I'm the
man who always felt sane, balanced, healthy in all situa-
tions, who always scorned mediums and table tappers,
priests and psychoanalysts.

The fog was beginning to lift, and he stopped to stare
at the distant smudge of mountains that stood guard over
the eastern approaches of the city. Planes had to come in
steeply over them and circle the city and land from the
westward side. A strip of blue appeared above the mountains and widened and widened, and the fog melted away
in wisps among the ugly, fat palm trees that lined the street,
and soon the sun was shining on the dewy lawns, and the
sky looked clear and blue from Beverly Hills to Scotland.

He went back to his hotel and lay down without even
taking his shoes off. Some time later he woke up.
Vaguely, in the moment before waking, there was a confusion of planes going down in puffs of smoke, like the
newsreel of an air battle, and Sally's voice over it, regretfully saying, as she always did at bedtime, "Do I
really have to go to sleep now? I'm terribly wide awake."

He looked at the clock. It was one-forty in New York.
They were at the airport now, and the big plane was waiting on the field, with the mechanics fiddling on it and
the men checking the gas tanks. The hell with it, he
thought. I don't care how foolish I seem.

He picked up the phone. "LaGuardia Field, New
York," he said.

"There will be a slight delay," the operator sang. "I
will call you."

"This is very important," Roy said. "Urgent."

"There will be a slight delay," the operator said in exactly the same tones. "I will call you."

He hung up and went to the window and stared out. The sky stretched, radiant and clear, over the hills toward New York. I'll tell her the whole thing, he thought, idiotic or not. Forbid her to get on the plane. We can laugh about it later. I'll take the first plane back myself and fly back with them. That'll prove to her it has nothing to do with anything here.

He went and got out his valise and put three shirts in it, then picked up the phone again. Five minutes later he got the airport, but it took another five minutes to get through to the station manager for the airline.

"My name is Gaynor"—Roy's voice was high and hurried—"and this is a very unusual request, so please listen carefully."

"What was that name, sir?"

"Gaynor. G-a-y-n-o-r."

"Oh, yes, Gaynor. Like the dive." The distant voice laughed politely at its own joke. "What can I do for you, sir?"

"My wife and child—"

"You will have to speak louder, please."

"My wife and child!" Roy shouted. "Mrs. Alice Gaynor, on the two-o'clock flight to Los Angeles. I want you to stop them—"

"What did you say?"

"I said I wanted you to stop them. They are not to take the plane. My wife and child. Mrs. Alice Gaynor. The two-o'clock flight to Los Angeles—"

"I'm afraid that's impossible, Mr. Gaynor." The voice was puzzled but polite.

"It can't be impossible. All you have to do is announce it over the public-address system and—"

"Impossible, sir. The two-o'clock flight is just taking off at this moment. I'm terribly sorry. Is there anything else I can do for you?"

"No," Roy said flatly, and put the phone down. He sat on the edge of his bed for a moment, then got up and went to the window. He looked out at the bright sky and the green-and-yellow mountains. He remained standing there, staring at the mountains, waiting for the call from the airline.

The Kiss at Croton Falls

FREDERICK MULL WAS A HUGE ROLLICKING MAN, WITH A
russet mustache, but when they took the trolleys off
Third Avenue and put him on a pension he sickened and
died, he who had never missed a day of work in his life
except for drunkenness or wounds incurred in the kind of
arguments a man from time to time could not avoid on
evenings out with high-spirited and honorable compan-
ions. It was bad enough when they took away his conductor and made him make his own change in the front
of the trolley, with all the traffic of New York charging
and howling around him, but when they put the buses
on and told him he'd have to learn how to drive if he
wanted to stay with the company, he knew and the company knew he was finished.

All this shows how long ago it all was, when there was
snow in the city every winter and the lakes froze over and
all the comfortable brown buildings hadn't been torn
down for gray and glass office slabs and it didn't take all
day to go from the Bridge to Yorkville by surface trans-
portation.

He had his faults. He drank whisky when he could afford it and beer when he couldn't and they carried him
home to his wife one night with a concussion that lasted
two days that he got defending the hanging of Roger
Casement in a bar owned by a man named Mulloy near
Fortieth Street. His father had fought in the Union Army,
under McClellan, and he was an unswerving patriot. He
was part-everything, he said, because has father's family
had come from the Midlands and his mother was one-
eighth Indian. He had a slow, barrelling baritone and
when he had drunk one or two he would sing "Flow
Gently, Sweet Afton" and "Good King Wenceslaus" and
"Oh, Susannah." But most of all he was partial to "John
Brown's Body Lies A-Mouldering in the Grave," and
"Who Is Sylvia?"

According to his wife, he also had a weakness for
women.

The sole basis for this belief came from something that

happened in the summer of 1921, when they were at a hotel at Croton Falls, recovering from the birth of their daughter, and Mrs. Mull looked out of her window on a moonlit night and saw her husband kissing a red-headed woman whose husband was not due to arrive until Labor Day. Mr. Mull's story was that before he knew what she was up to, the red-headed woman pinned him against a pillar after dinner, while he was quietly smoking his pipe, and threw her arms around him and kissed him, missing his mouth, in her anxiety, by a good margin. But Mrs. Mull would have none of that, and from that moment until the day he died, Mr. Mull enjoyed the reputation with his wife of being a wild, philandering ladies' man.

It was her contention that the women of the great city of New York rode on the Third Avenue trolley for the sole purpose of corrupting her husband. There was a story, it is true, that on a spring day in 1919 a widow in a veil walked forward along the aisle and slipped her address on an embossed card into his hand while she was waiting for the car to stop at Seventy-ninth Street, but there were many stories in those days about motormen and locomotive engineers and people like that, not all of them worthy of belief.

To forestall any other widows or soft-eyed virgins or dissatisfied wives with similar cunning tricks, his wife took to waiting along the route at odd and unsuspected hours for his trolley to appear. One or twice he saw her in time, standing there next to the elevated pillar holding their little dark-haired daughter, Clarice, by the hand and he merely passed her by. She would scream like a forsaken bride, shaking her fist after the yellow car rattling down the tracks toward the Bowery, with the taxi-drivers stopping their cabs to gawk at her in wonder, but naturally, she couldn't denounce him to the company. So she descended to guile and picked corners where there'd be sure to be at least eight or ten other passengers waiting that, for his job's sake, he couldn't dare sail by. Even years after she had given up the practice, he'd tighten visibly at the box when he approached Twenty-third Street, Thirty-fourth Street, or the back entrance of Bloomingdale's.

When she climbed into the car, she'd nod icily to Mr. Coombs, who was her husband's conductor the best part of the time, pay her nickel, march up the aisle toward the head of the car, daring any other woman who happened

to be sitting there to look at her. She'd never say a word
to her husband. She'd just sit there, boring holes in the
back of his head with her eyes, until he couldn't stand it
anymore and he'd draw the leather curtain they had
around the motorman's position to keep the reflection of
the lights within the car from confusing him on the night
run.

The night shifts were of course the worst. She'd sit up
for him in the dark cold kitchen with a blanket wrapped
around her like a fisherman's wife during a storm waiting
for the lighthouse keeper to come knocking on the door
with the bad news. And when he did come home she'd
pretend to be making coffee and getting out the biscuits,
but all the time she was sniffing him for perfume like a
hound on new tracks and her eyes would be going over
him for lipstick and signs of disarray like a pirate over a
bloodstained map.

He was a good-natured man and he made no complaint. He'd only been married that once and he supposed
that was what the institution was like.

He was content enough. He had his whisky on and off
the route and played with Clarice and taught her "Who Is
Sylvia?" He endured the reproaches of his wife as he endured the weather and traffic policemen, and in the end
he took it as a sign of love, which indeed it was, and he
would have been lonely and lost without it. Everything
considered, they lived together for nearly thirty years in
what would certainly pass in these days as happiness.

He lived to see his only daughter married to a good
man by the name of Smalley, who had a dependable job
as an insurance adjuster, and at the wedding he said to
the groom, "Ah, man, at least in your trade they'll never
tear the tracks out from under you."

Mr. Smalley was of a different breed from Mr. Mull,
which was only to be expected, since Mrs. Mull had spent
a good part of her life warning her daughter not to marry
a man like her father. Mr. Mull had heard many of these
warnings in his time and while he had not actively set
the seal of his approval upon them, he had been seen to
nod in quiet agreement with his wife's directives. He admired her intelligence vastly and took her word for gos-
pel in all questions of taste and affection.

The only pleasure Mr. Smalley took outside his home
was prevailing upon people who had broken their legs in
industrial accidents or who had lost their goods by fire to

settle for less than they had originally asked from the company. He had never been seen inside a saloon and he looked at his shoetops when he passed women in the street. He was a good provider, and while he did not seem capable of presenting his wife with an heir, he insisted upon her having a maid come in three afternoons a week to help with the cleaning and ironing.

When Mr. Mull died, Mrs. Mull mourned him truly, keeping his photograph on the mantelpiece, with his mustaches brushed, and saying to visitors, over a cup of tea, "Ah, nobody knows the life that man led me."

She dreamt about him constantly through the years, conversing with him in her sleep in wifely tones and walking over the next morning to her daughter's home to tell her about it. "Your father visited me again last night," Mrs. Mull would say, "and we had a nice long talk about the time we went up the river to Newburgh and the picnic steamer almost capsized in the rain." Or, "We had a serious talk last night and he promised to drink only beer until the Sunday after Easter." And sometimes Mrs. Mull would hurry over with her eyes shining, to say, "He was in very good spirits last night, not affected by drink or anything like that, you understand, but jolly, and he sang 'Flow Gently, Sweet Afton' and four verses of 'They're Hanging Danny Deever in the Morning.' "

Clarice took the reports of these conversations calmly. She had loved her father and thought him by far the most interesting man she had ever known and it seemed to her entirely natural that his memory died hard. And her mother was a lonely old woman, living in one room with very little to occupy her after an exhilarating lifetime of nagging an obstreperous and lovable man, and Clarice felt that these matter-of-fact nocturnal visits from the grave lightened her mother's solitude and gave point to her days.

But one morning the whole atmosphere changed. Her mother appeared early, white-lipped and angry. "He came again last night," she said, almost as soon as she walked through the door of Clarice's apartment.

"Did you have a nice visit?" Clarice asked, according to her usual formula.

"We did not," Mrs. Mull said. "We had a mortifying evening."

"Oh, Mother," Clarice said, "is that nice?"

"I would like to see what you would have done," said Mrs. Mull, "in my place."

"You must be careful not to hurt him," Clarice said soothingly. "Remember, he's an old man."

"Hurt him!" Mrs. Mull snorted. "Try and hurt that man. He has the hide of an elephant."

"What happened?" Clarice asked.

"The bell rang," said Mrs. Mull, "and there he was, standing there, with that smirk on his face he always has when he knows he's doing something that will annoy me."

"Now, Mother," Clarice began, "you mustn't read into things . . ."

"Read into things!" Mrs. Mull said. "Wait until you hear the story and then say read into things. Do you know what that man had the cold, icy courage to do last night?" She paused and Clarice dutifully said, "What?"

"Finally," Mrs. Mull said, "he overstepped the bounds. I'm a tolerant woman and I've learned to take the bad with the good, but even saints have their limits. And when I saw them standing there outside the door last night, I knew. . . ."

"What?" Clarice asked, puzzled. "What do you mean, *them?*"

"What I mean, exactly," Mrs. Mull said tightly, "is *them*. Your father and that red-headed woman in a crepe-de-Chine dress so tight you'd wonder how she could breathe the air or digest her food, and the child."

"What child?" Clarice asked faintly.

"A big, lumpish boy," said Mrs. Mull, "growing out of his clothes, with the same smirk on his face. Put a mustache on him and he could go down to the carbarn any day of the week and take out a car and run the full length of Third Avenue and nobody would know the difference."

"Now, Mother," Clarice said. She had heard, of course, of the red-headed woman on the porch at Croton Falls in the summer of 1921, but this was the first intimation of issue. "I never heard of any child."

"Neither did I," Mrs. Mull said, "until last night. Oh, he was the most deceptive man who ever walked the streets of the city. But last night he tore away the veil. Standing there, as cool as you please, with that woman's hand on his arm and that unmistakable child, saying,

'Bertha, I've brought some friends. Are there any refreshments in the house?' "

"And what did you do then?" Clarice asked, humoring her mother, but curious, also.

"Oh, I was polite," Mrs. Mull said. "I never held with making scenes before strangers and your father knows that and depends upon it. I gave her a cold bow and I took the boy's cap and I ushered them in with all civility and I made them tea and set out half a loaf of crumbcake that I had in the cupboard. I sat there, putting in a yes or no from time to time while that woman talked about Croton Falls and how she suspected they used margarine in the kitchen for cooking, although they swore they used butter. I'll tell the truth, I didn't go out of my way to make them comfortable, and they cut their visit mercifully short. I took the opportunity of getting your father off to one side for a moment and I told him, in no uncertain terms, that that was the last I wanted to see of that woman and their child of sin. I said, clear and definite, so there would be no misunderstanding in the future, that if he expected to see me again, he would have to make his visits alone."

"What did Father say to that?" Clarice asked.

"He didn't say anything," Mrs. Mull said. "Before he could open his mouth, she came into the hall and put her hand on his arm and said, 'Frederick, it's getting late, we're expected downtown,' and off they went together, after kindly thanking me for the tea, all unholy shameless three of them."

Clarice was a sensible girl and she said the right thing to restore order and harmony. "I don't think you have anything more to worry about now," she told her mother. "I'm sure he'll take the hint."

"He'd better," Mrs. Mull said fiercely, "or he'll find the door locked in his face."

For the next week or so, Mrs. Mull reported, all went well. Mr. Mull visited her three times, rather quiet and absent-minded, but alone. She herself had decided to be tolerant and keep her own counsel, and she had tactfully not brought up the subject of the red-headed woman and the unmistakable boy.

But then the devil came up in him again, and on a Saturday night he rang the bell and there he was with the smirk on his lips and the red-headed woman on his arm with every wrinkle of her corset showing as clear as

light through her skin-tight dress, and of course, that
lump of a boy, with his father's Saturday-night expression
built into his face.

"He stood there in the hallway," Mrs. Mull told Clarice
on the following Monday morning, "grinning and enjoying his guilt, saying, 'We were just passing by and we
thought maybe you'd be in the mood for a little company.' "

Mrs. Mull had had to wait until Monday to tell Clarice,
because Clarice had been in Providence for the weekend,
visiting the family of Mr. Smalley. The enforced delay
had enabled Mrs. Mull to arrange the details eloquently
in her mind and she started her story even before she
took off her hat in Clarice's living room.

"I took one look at him," Mrs. Mull said, "and I let
my eyes pass significantly over that woman and her
criminal son and it wasn't wasted on your father, you can
be assured of that. But he brazened it out. 'Aren't you
going to invite us in for a minute, Bertha?' he says, standing there between the two of them, like a prize bull at a
fair. 'I warned you, Frederick,' I told him, polite but final.
'Now go away and never come up these stairs again.'
'Now, Bertha,' he began, in that wheedling, sugary tone
he knows how to put on when there is a woman in question. But I cut him off quick. 'I told you to go away,' I
said, 'I wash my hands of you. I have stood enough.
Don't waste your time trying,' I said. 'This door is locked.'
And I closed it in his face, not slamming it, because I
wouldn't give the woman the pleasure of knowing I was
angry, but sharp and definite. I heard regretful whispering on the other side for a minute or two and then they
shuffled off and I went to bed. He came back an hour
later and he rang the bell and he called through the door.
'I'm alone now, Bertha, let me in for the love of God,'
but I made not a move and I said not a word. He rang
the bell all the night long and whimpered outside the door,
but my decision was made and I didn't let him know, even
by a whisper, that I so much as heard a sound. And in
the end, with the sun coming up, he gave a last, despairing ring, and he called, 'I'm going, Bertha, it's goodbye forever' and even though my heart fell down inside
me like a weight, I didn't answer him, because it's about
time he was taught a lesson. And that," Mrs. Mull said,
"is the end of your father."

Clarice started to tell her mother that she ought to give

him one more chance, but she gave up when she saw the
set of Mrs. Mull's jaw and made her a cup of tea and
tried to calm her as best she could and watched her put
on her hat, squarely on her head, like a soldier putting
on his helmet before a battle, and descend the stairs to
do her day's shopping, implacable and alone.

Clarice thought all day about her mother and about
how the love she bore her father could burn so fiercely
for forty years that she could find the strength to turn
him away from her door, even though he had been dead
so long, because of a kiss on a porch in Croton Falls in
1921. And when Mr. Smalley came home that night, she
looked at him coldly and knew, as he took off his shoes
and sat down mildly and faithfully in an easy chair,
putting on his glasses to read the evening newspaper,
that he never could inspire such passion in any woman,
and that ten days after he had been lowered into his
grave she would not be able to remember even his most
obnoxious mannerism.

"Ah," he said wearily, settling into his chair and folding his paper, "I've been busy today."

Clarice looked at him for a long, bitter moment. "Doing
what?" she asked. "Cheating the poor and doing sad souls
that have been destroyed by fire out of their rightful
damages?"

"Clarice . . ." Mr. Smalley said, looking up from his
newspaper, frightened and surprised, sensing a new disturbing note of passion in the marriage that he knew
would never be to his advantage. "What have I done?"

But Clarice did not answer. She was putting on her
coat, and she was out of the apartment, without a word,
on her way to a saloon on Third Avenue, not far from
the Bloomingdale corner.

Then We Were Three

MUNNIE BROOKS WAS AWAKENED BY THE SOUND OF TWO
shots outside the window. He opened his eyes and looked at
the ceiling. By the quality of the light, even through the
drawn curtains he could tell that it was sunny outside. He
turned his head. In the other bed Bert was still asleep. He
slept quietly, the blankets neat, in control of his dreams.

Munnie got out of his bed and, barefooted, in his pajamas, went over to the window and parted the curtains.

The last mists of morning were curling up from the fields, and far off and below, the sea was smooth in the October sunlight. In the distance, along the curve of the coast, the Pyrenees banked back in green ridges toward a soft sky. From behind a haystack more than a hundred yards away, beyond the edge of the hotel terrace, a hunter and his dog appeared, walking slowly, the hunter reloading. Watching him, Munnie remembered, with mild, gluttonous pleasure, that he had had partridge, newly killed and plump with the summer's feeding, for dinner the night before.

The hunter was an old man, dressed in fisherman's blue and wearing fisherman's rubber boots. He moved solidly and carefully behind his dog, through the cut stubble. When I am an old man, thought Munnie, who was twenty-two, I hope I look and feel like that on an October morning.

He opened the curtains wider and looked at his watch. It was aften ten o'clock. They had been up late the night before, all three of them, at the casino in Biarritz. Earlier in the summer, when they had been on the Côte d'Azur, a paratroop lieutenant on leave had showed them a foolproof system for beating the roulette table, and whenever they could, they frequented casinos. The system took a lot of capital and they had never made more than 8000 francs in one night among them on it, and sometimes it meant sitting up till three o'clock in the morning following the wheel, but they hadn't lost yet, either, since they met the lietuenant. It had made their trip unexpectedly luxurious, especially when they got to places where there was a casino. The system ignored the numbers and concentrated on the red and the black and involved a rather complicated rhythm of doubling. The night before they had won only 4500 francs and it had taken them until two o'clock, but still, waking late, with the weather clear and an old man hunting birds outside your window, the thousand-franc notes on the dresser added a fillip of luck and complacency to the morning.

Standing there, feeling the sun warm on his bare feet and smelling the salt and hearing the distant calm mutter of the surf, remembering the partridge and the gambling and everything else about the summer that had just passed, Munnie know he didn't want to start home that morning as they had planned. Staring down at the hunter following his dog slowly across the brown field on the edge of the sea, Munnie knew that when he was older he would look back upon the summer and think, Ah, it was wonderful when I was young. This double ability to enjoy a moment with the immediacy of youth and the reflective melancholy of age had made Bert say to him, half seriously, half as a joke, "I envy you, Munnie. You have a rare gift—the gift of instantaneous nostalgia. You get twice your investment out of everything."

The gift had its drawbacks. It made moving away from places he liked difficult for Munnie and packed all endings and farewells with emotion, because the old man who travelled within him was always saying, in his autumnal whisper, It will never be like that again.

But putting an end to this long summer, which had stretched into October, was going to be more painful than any other finish or departure that Munnie had known. These were the last days of the last real holiday of his life, Munnie felt. The trip to Europe had been a gift from his parents upon his graduation from college and now when he went back, there they would all be on the dock, the kind, welcoming, demanding faces, expecting him to get to work, asking him what he intended to do, offering him jobs and advice, settling him lovingly and implacably into the rut of being a grownup and responsible and tethered adult. From now on all holidays would be provisional, hurried interludes of gulped summertime between work and work. The last days of your youth, said the old man within. The boat docks in seven days.

Munnie turned and looked at his sleeping friend. Bert slept tranquilly, extended and composed under his blankets, his sunburned long thin nose geometrically straight in the air. This would change, too, Munnie thought. After the boat docked they would never be as close again. Never as close as on the rocks over the sea in Sicily or climbing through the sunny ruins at Paestum or chasing the two English girls through the Roman nightclubs. Never as close as the rainy afternoon in Florence when they talked, together, for the first time, to Martha. Never as close as on the long, winding journey, the three of them packed into the small open car, up the Ligurian coast toward the border, stopping whenever they felt like it for white wine or a swim at the little beach pavilions with all the small, brightly colored pennants whipping out in the

hot Mediterranean afternoon. Never as close as the con-
spiratorial moment over the beers with the paratrooper in
the bar of the casino at Juan-les-Pins, learning about the
unbeatable system. Never as close as in the lavender,
hilarious dawns, driving back to their hotel gloating over
their winnings, with Martha dozing between them. Never
as close as on the blazing afternoon at Barcelona, sitting
high up on the sunny side, sweating and cheering and
shading their eyes as the matador walked around the ring
holding up the two bull's ears, with the flowers and the
wineskins sailing down around him. Never as close as
at Salamanca and Madrid and on the road through the
straw-colored, hot, bare country up to France, drinking
sweet, raw Spanish brandy and trying to remember how
the music went that the gypsies danced to in the caves.
Never so close, again, finally, as here in this small white-
washed Basque hotel room, with Bert still asleep, and
Munnie standing at the window watching the old man
disappear with his dog and his shotgun, and upstairs in
the room above them, Martha, sleeping, as she always
did, curled like a child, until they came in, as they always
did, together, as though they didn't trust themselves or
each other to do it alone, to wake her and tell her what
they planned to do for the day.

Munnie threw the curtains wide open and let the sun
stream in. If there's one boat that I have a right to miss
in my life, he thought, it's the one that's sailing from
Le Havre the day after tomorrow.

Munnie went over to Bert's bed, stepping carefully over
the clothes that were crumpled on the floor. He poked
Bert's bare shoulder with his finger. "Master," he said,
"rise and shine." The rule was that whoever lost in tennis
between them had to call the other Master for twenty-four
hours. Bert had won the day before 6-3, 2-6, 7-5.

"It's after ten." Munnie poked him again.

Bert opened both eyes and stared coldly at the ceiling.
"Do I have a hangover?" he asked.

"We only had one bottle of wine amongst us for dinner," said Munnie, "and two beers after."

"I do not have a hangover," Bert said, as if the news
depressed him. "But it's raining outside."

"It's a bright, hot sunny morning," Munnie said.

"Everybody always told me it rained all the time on the
Basque coast," said Bert, lying still, complaining.

"Everybody is a liar," Munnie said. "Get the hell out of bed."

Bert swung his legs slowly over the side of the bed and sat there, thin, bony and bare from the waist up, in his pajama pants that were too short for him and from which his big feet dangled loosely. "Do you know why American women live longer than American men, Fat Man?" he asked, squinting at Munnie in the sunlight.

"No."

"Because they sleep in the morning. My ambition," Bert said, lying back on the bed again, but with his legs still over the side, "is to live as long as the American Woman."

Munnie lit a cigarette and tossed one to Bert, who managed to light it without lifting his head from the blanket. "I had an idea," Munnie said, "while you were wasting the precious hours of your childhood sleeping."

"Put it in the suggestion box." Bert yawned and closed his eyes. "The management will give a buffalo-hide saddle to every employee who presents us with an idea that is put into practice by the . . ."

"Listen," Munnie said eagerly. "I think we ought to miss that damned boat."

Bert smoked in silence for a moment, narrowing his eyes and pointing his nose at the ceiling. "Some people," he said, "are born boat-missers and train-missers and plane-missers. My mother, for example. She once saved herself from getting killed by ordering a second dessert at lunch. The plane left just as she got to the field and came down in flames thirty-five minutes later. Not a single survivor. It was ice-cream, with crushed fresh strawberries . . ."

"Come on, Bert." Sometimes Munnie got very impatient with Bert's habit of going off on tangents while he was making up his mind. "I know all about your mother."

"In the springtime," Bert said, "she goes mad for strawberries. Tell me, Munnie, have you ever missed anything in your life?"

"No," Munnie said.

"Do you think it's wise," Bert asked, "at this late stage, to fiddle with the patterns of a lifetime?"

Munnie went into the bathroom and filled a glass with water. When he came back into the bedroom, Bert was still lying on the bed, his legs dangling over the side, smoking. Munnie stood over him, then slowly tipped the glass over Bert's bare brown chest. The water splashed a little and ran in thin trickles over Bert's ribs onto the sheets.

"Ah," Bert said, still smoking. "Refreshing."

They both laughed and Bert sat up.

"All right, Fat Man," Bert said. "I didn't know you were serious."

"My idea," said Munnie, "is to stay here until the weather changes. It's too sunny to go home."

"What'll we do about the tickets?"

"We'll send a telegram to the boat people and tell them we'll take passage later. They've got a waiting list a mile long. They'll be delighted."

Bert nodded judiciously. "What about Martha?" he asked. "Maybe she has to get to Paris today."

"Martha doesn't have to go anyplace. Anytime," Munnie said. "You know that."

Bert nodded again. "The luckiest girl in the world," he said.

Outside the window there was the sound of the shotgun again. Bert turned his head, listening. There was a second report. "My," Bert said, running his tongue over his teeth, "that was wonderful partridge last night." He stood up, looking, in his flapping pajama pants like a boy who would be a good prospect for the college crew if he could be induced to eat heavily for a year. He had been chubby until he went into the Army, but by the time he got out in May, he was long and stringy and his ribs showed. When she wanted to make fun of him, Martha told him he looked like an English poet in his bathing trunks. He went to the window and Munnie crossed over and stood beside him, looking out over the mountains and the sea and the sunlight.

"You're right," Bert said. "Only an idiot would dream of starting home on a day like this. Let's go tell Martha the party's still on."

They dressed quickly, in espadrilles and cotton trousers and tennis shirts and went upstairs together and into Martha's room, without knocking. The wind was making one of the shutters rap against the window, but Martha was still asleep, curled around herself, only the top of her head showing above the blanket, the hair dark and tangled and short. The pillow was on the floor.

Munnie and Bert stood in silence for a moment, looking down at the curled, blanketed figure and the dark head, each of them convinced that the other did not know what he was thinking.

"Awake," Bert said softly. "Awake to glory." He went over to the bed and touched the top of Martha's head. Watching him, Munnie could feel the tips of his own fingers twitching electrically.

"Please," Martha said, her eyes still closed. "It's the middle of the night."

"It's nearly noon," Munnie said, lying by nearly two hours, "and we have to tell you something."

"Tell it to me," said Martha, "and get out of here."

"The Fat Man here," said Bert, standing at her head, "has come up with an idea. He wants us to stay here until it begins to rain. How do you feel about it?"

"Of course," Martha said.

Bert and Munnie smiled at each other, because they felt they understood her so well. "Martha," said Bert, "you're the only perfect girl alive."

Then they went out of the room to give her a chance to get dressed.

They had met Martha Holm in Florence. They seemed to have the same ideas about which museums and which churches to go to and they kept bumping into her and she was alone and obviously American and as Bert said, they didn't come prettier, and finally they started talking to each other. Maybe it was because they had first seen her in the Uffizi Gallery among the Botticellis that gave Munnie the idea, but he thought, privately, that, aside from the fact that her hair was short and dark and irregularly cut, she looked like the Primavera, tall, slender, and girlish, with a long narrow nose and deep, brooding, dangerous eyes. He felt extravagant and embarrassed to be thinking things like this about a twenty-one-year-old American girl who wore slacks and had gone a year to Smith, but he couldn't help himself. He never told Martha about it and of course he never said a word on the subject to Bert.

Martha knew a lot of people in and around Florence (later on, it turned out that she knew a lot of people in and around everyplace) and she got them invited to a tea in Fiesole at a villa where there was a swimming pool and to a party at which Munnie found himself dancing with a Contessa. Martha had been in Europe for nearly

two years and she was wonderful at telling you what
places to go to and what places were traps, and she spoke
Italian and French, and she was ready when you told her
to be ready, and she didn't scream for pity when she had
to walk a few blocks on her own two feet, and she
laughed at Bert's and Munnie's jokes and made some of
her own, and she didn't giggle, weep or sulk, which put
her several notches above every other girl Munnie had
ever known. After they had been together for three days
in Florence and were due to start for Portofino and
France, it seemed unbearable just to leave her behind. As
far as Munnie and Bert could tell, she had no plans of
her own. "I tell my mother," Martha explained, "that I'm
taking courses at the Sorbonne, and it's almost true, at
least in the wintertime."

Martha's mother lived in Philadelphia, after three
divorces, and every once in awhile, Martha said, she sent
back a photograph, so that when she finally did arrive
back home, there wouldn't be an embarrassing moment
on the dock when her mother wouldn't recognize her.

So Munnie and Bert talked it over very seriously and
sat at a café table with Martha in the Piazza del Signoria
and ordered coffee and put it up to her.

"What we've decided," Bert said, with Munnie sitting
beside him, silently agreeing, "is that the Brooks-Carboy
unguided tour of Europe could use you, as interpreter,
hotel-finder, and chief taster of foreign foods. Aside from
supplying a welcome feminine touch. Are you interested?"

"Yes," Martha said.

"We'd like to know if we could mesh schedules, more
or less," Munnie said.

Martha smiled. "I'm on a schedule of drift," she said.
"Didn't you know?"

"Does that mean," Munnie asked, because he liked to
have everything absolutely clear, "that you want to come
along?"

"It means that I want to come along very much," said
Martha, "and I was hoping you'd ask me." She looked at
each of them for exactly the same number of seconds,
cheerful, grateful, ready for anything.

"Now," said Bert, "Munnie and I have talked it over
and we're going to lay it on the line. Something like this
has to be planned out in advance or there comes a dark
and hideous night of disaster. We've thought up a good,

workable set of rules and if you agree, off we go tomorrow. If not—no harm done—and we hope you spend a
pleasant summer."

"Get to it, Bert," Munnie said, impatiently. "Don't
recite the preamble to the Constitution."

"Rule Number One," Bert said, with Martha sitting
still, nodding, gravely listening, "rule number one is basic.
No entanglements. Munnie and I're old friends and we've
planned this summer for years and we've been having a
wonderful time and we don't want to wind up fighting
duels with each other or anything like that. Now, I know
women . . . ." He paused, daring either of them to smile.
They didn't smile.

"He wouldn't have said that," Munnie explained, "before the Army."

"What do you know about women?" Martha asked,
being serious.

"What I know is that women're always busy choosing,"
Bert went on. "They come into a room and if there're
five men present, their minds get to work like a business
machine, punching holes. First Choice, Second Choice,
Acceptable, Perhaps, Impossible."

"Oh, my." Martha began to laugh. She covered her
mouth with her hand apologetically and tried to straighten
her face. "Forgive me. Munnie . . . do you believe this?"

"I don't know," he said embarrassedly. "I haven't
had Bert's advantages. I wasn't in the Army."

"I'll even tell you how you'd choose," Bert said, "between Munnie and me, so you won't have to wonder or
waste your time."

"Tell me," Martha said. "Do tell me."

"In the beginning," said Bert, "the tendency is to choose
me. I'll go into the reasons some other time. Then, after
a while, the switch sets in, and Munnie gets the final decision."

"Poor Bert," Martha said, chuckling. "How awful for
you! Only winning the opening game of the season all
the time. Why are you telling me all this?"

"Because you've got to promise not to choose anybody," Bert said. "And if you *do* choose, you have to go
to the grave with your secret."

"To the grave," Martha repeated, trying to be solemn,

"Until the boat sails," Bert said, "we treat each other
like brothers and sister, and that's all. *D'accord?*"

"*D'accord,*" Martha said.

"Good." Bert and Munnie nodded at each other, pleased with how reasonable everybody was.

"Rule Number Two," Bert said, "if after a while we get to feel you're a nuisance—we say farewell and you leave. No tears. No recriminations. No scenes. Just a friendly shake of the hand and off to the nearest railroad station. *D'accord?*"

"*D'accord* two times," Martha said.

"Rule Number Three—everybody pays exactly one third of the expenses."

"Of course," said Martha.

"Rule Number Four," Bert went on, like the director of a company explaining a plan of operations to his board, "everybody is free to go wherever he or she wants to, and with anyone else whoever, and no questions asked. We are not an inseparable unit, because inseparable units are boring. O.K.?"

"A free, loose confederation of sovereign states," Martha said. "I got it. Whomever."

They all shook hands on it, surrounded by the looming oversized statues, and started out together early the next morning, after figuring out a way to squeeze Martha into the car and strap her baggage onto the back, and it all couldn't have worked out better. There hadn't been a single argument all summer, although they had discussed, among other things, sex, religion, politics, marriage, the choice of careers, the position of women in modern society, the theatre in New York and Paris, and the proper size of bathing costumes for young girls on the beaches of Italy, France and Spain. And when Bert had taken up with a plump little blonde American girl in St. Tropez for a week or so, it hadn't seemed to disturb Martha for a minute, even when the girl moved into the hotel they were staying at and frankly installed herself in the room next to Munnie's and Bert's.

The truth was, nothing seemed to disturb Martha very much. She greeted the events of each day with a strange and almost dreamlike placidity. She seemed to make no decisions herself and whatever decisions the others made, regardless of how they turned out, she accepted with exactly the same good-natured, smiling rather vague approval. Linked in Munnie's mind with this pleasant will-lessness was Martha's extraordinary talent for sleeping. If nobody went in to awaken her in the morning, she would sleep on till noon, till two o'clock in the afternoon, even if she had gone to bed early the evening before. It wasn't anything physical, either, because she didn't need the sleep and never suggested, herself, that it was time to go to bed, no matter how late they stayed up at night or at what hour she had arisen in the morning. She never wrote any letters and rarely received any, since she hardly ever remembered to leave a forwarding address when they moved. When she needed money she would wire the bank in Paris that handled her allowance, and when it came she spent it carelessly. She took almost no interest in clothes and the reason she cut her hair short the way she did, she told Bert and Munnie, was that she didn't want to be bothered having to comb it all the time.

When the three of them talked about what they would like to do with their lives, she was vaguer than ever. "I don't know," she said, shrugging, smiling, seeming to be mildly and indulgently puzzled about herself. "I suppose I'll just hang around. Wait and see. For the moment, I'm on a policy of float. I don't see anybody else our age doing anything so damned attractive. I'm waiting for a revelation to send me in a permanent direction. I'm in no hurry to commit myself, no hurry at all . . ."

In a curious way, Martha's lack of direction made her much more interesting to Munnie than all the other girls he had ever known, the positive but limited girls who knew they wanted to be married and have babies and join a country club, the girls who wanted to go on the stage and be famous, the girls who wanted to become editors or deans of women's colleges. Martha hadn't settled for anything yet, Munnie felt, because nothing good enough had come up. And there was always the chance, he believed, that when she finally did commit herself it would be for something huge, original and glorious.

The only way that the plans hadn't worked out as outlined in Florence had been that, except for the week of the plump blonde in St. Tropez, they had been an inseparable unit, but that was only because all three of them enjoyed being with one another better than being with anyone else. It wouldn't have worked if Martha had been a different kind of girl, if she had been a coquette or greedy or foolish, and it wouldn't have worked if Munnie and Bert hadn't been such good friends and hadn't trusted each other so completely, and finally, it wouldn't have worked if they had all been a little older. But it *had* worked, at least up until the first week of October, and with luck,

it would continue to work, until they kissed Martha goodbye and got on the boat train, and started for home.

They lay on the deserted beach until nearly two o'clock
and then took a swim. They had a race, because the water
was cold, and it was the best way to keep warm. The race
was a short one, only about fifty yards, and Munnie
was completely out of breath by the time he finished, trying to keep up with Martha. Martha won easily and was
floating serenely on her back when Munnie came up to
her, blowing heavily and fighting to get air in his lungs.

"It would be a different story," Munnie said, grinning,
but a little ashamed, "if I didn't have asthma."

"Don't be gloomy about it," Martha said, kicking her
legs gently. "Women're more naturally buoyant."

They both stood up and watched Bert plowing doggedly
up toward them.

"Bert," Martha said, as he reached them and stopped,
"you're the only man I know who looks like an old lady
driving an electric automobile when he swims."

"My talents," said Bert, with dignity, "run in another
direction."

They went in then, shouting and pink from the cold
water and waving their arms. They dressed on the beach,
under the big towel, one after another, for modesty's sake.
Martha wore slacks that came down only to the middle
of her calf and a fisherman's jersey, striped blue and white.
Watching her arrange her clothes with light, careless movements, Munnie felt that never in his life would he see
again anything so gay and obscurely touching as Martha
Holm, dressed in a sailor's striped shirt, on a sunny beach,
shaking the sea water out of her short, dark hair.

They decided to have a picnic rather than to go to a
restaurant for lunch and they got into the little two-seater
MG that Munnie's brother had left for him, when he had
had his summer in Europe the year before. With Martha
sitting on the cushioned brake in the middle they went into
town and bought a cold chicken and a long loaf of bread
and a piece of Gruyère cheese. They borrowed a basket
from the fruit dealer from whom they bought a huge
bunch of blue grapes and picked up two bottles of pink
wine and got back into the car and drove all around the
harbor to the old fort, which had been besieged and which
had fallen at other times but which was used now in the
summertime as a school to teach young people how to

sail. They parked the car and walked out along the broad, bleached top of the sea wall, carrying the basket and the wine and the big, slightly damp towel, to serve as a table-cloth.

From the wall they could see the wide stretch of the oval harbor, empty now except for a dory with a homemade sail heading toward the point of Saint Barbe, and the deserted beach and the white and red buildings of Saint Jean de Luz. The boatyard near the fort was crammed with small blue Snipe-class boats, lashed down and on blocks for the winter, and from somewhere in the distance came the faint sound of hammering, lonely and out-of-season, where a single workman was putting new planks into the bow of a small fishing vessel. Out at sea, almost lost against the gray-blue wash of the horizon, the boats of the tuna fleet bobbed in the swell. The tide was out and the waves rolled in, white and spumy, but not ominous, over the slanting uncovered rocks on which the sea wall was built. Close to the wall, on the bay side, the ruined, circular bastions of the old wall, which the sea had broken in another century, loomed out of the quiet water, ir-regular, crumbling, useless, looking somehow Roman and reminding Munnie of aqueducts that had brought mountain water to cities that had long since vanished and dungeons in which the last prisoners had died five hundred years before.

They didn't go all the way out to the end of the wall, which was separated from the middle section of the break-water by a wide channel through which the shipping entered and left the harbor. Even on the calmest day, Munnie felt something wild and dangerous out there on the flat point of stone, where the full force of the unbroken ocean probed, however quietly, at the guarded waters of the bay and the land beyond. Munnie suffered a little from vertigo and when he looked down the sheer sides of the wall into the shifting green depths and the fringe of foam he had a helpless picture of himself caught there be-low, or plunging down to fight against the tides and the rocks and the waves coming and going and crossing each other with upcurling tips of spray. He didn't say anything about it, of course, but he was grateful when Martha said, "This is good enough," before they had gone very far, and he carefully helped weight the towel down as a table-cloth squarely in the middle of the wall.

There was a little wind, capricious and sporadically

chilly, but Bert took off his shirt, to maintain his tan. Munnie, who had a soft, rather full growth of fuzzy reddish hair on his chest, and who was embarrassed by it, said that the wind was too cold for undressing. Bert glanced at him ironically, because he knew how Munnie felt about his chest, but he didn't say anything.

As Martha cut up the chicken and arranged the cheese and bread and grapes on pieces of paper in the center of the towel, where they could all get at them neatly, Bert cocked his head, listening to the distant, slow, rhythmic hammering from the boatyard. "Whenever I hear that noise in a place like this," he said, "it reminds me of the end of *The Cherry Orchard*. Everything melancholy and closed up and ready to die and the autumn setting in . . ."

"Whenever I hear it," Martha said, arranging the grapes, "I think, 'Divorce, divorce.'"

"That's the difference," said Bert, "between Russia and America." He walked over to the edge of the wall and stood there, his toes dangerously over the brink, staring out at the horizon, a tall, spare, loose-limbed figure, reciting, his arms ritually upraised, "Break, break, break, On thy cold gray stones, Oh, sea, And I would that my heart could utter, The thoughts that arise in me . . ."

"Lunch is on," Martha said, sitting cross-legged and pushing her sleeves above the elbows, her bare arms, under the bunched jersey, brown and surprisingly full and solid for such a slender girl. She took a piece of chicken and bit into it and said, "It's the only kind of picnic that makes picnics worth while. And no ants."

Munnie drank some of the wine from the bottle, because they had neglected to bring glasses, and broke a piece of bread off the long loaf and took some of the dark meat. Bert sat on the other side of Martha, folding his long legs down in slow motion. He reached for a piece of chicken, and said, as he munched at it, "Do you think a bright, sober young American would make a fortune setting up a factory in France to manufacture paper plates and paper cups?"

"It would spoil all the ineffable medieval charm," Martha said.

"Oh, that old, lowdown, ineffable, medieval, greasy-paper charm," Bert said. "Trust a woman to notice things like that, eh, Munnie?" He lifted his eyebrow in an exaggerated, theatrical leer. "God, isn't it lucky we walked into that gallery in Florence and found Martha? Otherwise, you know what our summer would've been like? We'd have been delivered over to all the female riffraff of Europe—all those Italian movie starlets, bursting out of their shirtwaists, all those skinny French models, all those hungry-eyed, golden-brown American divorcees, smelling from Arpège. God, Munnie, doesn't it make you feel as though Something was watching over you that day in the museum? Tell me the truth, Fat Man, doesn't it make you feel supernaturally serene?"

"Where did you ever learn to talk like that?" Martha asked, sitting cross-legged, placidly lifting the wine bottle to her lips.

"My grandfather was a Baptist preacher in Memphis, Tennessee," Bert said, "and he taught me to fear the Lord, read the Bible, relish corn, and speak in balanced sentences." He stood up and waved the drumstick of the chicken at the Atlantic Ocean. "Repent, ye sinners, because ye have swum in the warm waters, and ogled the virgins . . ." He made a bow in Martha's direction. "And ye have played at the tables and ye have neglected to send postcards home. Repent, because ye have found pleasure and ye have missed the boat."

"Do you want some cheese?" Martha asked.

"With mustard." Bert sat down again. He peered thoughtfully at Munnie. "What do you think, Munnie?" he asked. "Are we really as happy as we feel or do we only *think* we're this happy? The philosopher's everlasting cud —illusion or reality. Is this wall stone?" he demanded oratorically. "Is this ocean blue, this water wet? Is this girl beautiful? Is this money we have in our pockets or is it really coupons for prizes that were given away in Duluth in 1922 by a tobacco company that went bankrupt the first Thursday after the crash? Is this the good wine of France we're drinking or is it vinegar spiked with blood and seawater? Rosé de Béarn," he said, reading the label on the bottle. "It seems real, doesn't it, but *is* it? Are we three over-privileged, white-toothed, splendid young American princes, visiting our greatest colony, or are we, without knowing it, pitiful refugees, in flight, with our backs to the sea? . . . Have you read a newspaper this morning, do you know the answer? Are we friends and brothers, or will we betray each other by sunset? Search the lady for daggers."

"Holy man," Martha said, "the self-starter got loose."

Munnie smiled dreamily, in appreciation of Bert's performance. He himself was literal and direct and always said exactly what he meant and no more. But he was entertained by Bert's flights of rhetoric and appreciated Bert much the way a man with no talent, but a love for music, appreciates a friend who is a skillful pianist and who generously performs at just the right moments, without being asked. It went all the way back to the time when they were both sixteen and in school together and Bert used to make scandalous improvisations in blank verse about the assumed sexual habits of the middle-aged and slightly bald lady who taught them chemistry. It got Bert into trouble from time to time because he was recklessly brave and once he started he let himself be carried away and say outrageous things, no matter who was listening. Just this summer, they had had to fight four young Germans in a *brasserie* in Nice and run from the police because of one of his performances. Bert had struck up a conversation with the young men and asked them where they came from and they had said, after a little hesitation, that they were Swiss. "What part of Switzerland?" Bert had asked blandly. "Dusseldorf? Hamburg?"

The Germans, who were large, solid men, had looked uncomfortable and turned away from him toward the beers that were standing on the bar in front of them, but Bert wouldn't leave it alone. "The part of Switzerland I find most charming," Bert said loudly, "is Belsen. So rural, so cosy, so full of memories. What I always have said is that Switzerland would have won the war if it hadn't been stabbed in the back by the watchmakers. And a good thing, too."

"Cut it out," Munnie had whispered, and Martha had shaken her head warningly too, and pulled at Bert's arm. "There're four of them. They'll murder us."

But Bert had gone right on. "I'm proud to tell you gentlemen," he said, smiling broadly, "that I have always been a believer in a Greater Switzerland and there are plenty of good, red-blooded Americans who go right along with me." The Germans were muttering among themselves by now and Munnie took off his watch and slipped it into his pocket because he didn't want it broken when the fight began.

"Shut up, Bert," Martha said. "They're going to hit you with a beermug."

"Now boys," Bert went on, lifting his glass, "I'd like you to join me in a toast to the greatest little old Swiss of

them all, that kindly, sweet old lovable fellow, Adolf
Hitler, and after that we'll all join in singing Switzerland
Über Alles. I'm sure you know the words . . ."

Munnie had edged around by now and when the first
German swung, he grabbed the man's arm and clubbed
him twice with his right hand. The Germans were slow,
but strong, and very angry, and by the time Munnie
dragged Bert to the door, he had a bloody nose and Bert's
coat collar was half torn off and all the waiters were
screaming for the police.

The three of them ran through the back streets of Nice,
hearing confused shouting dying down behind them. Bert
was chuckling as he ran, and shaking his right hand, which
was numb from a German skull, and he kept saying to
Munnie, "What part of Switzerland you from, Bud? Leip-
zig? Nuremberg?"

A half hour later, when they were sitting safely in a bar
along the Promenade des Anglais, it had begun to seem
funny to Martha and Munnie, too, and for the rest of the
summer, whenever any one of them did something that
seemed objectionable or foolish, the others would ask, incredulously, "What part of Switzerland are *you* from?"

Now Bert was sitting, waving the wine bottle gently,
beaming out at the bay. "I think I am going to start a new
kind of travel service. Out-of-season tours to slightly run-
down resorts. I'll write a brochure, entitled 'Know bliss!
Be Unfashionable! Get Away from Your Fellow Man on
Your Next Vacation!' Do you think your father would be
inclined to put up the dough to get us started, Munnie?"

Bert had an unshakable belief that Munnie's father was
enormously wealthy and avid for unusual business opportunities, which Bert was happy to find for him. The
opportunities had included the planting of an avocado
grove near Grasse, and the building of a 4000-foot télé-
phérique for skiing in a village of twenty-two houses in the
Spanish Pyrenees. All of Bert's projects, aside from in-
volving great outlays of capital on the part of Munnie's
father, also included the necessity of Bert's remaining
permanently in Europe as manager.

"Munnie," Bert said, "don't you think we ought to send
your father a cable?"

"No," said Munnie.

"The chance of a lifetime," Bert said. "What does he
want to hold onto all that money for? The inheritance
people'll just take it from him in the hideous end. Well,

I'll find something. That's not the only way to turn a
dollar." He peered speculatively at Martha, who was eating
the grapes by now. "Martha," he said, "do you know that
you represent a source of vast potential income?"

"I'm going to donate my body to science," Martha said,
"at the age of eighty-five."

"The essential thing," said Bert, "is not to marry an
American."

"Report that man to a committee," Martha said.

"America is not the place for a pretty woman," Bert
went on. "The houses're getting too small, the help too
expensive, a beauty suddenly finds herself in a cosy little
nest in Scarsdale surrounded by television sets and labor-
saving devices and invitations to join the Parent-Teachers
Association. A beautiful woman does better in a country
which is decaying a little, and rather uneconomically run
—like France. You could marry a nice forty-five-year-old
man with a clean mustache and large, rolling feudal estates
on the banks of the Loire. Wonderful shooting in the
autumn and good, light wines grown on the property
and dozens of servants taking off their caps and bowing
when the station wagon went by. Your husband would
adore you and invite all your friends down to keep you
happy and he'd leave you alone a good deal of the time
when he went up to Paris to attend to his affairs and have
his doctor probe his liver."

"Where do you fit into this picture?" Martha asked.

"He'd be one of the friends invited to keep you happy,"
Munnie said. He wasn't enjoying the conversation. Even
though Bert was joking, Munnie knew that actually Bert
would approve if Martha *did* go out and marry an old
man with a lot of money. Just the other day, when they
had been talking about the careers that might lie ahead of
them, Bert had said, "The important thing is to recognize
your gift and then use it. And the best way to use it is to
keep you from the insufferable boredom of work. Now
your gift—" he had grinned at Martha "—your gift is
beauty. That's easy. You use it on a man and the sky's the
limit. My gift is a double one, but in the long run less
hopeful. I have charm . . ." He grinned more widely,
making fun of himself, "and I don't give a damn. Still, if
I'm clever enough and don't rise to the wrong bait, I may
go a long way on it. As for Munnie . . ." He shook his
head doubtfully. "His gift is virtue. Poor sod. What can he
do with that?"

Now, sitting on the corner of the towel, picking the grapes appreciatively off their stems, one by one, Bert was shaking his head. "No," he said, "I won't be one of the invited friends. I'm a permanent fixture. I'm the overseer of the estates, the curious American with no ambition who likes to live in France on the banks of the pretty river. I walk around in an old tweed jacket smelling a little from horses and new wine barrels, loved by one and all, making wry comments on the state of the world, playing backgammon in front of the fire with the mistress of the house when her husband is away, and going up the stairs later, with the last glass of Armagnac in my hand, to entertain her in my wry, American way in the ancestral bed . . ."

"Ah," Martha said, "how idyllic!"

"Every age," Bert said gravely, "to its own particular idyll. This is the year, among the wars."

Munnie felt very uncomfortable and when he looked over at Martha he felt even more uncomfortable, because she was laughing. They had laughed together at a lot of things since Florence, and they had covered all the subjects, but Munnie didn't want to hear Martha laughing now at this.

He stood up. "I think I'm going down the wall a way," he said, "and take a siesta. Wake me when you want to go."

He walked about thirty yards, carrying a sweater to use as a pillow, and as he stretched out on the smooth sun-warmed stone, he heard Martha and Bert laughing together, the laughter private and small in the wide, bright emptiness.

Closing his eyes against the glare of the sun, listening to the distant laughter, Munnie realized that he was in pain. The pain was not localized and it had a curious, evasive quality. Just when Munnie felt, *There, I've got it, it's in my throat,* it slipped away, not to disappear, but to put vague, sharp, almost detectable fingers somewhere else. Then, lying there, with the curtain of heat on his eyelids, Munnie understood that what he was feeling was not pain, but sorrow.

The sorrow was deep and complex, and was composed of many elements—a sense of deprivation, a shadow of impending departure, a nostalgia for memories that were moving irrevocably away from innocence, a confusion of emotion more profound than anything he had ever experienced before in his life. Engulfed and shaken as he was,

Munnie also knew that if, telepathically affected, Martha would stop laughing with Bert and get up and walk the thirty yards along the wall to where he lay, and if she were to sit down beside him and touch his hand, all would instantaneously be well.

But she didn't move, and he heard her laugh more loudly at something that Bert had said and which Munnie couldn't hear.

Suddenly, Munnie knew what he was going to do. As soon as he was on the boat, and all bargains were over, all rules no longer in effect, he was going to write Martha and ask her to marry him. Clumsily, he began to compose the letter in his mind. *This will come as a surprise to you, I suppose, because all summer long I never said a word, but I didn't realize for a long time what had been happening to me, and besides there was the arrangement you and Bert and I made in Florence to keep everything on a purely friendly basis, which I am happy we did. But now I'm on the boat and I feel free to tell you how I feel about you. I love you and I want to marry you. I don't know how you feel about me, but maybe the arrangement kept you from saying anything, just the way it did me. Anyway, I hope so. I am going to get a job and get settled just as soon as I get home, and then you could come back and meet my family and all that . . ."*

The letter stopped writing itself inside his head. He thought of his mother sitting down having tea with Martha, saying, "You say your mother lives in Philadelphia? And your father . . . oh . . . Do try one of these cakes. And you say you met Munnie in Florence and then just you and he and Bert went all around Europe for the rest of the summer all together . . . Lemon, cream?"

Munnie shook his head. He'd handle his mother when the time came. He went back to writing the imaginary letter.

You said once that you didn't know what you wanted to do with yourself, that you were waiting for some kind of revelation to send you in a permanent direction. Maybe you'll laugh at me for offering myself as a revelation, but maybe you'll feel that marrying me will . . .

Munnie shook his head disgustedly. God, even if she was crazy in love with him, he thought, a sentence like that would queer it forever.

I don't know about you and other men, he went on jumpily in his head. *You never seemed interested in any-*

*body else while you were with us and you never mentioned
anybody else in any particular way and as far as I could
tell you never showed any preference between Bert and
me . . .*

Munnie opened his eyes and turned his head to look at
Bert and Martha. They were sitting close together, almost
head to head, facing each other, talking in low, serious
voices.

He remembered Bert's description of what he called his
gift. I have charm and I don't give a damn. Well, Munnie
thought, with satisfaction, even if she overlooked the
egotism, that can't have attracted her so much. And besides, there was that open and avowed blonde in St.
Tropez. If Bert had planned to do anything with Martha,
or if Martha, as Bert had predicted, was interested in making a choice, that certainly would have put an end to it,
wouldn't it? Bert, Munnie decided, could be the amusing,
bachelor friend of the family. The best kind.

Munnie dozed a little, a succession of warm and delicious images pouring through his mind. Martha coming off
the airplane at Idlewild, because after getting his letter
the boat was too slow, and walking away from the runway
into his arms. Martha and he waking late on a Sunday
morning in their own apartment and deciding to doze for
another hour and then go out to breakfast. Martha coming
into a party on his arm and a slight, approving, envious,
subtle hush sweeping the room for a moment, because she
was so beautiful. Martha . . .

Someone was shouting. Far off, someone was shouting.

Munnie opened his eyes and blinked, thinking, puzzled.
Now, why did anyone shout in my dream?

The cry came again and Munnie stood up and looked
out at the bay. In the water, at least three hundred yards
away, was a small boat. It was the dory they had seen
before. It had capsized and it was low in the water and
there were two figures clinging to it. As he watched, he
heard the cry again, wordless, desperate. A hand and arm
flashed in the sunlight, waving.

Munnie turned and looked over at Bert and Martha.
They were stretched out, their heads together on the towel,
their bodies making a wide V, sleeping.

"Bert!" Munnie called. "Martha! Get up!"

Bert stirred, then sat up, rubbing his eyes. The shout
came again, wailing, from the bay.

"Out there," Munnie said, pointing. Bert swung around,

still sitting, and looked at the capsized boat and the two almost-submerged figures clinging to it, a man and a woman. "Good God," Bert said. "What do they think they're doing there?" He nudged Martha. "Wake up," he said, "and watch the shipwreck."

The boat lay almost motionless in the water, only shifting a little as the two figures moved, changing their positions. As Munnie watched, he saw the man push off from the boat and start to swim toward the beach. The man swam slowly and every thirty seconds he stopped and shouted and waved. After each stop he slid under, then reappeared, splashing and frantic.

"Oh, my," Bert said. "He's leaving her out there!"

Bert was standing by now, with Martha at his side, peering across the bay. The man had a good three hundred yards to go before he could touch down on the beach and with his screaming and waving and going under twice a minute, it didn't look as though he was going to make it. The woman who had been left hanging onto the boat shouted from time to time, too, and her voice sounded shrill and angry as it floated across the glittering quiet water.

Finally, Munnie could make out what the swimmer was shouting. *"Au secours! Je noye, je noye!"* Munnie felt a little flicker of annoyance with him. It seemed melodramatic and overdone to be shouting "I'm drowning," especially in such a powerful voice, on a peaceful afternoon in the calm, sunny bay. He went over to the edge of the wall, joining Bert and Martha.

"He seems to be doing all right," Bert said. "He's got a nice, strong stroke there."

"He's going to have to do a little explaining later," Martha said, "leaving his girl friend out there like that."

As they watched, the man went under again. He seemed to stay under a long time and Munnie began to feel his mouth get very dry, watching the spot where the man had disappeared. Then the man surfaced again, this time with his shoulders and arms bare, white and glistening against the deep blue water. He had taken off his shirt underwater and a moment later the shirt came up and floated away, billowing soddenly. The man shouted again. By now it was plain that he was calling directly to the three of them, standing on the wall. The man started swimming again, thrashing heavily.

Munnie scanned the beach and the wharf on which the

Snipes were put up on blocks for the winter. There wasn't a boat of any kind he could use, or even a length of rope. He listened for the sound of the hammer they had heard when they had first come onto the wall. Then he realized it had stopped a long time ago, while they were still eating. Far across, on the other side of the bay, there was no movement in front of the houses that faced the water and there were no swimmers or fishermen or children playing anywhere in sight. The entire world of stone, sand and sea that afternoon seemed to be given over to the three of them standing on the wall, and the woman clinging to the bottom of the capsized boat calling shrilly and angrily to the half-naked man struggling in the water and moving slowly and painfully away from her.

Why couldn't this have happened in August? Munnie thought irritably. He looked down at the water rippling in gentle regular swells against the base of the wall. It wasn't very deep now, with the tide out, four or five feet at the most, and huge chunks of rock and concrete broke the surface irregularly. If you jumped it was a drop of at least fifteen feet and there would be no avoiding the rocks.

Munnie looked, almost embarrassedly, across at Martha and Bert. Martha was squinting and there were lines on her forehead. She was biting her thumbnail absently like a little girl puzzling over a problem in school. Bert seemed critical and mildly interested, as though he were watching the performance of an acrobat in a third-rate circus.

"The damn fool," Bert said mildly. "If he couldn't handle a boat any better than that you'd think he'd have had the sense to stick close to the shore."

"Frenchmen," Martha said. "They think they can do anything." She went back to chewing on her nail.

The man called again, aiming at them.

"What're we going to do?" Munnie asked.

"Bawl the stupid bastard out," Bert said, "when he comes ashore, for being such a lousy sailor."

Munnie peered at the swimmer. He was going more slowly now and he seemed to be settling deeper in the water after each stroke. "I don't think he's going to make it," Munnie said.

"Well," said Bert, "that'll be too bad."

Martha said nothing.

Munnie swallowed drily. Later on, he thought, I won't be able to bear remembering today, standing here, watching a man drown.

Then another picture flicked before his eyes. It was sharp and clear and there was nothing missing. It was of Bert and Martha and himself standing in front of a French policeman, seated at a desk, with his cap on, scratching away with a leaking fountain pen in a little black book.

"So," the policeman was saying, "you wish to report a drowning?"

"Yes."

"So—you saw this gentleman, some distance from the shore, waving at you, and then he disappeared?"

"Yes."

"And the lady?"

"The last we saw of her she was still holding onto the boat, floating out to sea."

"Ah. And—uh—what steps did you take, personally?"

"We . . . we came here and reported it."

"Oh, yes. Of course." More scratching in the book. A hand reaching out. "Your passports, please." A quick riffling through the pages and one short, coldly smiling glance as the policeman tossed them on the desk. "Ah, Americans, all of you . . ."

The man out in the water went under again for a second.

Munnie tried to swallow again. This time he couldn't manage it.

"I'm going to get him," he said. But for a moment he didn't move, as though, somehow, just saying it would fix everything, put the man on dry land, right the boat, stop the screams.

"It's two hundred and fifty yards at least from the beach," Bert said, very calmly. "And then two hundred and fifty yards back, or a little less, with a crazy Frenchman holding onto your neck."

Munnie listened gratefully. "Yes," he said. "At least."

"You never swam five hundred yards in your life," Bert said, sounding friendly and reasonable.

The man screamed again and now his voice was hoarse and terrified.

Munnie started walking swiftly along the wall, back to where there was a narrow flight of steps leading down to the little beach in front of the fort. He didn't run because he didn't want to be out of breath when he went into the water.

"Munnie!" he heard Bert call behind him. "Don't be a damn fool!"

Even as he started down the steep flight of steps, slippery with moss, Munnie noticed that Martha hadn't said anything. When he got down to the beach, he trotted across it, at the water line, to get to the point nearest the man. He stopped, breathing heavily, and waved at the swimmer, encouraging him. Now, down at water level, it looked a good deal more than two hundred and fifty yards. He kicked off his shoes and tore off his shirt. The wind felt cold on his skin. He took off his pants, tossing them to one side on the sand, and stood there in his shorts. He hesitated. They were old shorts and they had torn at the crotch and he had mended them, clumsily, himself. He had a sudden picture of his body washed ashore and people noticing the shabby mending job and smiling a little. He unbuttoned the shorts, his fingers fumbling thickly at the buttons and let the shorts drop to the sand. As he walked deliberately into the water, he thought, She's never seen me naked, I wonder what she thinks.

- He scraped his toes on a rock and the pain made the tears come into his eyes. He kept walking until the water was up to his chest, then pushed off and began to swim. The water was cold and his skin felt tight and frozen almost at once. He tried not to swim too fast, so that he would have some strength left when he reached the drowning man. Whenever he looked up to see how far he'd gone it seemed to him that he had hardly moved at all, and it was hard to keep going in a straight line. Somehow he always seemed to be veering to his left, in the direction of the wall, and he had to keep correcting himself all the time. Once, he looked up at the wall, searching for Bert and Martha. He couldn't see them and he had a moment of panic. What the hell have they done? he thought. They've left. He turned over on his back, losing precious seconds, and saw them on the beach, standing at the water's edge, watching him. Of course, he thought.

He turned over and kept on swimming methodically toward the Frenchman. Whenever he picked his head out of the water, the Frenchman seemed to be screaming, and just as far away as ever. He decided not to look again for awhile. It was too discouraging.

Then his arms began to feel tired. It can't be, he thought. I haven't even gone fifty yards yet. Still, the muscles between his shoulders and his elbows seemed to be contracted, twisting his bones, and there was a deep ache of weariness in the back of his arms. His right hand began to cramp a little, too, and he let it flutter loosely through the water, which slowed him down, but he didn't know what else to do about it. The cramp reminded him that he had eaten not very long before and had a lot of wine and grapes and cheese. As he swam, with the water a green blur in his eyes and the slow, steady push of it going past his ears, he remembered his mother, in all the summers of his boyhood, on the shores of the lake in New Hampshire, saying, "No swimming for at least two hours after meals." Sitting on a little wooden chair, under a striped umbrella, watching the children play on the narrow, pebbly beach.

The back of his neck and the base of his skull started to ache now, and his thoughts wavered across his consciousness, disconnected and slippery. He had never liked swimming much, he remembered. He just went in to cool off and play around. Swimming had always seemed like a boring sport. The same old thing, over and over again, lift one arm, lift the other arm, kick, lift one arm, lift the other arm, kick, never really get anyplace. And he had never learned to keep the water out of his ears and sometimes he'd feel deaf for hours and the water wouldn't come out until he'd gone to bed and slept on one side for a long time.

His arms began to feel numb and he rolled more and more, in an effort to get his shoulders into the job, and he seemed to be swimming lower in the water than he ever had before. There's no sense in wasting time, he thought, making himself worry about something else besides his arms, I might as well figure out what to do once I get there. Laboriously, he tried to phrase what he would say to the man in French when he approached him. *Monsieur, j'y suis. Doucement. Doucement.* He would stay off from the man and try to calm him down before grabbing him. Dimly, he remembered having seen a demonstration of life-saving at a pool when he was fourteen years old. He hadn't paid much attention, because the boy behind him had surreptitiously kept flicking at him with a wet towel. But there was something about letting yourself sink if the drowning man put his arms around your neck, then twisting and putting your hand under his chin and pushing back. He hadn't believed it when he was fourteen years old and he didn't believe it now. It was one of those things that looked good in practice, on dry land. Then there were all the stories about hitting people on the chin and knocking them out. More dry land. He had never knocked anybody out in his whole life. His mother hated fighting.

Monsieur, soyez tranquille. Roulez sur votre dos, s'il vous plaît. Then he'd go in and grab him by the hair and start towing him, sidestroke. If the man understood him. He had an awful lot of trouble getting Frenchmen to understand his accent, especially here in the Basque country. Martha had no trouble at all. They all said what a charming accent she had. Well, why not, after all that time at the Sorbonne? She should have come with him as an interpreter, if for nothing else. *Tournez sur votre dos.* That was better.

He swam heavily and slowly, his eyes beginning to smart from the salt water. When he lifted his head there were white and silver spots before his eyes and everything seemed to be blurred and he couldn't really see anything much. He kept on swimming. After fifty strokes he decided he'd stop and tread water and look around. The idea of treading water now seemed like the greatest pleasure ever vouchsafed the human race.

He started to count the strokes. Fourteen, fifteen, sixteen . . . Lord, he thought, what if he's bald? He tried to remember what the man's head had looked like, far out, splashing away from the overturned boat. There had been a funny pale gleam. Bald, Munnie decided desperately. Nothing is going to go right.

He started counting strokes all over again. By the time he got to thirty-five he knew he would have to stop for awhile. He made himself do five more, then stopped and rolled over on his back, gasping and blowing water and looking up at the sky. He got his breath back and turned again and trod water, searching for the Frenchman.

He blinked his eyes and rubbed them with the back of his hand, sinking up to his mouth as he did so. The Frenchman wasn't there. Oh, God, he thought, he went down.

Then he heard the chugging and twisted in the water. A fishing boat was bearing away from the spot where Munnie had last seen the Frenchman, and was going toward the overturned dory. Munnie trod water, watching while the tuna boat stopped, and two fishermen reached down and pulled the woman on board. The tuna boat, Munnie realized, must have been coming up from the south, concealed by the little headland on which the fort was built, and must have coasted along the seaward side of the wall and entered the channel while he was swimming blindly out from the beach.

The men on the tuna boat threw a line onto the dory,

then swung around and headed for Munnie. He waited for it, fighting his lungs. The tuna boat, painted blue, and slow and old, approached him, looking big and safe as it drew nearer. Munnie saw grinning, tanned wide faces, capped by blue berets in the bow, and he waved, with great effort, as the tuna boat slowed down and came to a stop next to him.

"*Ça va?*" a fisherman shouted, grinning down at him. A cigarette, burned almost to the end, hung plastered to his lips.

Munnie managed to smile. "*Ça va bien,*" he called. "*Très bien.*"

The man who had been rescued came to the rail, still naked to the waist, and peered curiously down at Munnie. Munnie saw that he had plenty of hair. The Frenchman didn't say anything. He was a fat young man with a hurt and dignified expression on his face. At his side appeared a woman. She had been heavily made up and the seawater had done a great deal of damage to the rouge and mascara. She stared furiously down at Munnie, then turned to the Frenchman. She grabbed him by both ears and shook him. "*Crapaud!*" she said loudly. "*Espèce de cochon.*"

The Frenchman closed his eyes and allowed his head to be shaken, keeping his face sad and dignified. The fisherman grinned more broadly.

"*Alors,*" one of the fishermen said, throwing a line out toward Munnie, "*allons-y.*"

Munnie looked longingly at the line. Then he remembered that he was naked. He shook his head. One thing that was not going to happen to him that afternoon was to be fished out of the sea naked in front of that woman pulling her friend's ears and calling him a pig and a toad. "I'm O.K.," Munnie said, up to the brown, tough, amused faces, used to all sorts of comical, salty accidents and escapes. "*Je suis O.K.* I want to swim. I mean—*Je voudrais bien nager.*"

"O.K., O.K.," the fishermen said, laughing, as though what he had said was enormously witty. They pulled in the line and waved and the tuna boat swung around and started in toward the harbor, towing the dory. As it went, over the sound of the engine, Munnie could still hear the sound of the woman screaming.

Well, Munnie thought, watching the boat sail off, at least they understood me.

Then he turned and looked at the beach. It looked miles

away and Munnie was surprised that he had swum that far. He had never swum that far before in his life. On the beach, at the water line, with the tower of the fort behind them, Bert and Martha were standing, small, sharp figures, throwing long shadows now in the declining sun.

Taking a deep breath, Munnie started to swim in.

He had to turn over and float every ten yards or so and for awhile it seemed to him that he wasn't moving at all, only going through the motions of swimming, but finally, putting his feet down, he touched bottom. It was still fairly deep, up to his chin, and he pulled his feet up and stubbornly kept on swimming. And as a gesture, which he didn't try to understand, even as he did it, he swam all the way in, making himself spurt and do a proper crawl, until the water was so shallow that his finger-tips scraped the sand.

Then he stood up. He wavered a little, but he stood up and, making himself smile, walked slowly, naked, with the water streaming off him, toward where Bert and Martha stood next to the little pile of his clothes on the beach.

"Well," Bert said as Munnie came up to them, "what part of Switzerland are *you* from, Bud?"

As he bent over and picked up the towel and began to dry himself, shivering under the rough cloth, Munnie heard Martha laugh.

He rubbed himself dry. He took a long time, shivering badly, too weary and not interested enough to try to cover his nakedness. They drove back to the hotel in silence and when Munnie said that he thought he'd lie down and try to rest for awhile, they both agreed that it was probably the best thing to do.

He slept uneasily, his ears half deaf and stopped with water and the blood pounding in them like a distant, fitful sea. When Bert came in and said it was time for dinner, Munnie told him he wasn't hungry and that he wanted to rest. "We're going to the Casino after dinner," Bert said, "Should we stop by and pick you up?"

"No," Munnie said. "I don't feel lucky tonight."

There was a little silence in the darkened room. Then Bert said, "Good night. Sleep well, Fat Man," and went out.

Alone, Munnie lay staring at the shadowed ceiling, thinking. *I'm not fat. Why does he call me that? He only started it in the middle of the summer.* Then he slept again and only awakened when he heard the car drive up outside the hotel and the steps going softly up the stairs, past his door, to the floor above. He heard a door open and close gently upstairs and he made himself shut his eyes and try to sleep.

When he awoke the pillow was wet, where the water had run out of his ears, and he felt better. When he sat up the blood stopped pounding inside his head, too. He turned on the lamp and looked at Bert's bed. It was empty. He looked at his watch. It was four-thirty.

He got out of bed and lit a cigarette and went to the window and opened it. The moon was just going down and the sea was milky and was making an even, grumbling sound, like an old man complaining about the life that lay behind him.

For a moment, he wondered where he would have been at this hour if the tuna boat hadn't come in around the breakwater. Then he doused his cigarette and began to pack. It didn't take long, because they had been travelling light all summer.

When he finished he made sure that the extra key for the car was on his ring. Then he wrote a short note for Bert, telling him that he'd decided to take off for Paris. He hoped to get to Paris in time to catch the boat. He hoped this wouldn't inconvenience Bert too much and he knew that Bert would understand. He didn't mention Martha.

He carried his bag out to the car through the dark hotel and threw the bag into the empty space next to the driver's seat. He put on a raincoat and a pair of gloves and started the car and drove carefully out the driveway, without looking back to see whether the sound of the engine had awakened anyone or whether anyone had come to a window to watch him leave.

There was mist in the low places on the road, and he drove slowly, feeling it wet against his face. With the sighing regular noise of the windshield wipers and the steady, damp light of the headlights on the road ahead of him almost hypnotizing him, he drove mechanically, not thinking of anything at all.

It was only far past Bayonne, when the dawn had broken and he had cut off the lights and the road stretched gray and glistening through the dark pine aisles of Les Landes, that he allowed himself to remember the day and night that had just passed. And then all he could think was, It's my fault. I let the summer go on one day too long.

The Sunny Banks of the River Lethe

HUGH FORESTER ALWAYS REMEMBERED EVERYTHING. HE remembered the dates of the Battle of New Cold Harbor (May 31-June 12, 1864); he remembered the name of his teacher in the first grade (Webel; red-haired; weight, one-forty-five; no eyelashes); he remembered the record number of strikeouts in one game in the National League (Dizzy Dean, St. Louis Cards, July 30, 1933, seventeen men, against the Cubs); he remembered the fifth line of "To a Skylark" (Shelley: "In profuse strains of unpremeditated art"); he remembered the address of the first girl he ever kissed (Prudence Collingwood, 248 East South Temple Street, Salt Lake City, Utah; March 14, 1918); he remembered the dates of the three partitions of Poland and the destruction of the Temple (1772, 1793, 1795, and 70 A.D.); he remembered the number of ships taken by Nelson at the Battle of Trafalgar (twenty), and the profession of the hero of Frank Norris's novel *McTeague* (dentist); he remembered the name of the man who won the Pulitzer Prize for history in 1925 (Frederic L. Paxson), the name of the Derby winner at Epsom in 1923 (Papyrus), and the number he drew in the draft in 1940 (4726); he remembered the figures for his blood pressure (a hundred and sixty-five over ninety; too high), his blood type (O), and his vision (forty over twenty for the right eye and thirty over twenty for the left); he remembered what his boss told him when he was fired from his first job ("I'm getting a machine to do the job"), and what his wife said when he proposed to her ("I want to live in New York"); he remembered the correct name of Lenin (Vladimir Ilyich Ulyanov), and what caused the death of Louis XIV (gangrene of the leg). He also remembered the species of birds, the mean depths of the navigable rivers of America; the names, given and assumed, of all the Popes, including the ones at Avignon; the batting averages of Harry Heilmann and Heinie Groh; the dates of the total eclipses of the sun since the reign of Charlemagne; the

118

speed of sound; the location of the tomb of D. H. Lawrence; all of the *Rubáiyát of Omar Khayyám;* the popula-
tion of the lost settlement of Roanoke; the rate of fire
of the Browning automatic rifle; the campaigns of Caesar
in Gaul and Britain; the name of the shepherdess in *As
You Like It* and the amount of money he had in the
Chemical Bank & Trust on the morning of December 7,
1941 ($2,367.58).

Then he forgot his twenty-fourth wedding anniversary
(January 25th). His wife, Narcisse, looked at him
strangely over breakfast that morning, but he was reading
the previous night's newspaper and thinking, They will
never get it straight in Washington, and he didn't pay much
attention. There was a letter from their son, who was at the
University of Alabama, but he put it in his pocket without
opening it. It was addressed only to him, so he knew it was
a request for money. When Morton wrote his dutiful,
familial notes they were addressed to both his parents.
Morton was at Alabama because his marks had not been
high enough to get him into Yale, Dartmouth, Williams,
Antioch, the College of the City of New York, or the University of Colorado.

Narcisse asked if Hugh wanted fish for dinner and he
said yes, and Narcisse said that fish was criminally expensive, too, and he said yes, and she asked if anything was the
matter and he said no and kissed her and walked out of the
apartment to the 242nd Street subway station and stood all
the way down to the office, reading the morning newspaper.
Narcisse's parents had lived in France for some time and
that was where the name came from; by now he was used
to it. As he read his newspaper in the crowded car he
wished, mildly, that most of the people whom people
wrote about in the newspapers would vanish.

Hugh was the first one in the office, and he went to his
cubbyhole and sat at his desk, leaving the door open, enjoying the empty desks and the sound of silence. He remembered that Narcisse's nose had twitched at the breakfast
table and that she had seemed about to cry. He wondered
briefly why, but knew that he would be told in good time,
and dismissed it. Narcisse cried between five and eight
times a month.

The company for which he worked was putting out a
one-volume encyclopedia, absolutely complete, on Indian
paper, with seven hundred and fifty illustrations. There
was some talk of its being called the Giant Pocket Encyclo-

pedia, but no final decision had as yet been reached. Hugh was working on the "S"s. Today he had Soap, Sodium, Sophocles, and Sorrento before him. He remembered that Maxim Gorki had lived in Sorrento, and that of the hundred and twenty-three plays that Sophocles wrote, only seven had been discovered. Hugh was not actually unhappy at his work except when Mr. Gorsline appeared. Mr. Gorsline was the owner and editor-in-chief of the house, and believed in standing behind the backs of his employees, silently watching them at their labors. Whenever Mr. Gorsline came into the room, Hugh had the curious feeling that blood was running slowly over his groin.

Mr. Gorsline was gray-haired, wore tweed suits, had the face and figure of a picador, and had started with calendars. The house still put out a great variety of calendars —pornographic, religious and occasional. Hugh was very useful on calendars because he remembered things like the death of Oliver Cromwell (September 3, 1658) and the date on which Marconi sent the first wireless message across the Atlantic (December 12, 1901) and the date of the first steamboat run from New York to Albany (August 17, 1807).

Mr. Gorsline appreciated Hugh's peculiar talents and was relentlessly paternal about his welfare. Mr. Gorsline was a believer in homeopathic medicines and the health-giving properties of raw vegetables, particularly eggplant. He was also opposed to glasses, having thrown his away in 1944 after reading a book about a series of exercises for the muscles of the eyes. He had persuaded Hugh to discard his glasses for a period of seven months in 1948, during which time Hugh had suffered from continual headaches, for which Mr. Gorsline had prescribed minute doses of a medicine from a homeopathic pharmacy which made Hugh feel as though he had been hit in the skull with bird shot. Now whenever Mr. Gorsline stood behind Hugh, he stared at Hugh's glasses with the stubborn, Irredentist expression of an Italian general surveying Trieste. Hugh's health, while not actively bad, was shabby. He had frequent, moist colds, and his eyes had a tendency to become bloodshot after lunch. There was no hiding these lapses or the fact that in cold weather he had to make several trips an hour to the men's room. At such times, Mr. Gorsline would break his customary silence to outline diets designed to

improve the tone of the nasal passages, the eyes and the
kidneys.

During the morning, Mr. Gorsline came into Hugh's
room twice. The first time, he stood behind Hugh's chair
without saying a word for five minutes, then said, "Still on
sodium?" and left. The next time, he stood silently for
eight minutes, then said, "Forester, you're putting on
weight. White bread," and left. Each time, Hugh had the
familiar feeling in the groin.

Just before lunch, Hugh's daughter came into his office.
She kissed him and said, "Many happy returns of the day,
Daddy," and gave him a small oblong package with a bow
of colored ribbon on top of it. Clare was twenty-two and
had been married four years but she refused to stop saying
"Daddy." Hugh opened the package, feeling confused.
There was a gold-topped fountain pen in it. It was the
fourth fountain pen Clare had given him in the last six
years, two on birthdays and the third on Christmas. She
had not inherited her father's memory.

"What's this for?" Hugh asked.

"Daddy!" Clare said. "You're kidding."

Hugh stared at the pen. He knew it wasn't his birthday
(June 12th). And it certainly wasn't Christmas (December 25th).

"It can't be," Clare said incredulously. "You didn't *forget!*"

Hugh remembered Narcisse's face at breakfast, and the
twitching of her nose. "Oh, my," he said.

"You better load yourself with flowers before you set
foot in the house tonight," Clare said. She peered anxiously
at her father. "Daddy, are you all right?" she asked.

"Of course I'm all right," Hugh said, annoyed. "Everybody forgets an anniversary once in a while."

"Not you, Daddy."

"Me, too. I'm human, too," he said, but he felt shaken.
He unscrewed the top of the pen and wrote TWENTY-
FOUR YEARS, in capitals, on a pad, keeping his head
down. He now owned eight fountain pens. "It's just what
I needed, Clare," he said, and put it in his pocket. "Thank
you very much."

"You haven't forgotten that you promised to take me
to lunch, have you?" Clare had phoned the day before to
make the appointment for lunch, because, she told Hugh,
she had some serious problems to discuss.

"Of course not," Hugh said briskly. He put on his overcoat, and they went out together. Hugh ordered sole, then changed to a lamb chop, because he remembered that Narcisse had said at breakfast they were to have fish for dinner. Clare ordered roast chicken and Waldorf salad, and a bottle of wine, because, she said, the afternoons became less sad after a bottle of wine. Hugh didn't understand why a pretty twenty-two-year-old girl needed wine to keep her from being sad in the afternoons, but he didn't interfere.

While Clare was going over the wine card, Hugh took Morton's letter out of his pocket and read it. Morton was asking for two hundred and fifty dollars. It seemed that he had borrowed a fraternity brother's Plymouth and gone into a ditch with it after a dance and the repairs had come to a hundred and twenty-five dollars. There had been a girl with him, too, and her nose had been broken and the doctor had charged a hundred dollars for the nose and Morton had promised to pay. Then, there was ten dollars for two books in a course on ethics and fifteen dollars just, as Morton phrased it, to make it a round number. Hugh put the letter back in his pocket without saying anything about it to Clare. At least, Hugh thought, it wasn't as bad as last year, when it looked as though Morton was going to be kicked out of school for cheating on a calculus examination.

As Clare ate her chicken and drank her wine, she told her father what was troubling her. Mostly, it was Freddie, her husband. She was undecided, she said as she ate away steadily at her chicken, whether to leave him or have a baby. She was sure Freddie was seeing another woman, on East Seventy-eighth Street, in the afternoons, and before she took a step in either direction she wanted Hugh to confront Freddie man to man and get a statement of intentions from him. Freddie wouldn't talk to her. Whenever she brought the subject up, he left the house and went to a hotel for the night. If it was to be a divorce, she would need at least a thousand dollars from Hugh for the six weeks in Reno, because Freddie had already told her he wouldn't advance a cent for any damn thing like that. Besides, Freddie was having a little financial trouble at the moment. He had overdrawn against his account at the automobile agency for which he worked, and they had clamped down on him two weeks ago. If they had the baby, the doctor Clare wanted would cost eight hundred dollars, and there would be at least another five hundred for the hospital and nurses, and she knew she could depend on Daddy for that.

She drank her wine and talked on as Hugh ate silently. Freddie, she said, was also five months behind in his dues and greens fees at the golf club, and they were going to post his name if he didn't pay by Sunday, and that was *really* urgent, because of the disgrace, and Freddie had behaved like an absolute savage around the house ever since he received the letter from the club secretary.

"I told him," Clare said, with tears in her eyes and eating steadily, "I told him I would gladly go out and work, but he said he'd be damned if he'd let people say he couldn't support his own wife, and, of course, you have to respect a feeling like that. And he told me he wouldn't come to you for another cent, either, and you can't help admiring him for that, can you?"

"No," Hugh said, remembering that his son-in-law had borrowed from him, over a period of four years, three thousand eight hundred and fifty dollars and had not paid back a cent. "No, you can't. Did he know you were going to come and talk to me today?"

"Vaguely," Clare said, and poured herself another glass of wine. As she carefully harvested the last bits of apple and walnut from her salad, Clare said she didn't really like to burden him with her problems but he was the only one in the whole world whose judgment she really trusted. He was so solid and sensible and smart, she said, and she didn't know any more whether she really loved Freddie or not and she was so confused and she hated to see Freddie so unhappy all the time about money and she wanted to know whether Hugh honestly felt she was ready for motherhood at the age of twenty-two. By the time they finished their coffee, Hugh had promised to talk to Freddie very soon about the woman on Seventy-eighth Street and to underwrite either the trip to Reno or the obstetrician, as the case might be, and he had made a half promise about the back dues and the greens fees.

On the way to the office, Hugh bought an alligator handbag for Narcisse for sixty dollars and worried sharply, for a moment, about inflation as he wrote out the check and handed it to the salesgirl.

It was a little difficult to work after lunch, because he kept thinking about Clare and what she had been like as a little girl (measles at four, mumps the year after, braces from eleven to fifteen, acne between fourteen and seventeen). He worked very slowly on Sorrento. Mr. Gorsline came in twice during the afternoon. The first time he said, "Still on Sorrento?" and the second time he said, "Who the hell cares if that Communist Russian wrote a book there?"

In addition to the usual sensation in the groin, Hugh noticed a quickening of his breath, which was almost a gasp, when Mr. Gorsline stood behind him during the afternoon.

After work, he went into the little bar on Lexington Avenue where he met Jean three times a week. She was sitting there, finishing her first whisky, and he sat down beside her and squeezed her hand in greeting. They had been in love for eleven years now, but he had kissed her only once (V-E Day), because she had been a classmate of Narcisse's at Bryn Mawr and they had decided early in the game to be honorable. She was a tall, majestic woman who, because she had led a troubled life, still looked comparatively young. They sat sadly and secretly in sad little bars late in the afternoon and talked in low, nostalgic tones about how different everything could have been. In the beginning, their conversation had been more animated, and for a half hour at a time Hugh had recovered some of the optimism and confidence that he had had as a young man who had taken all the honors at college, before it had become apparent that a retentive memory and talent and intelligence and luck were not all the same thing.

"I think, very soon," Jean said while he was sipping his drink, "we'll have to give this up. It isn't going anywhere, really, is it, and I just don't feel right about it. I feel guilty. Don't you?"

Until then, it hadn't occurred to Hugh that he had done anything to feel guilty about, with the possible exception of the kiss on V-E Day. But now that Jean had said it, he realized that he probably would feel guilty from now on, every time he entered the bar and saw her sitting there.

"Yes," he said sadly. "I suppose you're right."

"I'm going away for the summer," Jean said. "In June. When I come back I'm not going to see you any more."

Hugh nodded miserably. The summer was still five

months away, but behind him he had a sense of something slipping, with a rustling noise, like a curtain coming down.

He had to stand in the subway all the way home, and the car was so crowded that he couldn't turn the pages of his newspaper. He read and reread the front page, thinking, I certainly am glad I wasn't elected President.

It was hot in the train, and he felt fat and uncomfortable jammed among the travellers, and he had a new, uneasy feeling that his flesh was overburdening him. Then, just before he came to Two hundred and forty-second Street, he realized that he had left the alligator bag on his desk in the office. He felt a little tickle of terror in his throat and knees. It was not so much that, empty-handed, he faced an evening of domestic sighs, half-spoken reproaches, and almost certain tears. It was not even so much the fact that he mistrusted the cleaning woman who did his office every night and who had once (November 3, 1950), he was sure, taken a dollar and thirty cents' worth of airmail stamps from the upper right-hand drawer. But, standing there in the now uncrowded car, he had to face the fact that twice in one day he had forgotten something. He couldn't remember when anything like that had ever happened to him before. He touched his head with his fingertips, as though there might be some obscure explanation to be found that way. He decided to give up drinking. He drank only five or six whiskies a week, but the induction of partial amnesia by alcohol was a well-established medical principle, and perhaps his level of tolerance was abnormally low.

The evening passed as he had expected. He bought some roses at the station for Narcisse, but he couldn't tell her about the alligator bag left on his desk, because he figured, correctly, that that would only compound the morning's offense. He even suggested that they return to the city for an anniversary dinner, but Narcisse had had the whole day alone to augment her self-pity and brood upon her martyrdom, and she insisted on eating the fish, which had cost ninety-three cents a pound. By ten-thirty she was crying.

Hugh slept badly and got to the office early the next morning, but even the sight of the alligator bag, left squarely in the middle of the desk by the cleaning woman, did not raise his spirits. During the day he forgot the names of three of Sophocles' plays *(Oedipus at Colonus,*

Trachiniae, and *Philoctetes)* and the telephone number of his dentist.

It started that way. Hugh began to make more and more frequent trips to the reference library on the thirteenth floor, dreading the trip through the office, because of the way his fellow-workers commenced to look at him, curious and puzzled, as he traversed the room again and again in the course of an hour. One day he forgot the titles of the works of Sardou, the area of Santo Domingo, the symptoms of silicosis, the definition of syndrome, and the occasion of the mortification of Saint Simeon Stylites.

Hoping it would pass, he said nothing about it to anyone —not even to Jean, in the little bar on Lexington Avenue.

Mr. Gorsline took to standing for longer and longer periods behind Hugh's desk, and Hugh sat there, pretending to be working, pretending he didn't look haggard, his jowls hanging from his cheekbones like gallows ropes, his brain feeling like a piece of frozen meat that was being nibbled by a wolf. Once, Mr. Gorsline muttered something about hormones, and once, at four-thirty, he told Hugh to take the afternoon off. Hugh had worked for Mr. Gorsline for eighteen years and this was the first time Mr. Gorsline had told him to take an afternoon off. When Mr. Gorsline left his office, Hugh sat at his desk, staring blindly into terrifying depths.

One morning, some days after the anniversary, Hugh forgot the name of his morning newspaper. He stood in front of the news dealer, staring down at the ranked *Times* and *Tribunes* and *News* and *Mirrors,* and they all looked the same to him. He knew that for the past twenty-five years he had been buying the same paper each morning, but now there was no clue for him in their makeup or in their headlines as to which one it was. He bent down and peered more closely at the papers. The President, a headline announced, was to speak that night. As Hugh straightened up, he realized he no longer remembered the President's name or whether he was a Republican or a Democrat. For a moment, he experienced what could be described only as an exquisite pang of pleasure. But he knew it was deceptive, like the ecstasy described by T. E. Lawrence on the occasion when he was nearly beaten to death by the Turks.

He bought a copy of *Holiday,* and stared numbly at the colored photographs of distant cities all the way down to

the office. That morning, he forgot the date on which John
L. Sullivan won the heavyweight championship of the
world, and the name of the inventor of the submarine.
He also had to go to the reference library because he
wasn't sure whether Santander was in Chile or Spain.

He was sitting at his desk that afternoon, staring at his
hands, because for an hour he had had the feeling that
mice were running between his fingers, when his son-in-
law came into the office.

"Hi, Hughie, old boy," his son-in-law said. From the
very first night his son-in-law had appeared at the house,
he had been unfalteringly breezy with Hugh.

Hugh stood up and said "Hello"—and stopped. He
stared at his son-in-law. He knew it was his son-in-law.
He knew it was Clare's husband. But he couldn't remember
the man's name. For the second time that day he experienced the trilling wave of pleasure that he had felt at the
newsstand when he realized he had forgotten the name
and political affiliations of the President of the United
States. Only this time it seemed to last. It lasted while he
shook hands with his son-in-law and all during the trip
down in the elevator with him, and it lasted in the bar
next door while he bought his son-in-law three Martinis.

"Hughie, old boy," his son-in-law said during the third
Martini, "let's get down to cases. Clare said you had a
problem you wanted to talk to me about. Spit it out, old
boy, and let's get it over with. What have you got on
your mind?"

Hugh looked hard at the man across the table. He
searched his brain conscientiously, but he couldn't think
of a single problem that might possibly involve them.
"No," Hugh said slowly. "I have nothing in particular on
my mind."

His son-in-law kept looking at Hugh belligerently while
Hugh was paying for the drinks, but Hugh merely hummed
under his breath, smiling slightly at the waitress. Outside,
where they stood for a moment, his son-in-law cleared his
throat once and said, "Now, look here, old boy, if it's
about—" but Hugh shook his hand warmly and walked
briskly away, feeling deft and limber.

But back in his office, looking down at his cluttered
desk, his sense of well-being left him. He had moved on to
the "T"s by now, and as he looked at the scraps of paper
and the jumble of books on his desk, he realized that he
had forgotten a considerable number of facts about Taci-

tus and was completely lost on the subject of Taine. There was a sheet of notepaper on his desk with the date and the beginning of a salutation: "Dear . . ."

He stared at the paper and tried to remember who it was he had been writing to. It was five minutes before it came to him; the letter was to have been to his son, and he had meant, finally, to enclose the check for the two hundred and fifty dollars, as requested. He felt in his inside pocket for his checkbook. It wasn't there. He looked carefully through all the drawers of his desk, but the checkbook wasn't there, either. Shaking a little, because this was the first time in his life that he had misplaced a checkbook, he decided to call up his bank and ask them to mail him a new book. He picked up the phone. Then he stared at it blankly. He had forgotten the telephone number of the bank. He put the phone down and opened the classified telephone directory to "B." Then he stopped. He swallowed dryly. He had forgotten the name of his bank. He looked at the page of banks. All the names seemed vaguely familiar to him, but no one name seemed to have any special meaning for him. He closed the book and stood up and went over to the window. He looked out. There were two pigeons sitting on the sill, looking cold, and across the street a bald man was standing at a window in the building opposite, smoking a cigarette and staring down as though he were contemplating suicide.

Hugh went back to his desk and sat down. Perhaps it was an omen, he thought, the thing about the checkbook. Perhaps it was a sign that he ought to take a sterner line with his son. Let him pay for his own mistakes for once. He picked up his pen, resolved to write this to Alabama. "Dear . . ." he read. He looked for a long time at the word. Then he carefully closed his pen and put it back in his pocket. He no longer remembered his son's name.

He put on his coat and went out, although it was only three-twenty-five. He walked all the way up to the Museum, striding lightly, feeling better and better with each block. By the time he reached the Museum, he felt like a man who has just been told that he has won a hundred-dollar bet on a fourteen-to-one shot. In the Museum, he went and looked at the Egyptians. He had meant to look at the Egyptians for years, but he had always been too busy.

When he got through with the Egyptians, he felt wonderful. He continued feeling wonderful all the way home in the subway. He no longer made any attempt to buy the newspapers. They didn't make any sense to him. He didn't recognize any of the people whose names appeared in the columns. It was like reading the Karachi *Sind Observer* or the Sonora *El Mundo*. Not having a paper in his hands made the long ride much more agreeable. He spent his time in the subway looking at the people around him. The people in the subway seemed much more interesting, much more pleasant, now that he no longer read in the newspapers what they were doing to each other.

Of course, once he opened his front door, his euphoria left him. Narcisse had taken to looking at him very closely in the evenings, and he had to be very careful with his conversation. He didn't want Narcisse to discover what was happening to him. He didn't want her to worry, or try to cure him. He sat all evening listening to the phonograph, but he forgot to change the record. It was an automatic machine and it played the last record of the second Saint-Saëns piano concerto seven times before Narcisse came in from the kitchen and said, "I'm going out of my mind," and turned it off.

He went to bed early. He heard Narcisse crying in the next bed. It was the third time that month. There were between two and five more times to go. He remembered that.

The next afternoon, he was working on Talleyrand. He was bent over his desk, working slowly but not too badly, when he became conscious that there was someone standing behind him. He swung in his chair. A gray-haired man in a tweed suit was standing there, staring down at him.

"Yes?" Hugh said curtly. "Are you looking for someone?"

The man, surprisingly, turned red, then went out of the room, slamming the door behind him. Hugh shrugged incuriously and turned back to Talleyrand.

The elevator was crowded when he left for the day, and the hall downstairs was thronged with clerks and secretaries hurrying out of the building. Near the entrance, a very pretty girl was standing, and she smiled and waved at Hugh over the heads of the homeward-bound office workers. Hugh stopped for an instant, flattered, and was tempted to smile back. But he had a date with Jean, and anyway he was too old for anything like that. He set his face and hurried out in the stream of people. He thought he heard a kind of wail, which sounded curiously like "Daddy," but he knew that was impossible, and didn't turn around.

He went to Lexington Avenue, enjoying the shining winter evening, and started north. He passed two bars and was approaching a third when he slowed down. He retraced his steps, peering at the bar fronts. They all had chromium on them, and neon lights, and they all looked the same. There was another bar across the street. He went and looked at the bar across the street, but it was just like the others. He went into it, anyway, but Jean wasn't there. He ordered a whisky, standing at the bar, and asked the bartender, "Have you seen a lady alone in here in the last half hour?"

The bartender looked up at the ceiling, thinking. "What's she look like?" he asked.

"She—" Hugh stopped. He sipped his drink. "Never mind," he said to the bartender. He laid a dollar bill on the counter and went out.

Walking over to the subway station he felt better than he had felt since he won the hundred-yard dash at the age of eleven at the annual field day of the Brigham Young Public School in Salt Lake City on June 9, 1915.

The feeling lasted, of course, only until Narcisse put the soup on the table. Her eyes were puffed, and she had obviously been crying that afternoon, which was curious, because Narcisse never cried when she was alone. Eating his dinner, conscious of Narcisse watching him closely across the table, Hugh began to feel the mice between his fingers again. After dinner, Narcisse said, "You can't fool me. There's another woman." She also said, "I never thought this would happen to me."

By the time Hugh went to bed, he felt like a passenger on a badly loaded freighter in a winter storm off Cape Hatteras.

He awoke early, conscious that it was a sunny day outside. He lay in bed, feeling warm and healthy. There was a noise from the next bed, and he looked across the little space. There was a woman in the next bed. She was middle-aged and was wearing curlers and she was snoring and Hugh was certain he had never seen her before in his life. He got out of bed silently, dressed quickly, and went out into the sunny day.

Without thinking about it, he walked to the subway

station. He watched the people hurrying toward the trains and he knew that he probably should join them. He had the feeling that somewhere in the city to the south, in some tall building on a narrow street, his arrival was expected. But he knew that no matter how hard he tried he would never be able to find the building. Buildings these days, it occurred to him suddenly, were too much like other buildings.

He walked briskly away from the subway station in the direction of the river. The river was shining in the sun and there was ice along the banks. A boy of about twelve, in a plaid mackinaw and a wool hat, was sitting on a bench and regarding the river. There were some schoolbooks, tied with a leather strap, on the frozen ground at his feet.

Hugh sat down next to the boy. "Good morning," he said pleasantly.

"Good morning," said the boy.

"What're you doing?" Hugh asked.

"I'm counting the boats," the boy said. "Yesterday I counted thirty-two boats. Not counting ferries. I don't count ferries."

Hugh nodded. He put his hands in his pockets and looked down over the river. By five o'clock that afternoon he and the boy had counted forty-three boats, not including ferries. He couldn't remember having had a nicer day.

The Wedding of a Friend

IT IS IMPOSSIBLE TO ATTEND A WEDDING WITHOUT A SENSE of foreboding or regret. Depending upon which side you are ranged, you are bound to have some unpleasant reservations about the bride or the groom, or perhaps both, and if you are cynical you are likely to remember other weddings you have witnessed and how the marriages eventually turned out. And if you are a man and the bride is beautiful, there is almost certain to be a moment during which you will feel a sharp, ignoble twinge of deprivation.

But at Ronny Biddell's wedding, although the bride was young and lovely and regarded Ronny with the most obvious bridal pleasure, I felt nothing but satisfaction and a strange kind of relief, a relief, I imagine, which must have been very close to the emotion felt by the brother of a matador who has watched a particularly dangerous fight, in which the matador has been upon the horns and has done foolhardy things all afternoon and has finally, exhausted and covered with blood, made a triumphant kill.

Ronny was not my brother and he was, of course, not covered with blood. He stood at the altar, ruddy, growing bald, sweating slightly, as he always did, a sturdy, round man in his tailcoat and striped trousers, looking, as he stood there, not quite being able to refrain from smiling a little, as though he had never been in danger in his life.

I was at the wedding by accident. I had arrived in London planning vaguely to look up Ronny, and had, in fact, made a desultory inquiry or two, but everyone in England seemed to have changed addresses several times since the war, and I had not taken the time to track him down. The truth was, too, that I was a little afraid of what I might find if I finally did locate him, and I invented excuses not to press the search too assiduously.

Then, one day, in a restaurant on Jermyn Street, I saw him across the room, sitting with a young, dark-haired girl of superlative beauty, who kept looking at Ronny with that narrowness and intensity of focus which is, in our era, in a crowded restaurant, the public advertisement of love. Fifteen minutes later I was being invited to the wedding.

Now I was sitting in the church, among the polished, strange British faces, listening to the ceremony, staring at Ronny's reddish scalp and his solid, polite shoulders, enjoying the curious feeling of relief for Ronny, who, unexpectedly, among all the men I had known during the war who had later suffered or vanished or failed to live up to the hopes we had entertained for them, had arrived at this shining and victorious moment.

I had met Ronny in London in 1943. He was at that time a lieutenant in the British Army, hazily attached to the same project to which I was assigned, one of those interallied missions which had very little to do with winning the war, but which served, while the armies waited for the invasion of Europe, as an occasion of Anglo-American good-will and co-operation at almost no military cost. Ronny at first sight looked like the sort or man who had been deprived, only because of his youth, of a colonelcy in the Indian Army. He wore a mustache, he boomed, he carried himself like a soldier and drank like one—he was in fact so markedly the type of regular colonial officer, at least to American eyes, that we called him, much to his enjoyment, the Beefeater. The flaw in the picture was that under the robust martial exterior he was hideously shy, especially with women. He had been brought up by aunts with so much circumspection that his respect for women at the age of twenty-eight was carried to an extreme which was, to all practical purposes, impotence.

He was childishly candid about himself with his friends and I knew all his history within two weeks of meeting him. He was abnormally susceptible to women—the sight of a pretty face across a theater lobby could make him blush, almost as though all the confused thoughts and emotions that flooded through him at the sight of the girl were somehow guiltily plain to her, at a distance of twenty feet, and to everyone else present. And once, when a girl whom I had invited to have dinner with Ronny and me kissed him good night on the cheek, he confessed that it kept him up, half smiling and half in despair, for the entire night. He also had an uncomfortable tendency to breathe brokenly, like a sufferer from asthma, when talking to a girl, and sometimes even when talking *about* a girl. In all that time in London, which, not to put too fine a point upon it, was a period of almost unprecedented *camaraderie* between the sexes, I never saw Ronny out with a girl of his own.

That is not to say that Ronny had never been involved with a woman. For two years before the war, he had lived in Paris, on a small income, wearing a beret, according to his report, and studying what he vaguely called Art. During that time the had met Virginie, or rather, as he later admitted, had permitted himself to be picked up by her in a café on a rainy evening and allowed to pay for her drink.

"Frenchwomen, my dear fellow," he confided in me, on the basis of his knowledge of Virginie, "are more in my line. Forthright. Not always playing that damned game with a man. Direct."

It developed that Virginie had not been as direct as all that. She was young, with black hair and what Ronny called drowning gray eyes and that French thing about the mouth. But she lived, so she said, with her family, who were so savagely devout that Ronny was not even permitted to meet them. After the numberless dinners, evenings at the opera and theater to which Ronny escorted her, she would leave him, severely, at the door. He himself lived with a family and he had to go through the salon to reach his room, and there never was any hope of inviting her there. He fell very much in love with her and had reached a point at which he was taking her out three nights a week and kissing her at her doorway and mentioning marriage when the war broke out.

There was a tearful and public parting in the Luxembourg Gardens and Ronny went back to England, promising a letter a day and a quick victory for the linked arms of their two countries. Healthy, willing and with no discernible military talent, he was enlisted as a private and put at a desk in a motor-repair depot near Salisbury. Feigning patriotism and an overwhelming desire to come to grips with the enemy, he pulled what wires he could to get himself transferred to a position of greater danger, and some months later happily found himself en route to France. He never got as far as Paris, but was set down at Rennes, where he was put behind a desk once more, again in a motor-repair depot. Virginie could not come to visit him, because of parental objections, but Ronny managed two leaves in Paris, where he made up for the ignominy of his trooper's uniform with prodigal tête à tête dinners with Virginie in the elegant restaurants and with substantial gifts bought from his dwindling income, in the most expensive shops.

Marriage was, for the moment, out of the question, but Ronny's ardor, fanned by two years of devotion, could no longer be stayed, and he so far forgot the maxims of his aunts as to press Virginie, finally, for a rendezvous. After a suitable hesitation, Virginie, taking into account the perils of the time and the patriotic claims of the poor boys in uniform who might be here today and God-knows-where tomorrow, relented. But after so much waiting, so many unassuaged sighs, so many whispered nighttime conversations under lampposts and outside darkened doors, she could not relent all in one piece or in a single moment. She agreed—but for the future. On his next leave in Paris, when they had had time to prepare themselves properly, she promised that the event would take place. Ronny went back to Rennes, blistered with anticipation, and put in, as soon as he dared, for another leave. The leave was promised him some three weeks in the future and he made thorough arrangements, through the mails, with a small but excellent hotel, for a two-room suite with bath and even went so far as to order the dinner and the wine for the crucial evening. Four years later, when he told me all this, he still remembered the exact menu and wines that he had ordered—smoked Scotch salmon, roast duck, cooked with peaches, salad and wild strawberries. The wines were a Haut-Brion, 1928, and a Veuve Cliquot, 1919.

Something of a hypochondriac, despite his robust appearance, and fearful that the prolonged state of tension under which he was living would bring him disastrously to sick parade and hospital, he began taking long, brisk, health-giving walks in the drab purlieus of Rennes and he gave up all drink, even wine, for the three weeks. As the day grew near, despite the fact that he no longer was able to sleep more than four or five hours a night, he began to feel that he would be able to arrive in Paris in acceptable condition.

His uniform glittering, his duties meticulously completed, all his rather extensive banking arrangements carefully made, Ronny was ready to take off for Paris when the German Army, after eight months of stationary and non-bellicose war on the Western front, struck through the Low Countries. All leaves, including Ronny's, were cancelled, and he spent the next twenty days praying, more fervently than any general in command of the engaged armies, for a stabilization of the front. As one turning movement, one counterattack after another was crushed and swept aside by the German armor, Ronny fell deeper and deeper into apathy. When the British Army, in accordance with the modern doctrine of saving the clerks first, loaded him on a truck to a port in Southern Brittany, where, without hearing a gun fired, he was put on a comfortable excursion steamer and carried across to England, Ronny had lost all interest in the war and hardly even bothered to listen to the ship's radio reports of the disintegration of the Allied Armies to the North.

For six months after that, Ronny sat on a hill in Sussex, serving a tank which was parked permanently in a meadow, since its engine had long since been removed to a more active unit. Neither the tank's immobility nor the fact that for a long time there were only four shells at the disposal of the crew in the event that the Germans appeared on the road below them served to disturb his melancholy tranquillity. Like those philosophers who have been driven into monasteries by a secret but overpowering disappointment, Ronny was for that period far past caring about such remote temporal matters as the passage of armies, death in battle, or the collapse of governments. He sat in the meadow beside the useless weapon, among the summer flowers, agreeable, silent, smiling distantly at his fellow-soldiers, rereading the curt letters he had received from Virginie before the fall of Paris, and going over and over again the communication to the hotel manager, with the menu of the celebration dinner, of which he had kept a copy.

When America entered the war and it began to seem as if, some time in the future, English armies would once more stand on the Continent, Ronny aroused himself and applied for O.T.C., under the sensible assumption that if he ever returned to Paris, in a military condition, he would be received more gratefully by Virginie if he were in the uniform of an officer. He worked conscientiously and won his commission, in an honorable middle place in his class, distinguishing himself among his fellow-officers only by signing his name to a petition for a Second Front which was being circulated at that time by the Communists, although he came from an unswervingly Tory family, and his personal politics would have been considered medieval even by the Duke of Wellington.

When I met him in London, in 1943, he was cheerful, lively and blindly pro-American, mostly because of the fact that with the arrival in England of each new troopship from the United States, the liberation of Paris became, in his eyes, more and more of a certainty. He admired, above all, the easy American familiarity, especially pronounced at that time, with the opposite sex, although he found it quite beyond his powers to emulate it. He was one of those unfortunate men in whom the conception of love, of sex, even, is irrevocably bound up with one woman—and the fact that he was separated from that woman by four years, the English Channel, and sixty divisions of the German Army, altered his attitude not at all, and, indeed, only served to strengthen it.

When it became plain that the Invasion was imminent, Ronny volunteered for a position of danger, garnering a promotion in the process, and managed to get himself set down on the beach on the first day. From then on he became the image of the perfect soldier, making his country's cause completely his own, cheerfully offering himself at all times for patrols, reconnaissance, liaison and attacks, although the mission of the unit to which he was attached was not primarily combat. But I think it could fairly be said that whatever one humble lieutenant in an obscure post could do to pierce the encircling lines and drive the German Army back toward the Rhine, Ronny did.

On the day that Paris fell, Ronny rode into the city amid the cheers and the snipers' fire with the first Allied troops. The driver of the small truck in which Ronny had made his entry into the capital was a forty-year-old corporal named Watkins, who, although the father of five children, was sympathetically romantic, and, under Ronny's direction, guided the truck along doubtful streets, sometimes dangerously deserted, sometimes swarming with celebrating Parisians, toward the address behind the Gare St. Lazare at which Ronny had last visited Virginie.

There is a whole tribe of men, who, at the end of a similar quest, would have found the lady waiting, perfumed and appropriately dressed, in her living room, ready to be embraced. Needless to say, Ronny was not one of those. Virginie was nowhere on the premises and there was no one there who even remembered her. In her old apartment was living a cranky couple from Caen who took the occasion, upon hearing Ronny speak French, to complain bitterly to him about certain bombings they had undergone from the R.A.F.

That evening, in the midst of the revelry which marked the first twenty-four hours of freedom for the city, Ronny moved absently, a fixed smile upon his lips, because he was too good and kindly a man to impose his sorrow upon his friend's pleasure, but facing tragically the conviction that for him love was over, once and for all, even before it had fairly begun.

Our unit, as though exhausted by the approach to Paris, remained there, under ambiguous orders, billeted in a small hotel off the Rue de Rivoli, while the lines of battle moved farther and farther off. Ronny had the room next to mine and night after night I heard his steady, military pacing up and down, like a guardsman who is making up his mind to face his colonel and tell him he has betrayed the honor of the regiment.

Then the miracle happened. While driving in the truck along the Boulevard des Italiens one afternoon, three or four days after our arrival in Paris, Ronny saw Virginie. She was on a bicycle and moving fast in the opposite direction and her hair was now blond, but Ronny, who had been scanning every female face in the city with the nervous persistence of a radar antenna, was not to be deceived.

He waved at Watkins, who was at the wheel of the truck, to turn around. Watkins, by now himself imbued with some of Ronny's passion, swung recklessly through the press of bicycles, jeeps and pedestrians and finally caught up with Virginie at the corner of the Rue Lafitte. Ronny jumped out of the truck while it was still moving but managed to hold his feet, calling Virginie's name wildly and reaching out for the handlebars of her bicycle. She recognized him almost immediately and they embraced in the middle of the street, with Watkins, grinning delightedly, and a good many others watching with interest. As Ronny admitted to me later, at that moment, standing there in the busy street, blocking traffic, with the sound of horns in his ears, holding Virginie in his arms, the war had reached its culminating point.

Virginie, it turned out, had an appointment that could not wait, but she took time for a hurried drink in a nearby café and a conversation which Ronnie could not repeat coherently when he tried to report it to me an hour later. They made a date for six o'clock at a bar near our hotel and kissed in parting, and Ronny, to whom loving was synonymous with giving, spent the rest of the afternoon collecting, from all possible sources, gifts for Virginie. He bought a pink scarf, although the rate of exchange was ruinous; he traded a pair of captured German binoculars for five yards of parachute silk; he managed to pry loose from a friend who had been hoarding them in his knapsack for two months, three cans of sardines; he ordered Watkins, who was more than willing, to impose mercilessly upon his connections with certain American mess-sergeants, and Watkins turned up with a box of ten-in-one rations and a five-pound can of orange marmalade, no mean accomplishment in a city in which everyone, soldiers and civilians alike, were on severely curtailed diets.

Ronny insisted that I meet the lady, although I tried to persuade him that on this first day, while the shock of the lost years was being absorbed, it would perhaps be better for him to be alone with her. But Ronny, whose concept of happiness was involved automatically with the idea of sharing, and who was understandably nervous about these first delicate moments with Virginie, insisted that I meet her, at least, even if I left after a few minutes.

When I got to the bar, shortly after six o'clock, Ronny was sitting tensely in a corner, sweating, alone, surrounded by his pile of gifts, looking anxiously at his watch.

"She's not here," he said, as I sat down. "I'm a fool. I should have told her I'd go and get her. She probably can't find the bar."

"She's been living in Paris all her life, hasn't she?" I said. "She'll find the bar."

"I don't know," Ronny said, keeping his eyes on the entrance. "And then there's the question of time. I said six o'clock but I don't remember whether I said French time or Army time." At that period, because of the manipulations with daylight-saving schemes that the Germans had introduced, in an effort to conserve fuel and lengthen the working day, the French were always an hour in advance of us. "Maybe she was here," Ronny said, troubledly, "and hung around and gave up and went home and like an idiot I never asked her for her address. . . ."

"Did you ask the bartender if he saw her?" I said.

"He says he hasn't seen anybody," Ronnie said. "But maybe she looked in and decided to wait outside. She's shy and sitting in here with a lot of soldiers might have . . ." He stopped and stood up, smiling tremulously. "Virginie," he said.

He shook hands formally with the girl and introduced us immediately, and carefully held her chair while she sat down.

"I'm terribly pressed, Ronneee," Virginie said. She had a full skirt and she settled herself in little ballooning movements. She was pretty enough, although the blond hair was a misfortune and she had a wary, speculative look about her, like a gambler measuring an opponent's luck before putting down his bet. She was a small, neat, clever-looking, big-city girl and it was hard to think of her saying good night so demurely and insistently at her door just four years before. "Would they have whisky?"

"Of course they have whisky," Ronny said, in the tone of a man who was prepared to distill it out of his own veins on the spot if necessary. He called to the bartender for a whisky and, clumsy and beaming in front of her, began shoveling his various gifts onto the table. "I brought you a few things. A scarf, and this silk is . . ."

"Ah," Virginie said, "the American rations." She ran her hand caressingly over the carton. "So ingenious." The look on her face changed subtly, the gambler deciding that the man opposite is not lucky. She smiled sentimentally and touched Ronny's hand. "The same old Ronneee," she said. "Always so thoughtful." She wrinkled her nose troubledly.

"But how am I to get it all home?" she said. "I only have a bicycle."

"I have a lorry," Ronny said, his happiness increased by this opportunity for further service. "I'll take you home."

"There is room for the bicycle, too?"

"Of course."

"Good," the girl said. "Now I can stay an additional fifteen minutes." She smiled softly at Ronny, although I still did not see the drowning look about the eyes that Ronny had described, or anything particularly French about the mouth. "I am so anxious to hear about the kind of war you have made and . . ." she looked at me significantly, "there are one or two things I wish to explain when we are alone."

I stood up. "I have to go along to dinner," I said.

"Americans," Virginie said, smiling charmingly, "are so tactful.

Ronny beamed, proud that his friend had won Virginie's approval. I left them, Ronny breathing hoarsely and talking in intimate whispers, Virginie sitting there, her eyes gently downcast, her fingers from time to time stroking the edges of the box of ten-in-one rations.

I was in my room, reading, later that night, when Ronny knocked on the door and came in. He was nervous and he had obviously had something more to drink and he could not sit still, but walked back and forth uneasily on the worn rug next to my bed.

"What do you think of her?" he asked.

"I. . . ."

"Isn't she marvelous?"

"Marvelous," I said.

"It's that thing about Frenchwomen," he said. "I'm spoiled forever for English girls."

"Well," I said, "maybe you . . ."

"Can you lay your hands on a carton of cigarettes?" he asked.

"Well," I said, "it's pretty difficult . . ."

"I'll pay, of course," he said hastily.

"Why do you need them?" I asked. "Does Virginie smoke?"

"No," Ronny said. "It's the man she's living with."

"Oh," I said, closing my book.

"He's a chain smoker," Ronny said. "But he only likes American cigarettes."

"I see."

Ronny made two more trips up and down the carpet. "That's why she was in a hurry," he said. "He's terribly jealous. What I mean is, after four years, and during a war and all, and she never knew whether I was alive or dead."

"Of course," I said.

"What I mean is, it would be childish to be surprised, wouldn't it?"

"I suppose so."

"He's one of those dark, intense types. He rather smouldered at me in the beginning." Ronny smiled briefly, and I could see that along with the disappointment of discovering that Virginie had been claimed in his absence there was a little sense of gratification that he had finally found someone who was jealous of him. "He was in the Underground or something like that and now that that's finished he just sits around the apartment all day, chain-smoking and keeping track of Virginie. Can't blame him, can you, with a girl as attractive as Virginie?"

"Well," I began.

"She doesn't love him, though," Ronny said, breathing heavily. "She told me in the truck going there. They live all the way up on top of Montmartre and that poor girl has to pedal up and down that hill in all weathers. She took him in when he was hiding from the police. Simple patriotism. And then one thing led to another. They've been together three years, but she isn't happy. I promised the cigarettes for tomorrow. Do you think you can manage it?"

"I'll try," I said. "In the morning."

"By Jove," he said, "after four years. Seeing her there riding down the Boulevard des Italiens on a bicycle. They opened the marmalade and it was pathetic to see how they spooned it up. I'm seeing her tomorrow afternoon. It's not as though they were married or she loved him or anything like that. What I mean is, it's not a violation of principle or taking advantage. I mean, I declared myself long before he appeared on the scene, didn't I? After all, if my leave hadn't been cancelled when the Germans went through Belgium . . ." He allowed himself a half-sigh, remembering that inconvenient invasion. "And I'm just meeting her in a bar. I can't go to their place, because he just sits there all day, chain-smoking, checking on her movements. Rum luck, eh?" He smiled wanly, moving to the door. "After four years. A man who sits home all day."

He went out and long after I had turned out the light I heard him striding steadily back and forth in his room, the boards creaking sadly through the long hours of the night in trouble and love.

For the next few days Ronny was of very little use to the British Army. Whenever Virginie had fifteen minutes that she could spare from her lover, Ronny would make himself available, meeting her in bars, in front of monuments, in the lobbies of hotels, and at the approaches to whatever bridges over the Seine Virginie had to cross in her various errands around Paris. There would be hurried, murmuring, serious talks, often with Virginie holding the handlebars of her bicycle and walking briskly with it down a street as Ronny strode alongside her, both of them followed, at a ceremonial pace, by Watkins, in the truck. Ronny would return from these tantalizing meetings red-faced, breathing hoarsely, with an obsessed glitter in his eyes, very much like the light that one might imagine as having shone in the eye of Captain Ahab as he was finally certain that he was closing in on the white whale. In the intervals of the day when he was not rushing to one point or another of the city to meet Virginie, Ronny devoted his energies to the amassing of treasure from the Allied Commissaries, which he delivered dutifully, by truck, to the apartment of Virginie and her lover. They had short, amiable conversations, the three of them, Ronny said, about what it had been like in Paris under the Germans and about how clumsily the Americans were conducting the war. Virginie's lover reserved his admiration for things American only to our cigarettes. The apartment, which was a small one, must have soon taken on the appearance of a small auxiliary depot of the Supply Services of two armies, with cases of bully beef, packaged rations, cans of coffee and cocoa powder, bottles of whisky, stacked cartons of cigarettes, and occasionally even loins of pork and cuts of beef piled all over the place, the substantial evidence of Ronny's devotion. I am sure that if by any chance Ronny, who until that time had been the most timid obeyer of regulations, had been investigated by the C.I.D., he would have run a fair chance of being sent to jail for ten years.

But neither this nor any other consideration could sway him for a moment. There was a continual procession of shifty-eyed sergeants carrying loaded barracks bags in and out of our hotel and Watkins was kept permanently in a state of readiness to drive Ronny to Virginie's apartment with each new acquisition. I know that Ronny dreamed of the hour when he would arrive, unannounced (Virginie

had no telephone), with his musette bag stuffed with cigarettes or bar chocolate, to find Virginie alone, finally, after
the six years. But this never happened. He often found
her lover, whose name was Emile, alone, and Emile would
sometimes even go so far as to offer Ronny a small drink
from the ration Scotch which Ronny had turned over to
the couple, but Virginie never.

Like a gambler who is deep in the hole who keeps
blindly doubling his bets to get even, Ronny poured his
gifts into the little apartment. He was not completely in-
genuous about what he was doing. "I'll tell you something," he confided to me. "That Emile doesn't really like
me. Everything else being equal, he'd tell Virginie that she
couldn't see me anymore. But this way, with the cigarettes
and the tinned bully beef and the whisky, he's torn.
Understand," Ronny said, "I wouldn't be doing this if he
treated Virginie well. But he treats her horribly and I feel
no compunctions."

"But you haven't done anything to feel any compunctions about," I pointed out.

"In due time, old man," Ronny said confidently. "All in
due time."

Then, the very next day, which was a Saturday, it turned
out that his confidence was justified. I was washing up in
my room, preparatory to going out for dinner, when Ronny
knocked and came in. I knew that he had had a date with
Virginie, in front of the Opera, and that she had said she
could only spare a quarter of an hour. Usually, when
he came from seeing Virginie, he was exceptionally red-
faced and booming, speaking in exhilarated half-sentences,
chuckling for no apparent reason, and moving restlessly,
with a nervous excess of energy. But tonight he seemed
pale and subdued and he spoke with a curious combina-
tion of languor and jumpily repressed emotion.

"Well," he said, "tomorrow is the day."

"What?" I asked, puzzled.

"I just saw her," he said. "I'm to come to the apartment tomorrow at three-fifteen. It's Sunday, and Emile is
going to the prize fights. He's interested in a middleweight.
It's the only moment in the week when he leaves her alone
for more than an hour at a time. There are people coming
in at four-thirty, though. It's rather split-second—one
hour and fifteen minutes." He smiled wanly, not looking at
all like the Indian colonel. "After six years. But a chap
must finally make a start, don't you think?"

"Yes," I said.

"It's almost inconceivable," he said. "Isn't it?"

"Almost," I agreed.

"My aunts would be amazed," he said.

"Would they?" I said noncommittally.

"There are chaps that do things like this every day of their lives, aren't there?"

"So I hear," I said.

"Amazing." He shook his head. "What time have you got?" he asked anxiously.

I looked at my watch. "Ten minutes to seven," I said.

He looked worriedly at his watch. "I have thirteen minutes to seven. Do you think my watch is slow?"

"I'm a little fast, I think."

He listened carefully to the ticking of his watch. "I'd better get the right time tomorrow morning," he said. "I told Watkins to meet me in front of the hotel at three sharp. He's more excited than I am." He smiled jerkily at the thought of the loyalty of Watkins. "Tell me, old man," he said, flushing a little, "is there anything I ought to know?"

"What?"

"I mean anything in particular?"

I hesitated, then decided that there wasn't enough time. "No," I said.

"Amazing," he said.

We sat in silence, not looking at each other.

"Curious," he said.

"What's curious?"

"Next January," he said, "I'm going to be twenty-nine years old."

I stood up and put on my tie. "I'm going down to dinner. Do you want to eat with me?"

"Not tonight, old man," he said. "I don't think I could eat tonight."

I nodded sympathetically, pretending to be more sensitive than I was, and went down to dinner. Ronny went into his room to write his weekly letter to his aunts.

The next morning I was on duty and the man who was supposed to relieve me didn't appear until well after two o'clock. I had lunch in a transient officers' mess and then, because it was a hot, sunny day, I walked leisurely, stopping often to enjoy the bright September sunlight on the old buildings and the quiet streets, toward the hotel. I was glad that I would be too late to see Ronny before he set out on his adventure. I had the feeling that it would be almost impossible to avoid saying the wrong thing at a moment like that, and I did not wish to complicate, by a slip of the tongue or an inadvertent smile, Ronny's climactic hour.

I reached the hotel at twenty minutes past three, and I was just going in, when Ronny came charging out of the open door. He was sweating heavily in his beautifully pressed battledress, and his face was red, his eyes were rolling, and his mouth was hanging open as if he had been bellowing. He grabbed me by both arms, his hands crazily powerful, crushing my shirt.

"Where's Watkins?" he shouted, although his face was no more than six inches from mine.

"What?" I asked, stupidly.

"Have you seen Watkins?" Ronny shouted, even more loudly, shaking me. "I'll kill the bastard."

"What's happened, Ronny?"

"Have you got a jeep?" he roared. "I'll have him court-martialed."

"You know I haven't got a jeep, Ronny," I said.

He dropped my arms and leaped out into the middle of the empty street and peered in both directions, wheeling around on his heels, waving his arms. "No transport," he cried. "No bloody transport!" He looked at his watch. "Twenty-five minutes past three." The numerals came out in a sob. "I'll have him transferred to the infantry, the swine!" He jumped back onto the sidewalk and began a short, running step, back and forth in front of the hotel entrance. "I should have been there ten minutes ago."

"Did you call the garage, Ronny?" I asked, trying to be helpful.

"He was there all morning," Ronny shouted, "washing the damn truck. Then he left about an hour ago. He's probably joy-riding in the Bois with his damned black-market friends."

This was a little unfair, since Watkins' by now extensive acquaintanceship in the black market had been built up solely in Ronny's service, but I didn't feel that this was the moment to see justice done to the reputation of the absent driver.

Ronny looked at his watch once more and moaned. "He's been driving for me for a year and a half," Ronny cried, "and he hasn't been a minute late yet. And he picks this day for it! Don't you know somebody with a jeep?"

"Well," I said doubtfully, "I guess I could rustle one up if you give me an hour or so."

"An hour or so!" Ronny laughed horribly. "There're people coming in at four-thirty! An hour or so!" He gazed wildly at the blank faces of the buildings and the calm, deserted street. "What a city! No Metro, no buses, no taxi! God, do you know anybody who has a bicycle?"

"I'm afraid not, Ronny," I said. "I wish I could help . . ."

"You wish you could help," he said, snarling, turning on me. "I don't believe you. I don't believe you for a minute."

"Ronny," I said, reproachfully. In all the time we had known each other, this was the first unfriendly word I had heard from him.

"Nobody gives a damn!" he shouted. "You don't fool me!" The sweat was pouring off him now and his face was alarmingly red. "The hell with you all! All right, all right," he shouted incoherently, waving his arms, "I'll go on foot."

"It'll take you at least a half hour," I said.

"Forty-five minutes," Ronny said. "What's the difference? If that bloody driver comes, tell him to come after me and watch for me on the street. He knows the route."

"Yes, Ronny," I said. "Good luck."

He looked at me bleakly, breathing hard. Then he said something obscene and short and started running. I watched him running heavily down the sunny street, past the shuttered windows, the sturdy khaki figure growing smaller and smaller, the sound of the thick boots on the pavement going farther and farther away, diminishing, in the direction of Montmartre. He turned a corner and the street was quiet, lost in its bright, Sunday stillness.

Somehow, I felt guilty, as though there were something I might have done for Ronny that I had callously left undone, and I stayed in front of the hotel, smoking, watching for Watkins and the truck. Finally, at ten minutes to four, I saw it turn the corner and come down our street. It was thoroughly washed and polished and looked as neat as any truck could possibly be expected to look which had made the entire campaign from the beaches to Paris. Watkins, too, I saw as he drove up, had taken great pains with himself. He had shaved himself painfully close and his skin was shining pink and raw, his hair was plastered down under his hat, and he had a sly, benignant, anticipatory smile on his face as he parked the truck in front of the hotel with an unaccustomed flourish. On the seat beside him, I saw, there was a large bunch of flowers.

He sprang out and saluted me smartly, still smiling. "Well," he said, "I'm a little early, but I thought, on a day like this, the lieutenant might be waiting for me on the pavement."

"Where the hell have you been, Watkins?" I asked, exasperated for Ronny's sake with the man's idiotic pleasure in himself.

"Been?" Watkins asked, puzzled. "Been?"

"The lieutenant called the garage nearly an hour ago," I said, "and they said you'd left."

"Well," Watkins said, "I thought it might be a pleasant touch if the lieutenant carried some flowers in for the lady and I took a little tour looking for them. Carnations," he said, pointing to them. "You'd be shocked if I told you what they ask for them . . ."

"Watkins," I said, "you're an hour late."

"What? Watkins' mouth fell open. He looked at his watch. "The lieutenant said specifically three o'clock, and I allowed a little extra time and it's not ten to three yet."

"It's ten to four, Watkins," I said.

"What?" Watkins closed his eyes, as though he could not bear to look at my face.

"It's ten to four," I said. "Weren't you told that as of last midnight, all clocks would be advanced one hour, to coincide with French time?"

"Oh," Watkins said in a whisper. "Oh, suffer me, suffer me." His face looked drained and loose, like the face of a man going under anesthesia. "I heard about it during the week, but I didn't spend the night in billets, and I was off duty this morning and nobody happened to mention it at the garage. Oh, suffer me, Mother . . . Where's the lieutenant now?"

"At this moment," I said, "he's probably just passing Sacre Coeur, on the dead run."

Watkins turned slowly, like a prizefighter who has been hit and is senselessly seeking the support of the ropes. He leaned against the door of the truck, his forehead pressed against the metal. When he lifted his head, I saw that there were tears in his eyes. There he stood, bowlegged and hunched over in his neat uniform, his scraggly, cruelly shaven, Cockney face twisted in grief as he thought of

Ronny pounding hopelessly up the hills of Montmartre.

"What can I do?" he asked brokenly. "What can I ever bloody well do?"

"Well," I said, "at least go wait for him so he doesn't have to walk home."

Watkins nodded mechanically. Then he got into the cab of the truck, carelessly knocking the carnations onto the floor, and started the motor. He drove off, looking neither to the right nor left.

Ronny got back to the hotel at six o'clock. I heard the truck drive up to the door and I looked out my window and saw him descend from the truck, slowly, without saying a word to Watkins, and move exhaustedly into the hotel. He came directly to my room and entered without knocking and sank into a chair, keeping his cap on his head. There were dark sweat stains around his collar and there were hollows under his eyes, as though he hadn't slept in weeks. I poured him a whisky and put the glass in his hand. He didn't even look up at me, but sat there, a round, diminished, rumpled figure, staring blankly ahead of him at the stained wall above the bed.

"You heard," he said finally.

"Yes."

"The Army," he said flatly. "Whenever anything good is liable to happen to you, the Army does something." He sat slumped in the chair, with his cap on, thinking of the declaration of war in 1939 and the collapse in Belgium less than a year later. He shook his head and took a long drink. "French time," he muttered, obscurely.

I poured some whisky into his glass.

"I've got to get out," he said. "I've been in this war long enough."

"What happened?" I asked, thinking that perhaps talking about it would help him.

"Nothing," he said. He chuckled once, shortly. "I got there at five minutes past four. Watkins caught up with me one block from the house. Did you see the flowers?"

"Yes," I said.

"That was thoughtful of him, wasn't it?"

"Yes."

"She was making canapés for her guests. Sardines. She had oil all over her fingers."

"Was she angry?"

"Not exactly," Ronny said. "When I told her what had

happened, she began to laugh. I thought she was going
to strangle, she laughed so hard. I never heard a woman
laugh like that in my whole life."

"Well," I said, trying to be comforting, "another time."

Ronny shook his head. "No. When she finally got
through laughing, she kissed my forehead and she said,
'It's fate, Chérie, we will remain good friends.'"

There was nothing to be said to this, and I poured myself a drink. We sat in silence.

"She asked me to help her with the canapés," Ronny
said. "I opened two tins of bully beef and I cut my finger."
He held up his right hand and I saw a nasty, jagged cut,
sticky with dried blood. "The only blood I've lost in the
whole damned war," he said. "Her friends came in early.
Four-fifteen. They devoured everything. I had to open
three more tins of bully. They kept complaining about the
American Army. Emile came in early, too. Four-thirty-
five." Ronny by now was as conscious of time as a railroad engineer. "His middleweight won," Ronny said bitterly, as though this was finally too much to bear. "A
knockout in the first round. He drank three glasses of
whisky to celebrate and he keep clapping me on the back
and calling me *mon petit Anglais* and showing me how it
was done. Three lefts, *mon petit Anglais,* like lightning,
to the nose, and a straight right, like a bomb, to the point
of the jaw. The other man didn't wake up for ten minutes.
He was feeling so good, Emile, he let Virginie say goodbye to me alone in the hallway." Ronny smiled wanly.
"She got sardine oil all over my battledress. And she gave
me some information. She said her conscience was bother-
ing her; the time had come to speak frankly. She was very
queer. When she talked it was as though she was having a
hard time to keep from laughing. She said she had known
Emile since 1937. She hasn't lived with her family since
she was fifteen years old. Her family lives in Nice. They've
never been to Paris. And Emile wasn't in the Underground.
I got *that* from her friends. He smuggled butter from
Normandy all during the war."

Ronny got up from the chair, slowly and painfully, like
a man whose bones are giving him trouble. "I've got to
get out," he said. "I've just got to get out." He turned and
faced me, looking at me with brooding intensity. "Don't be
surprised," he said mysteriously, "not matter what you
hear."

He went out slowly, the bones not moving very well in

the martial, chubby flesh. I heard him go into his room
and the springs creak as he lay heavily down in his bed.

The very next day, I noticed a change in Ronny. Whenever he moved, he gave off a strong smell of particularly
sweet toilet water, and he began to cultivate the habit of
wearing his handkerchief in his sleeve. He also began to
walk in a curious, short-stepped way and his speech suddenly took on a slight lisp, very disturbing in a man who
looked as though he should be leading a regiment of Sikhs.
He began to avoid me, too, and there were no longer the
long, candid conversations in my room at night. When I
invited him to have dinner with me, he giggled nervously
and said he was terribly busy these days.

Then, a week later, I was visited by a British Medical
Officer, a bleak, graying captain, who, it turned out, was a
specialist in psychic disorders and cases of combat fa-
tigue.

"I wonder if you could help me, Lieutenant," the captain said, after ascertaining that I had known Ronny for
almost a year. "It's about your friend, Lieutenant Biddell."

"Is anything wrong with him?" I asked, cautiously,
wishing Ronny had briefed me.

"I'm not sure," the captain said. "Would you say there
was something abnormal about him?"

"Well," I said, wondering how I might answer a question like that honestly without harming Ronny, "that
would be hard to say. Why? What's the matter?"

"Lieutenant Biddell has been to see me three or four
times this week," the captain said, "with a most unusual
story. Most unusual." The captain hesitated, then decided
to plunge ahead. "Well, there's no sense in being ambiguous. He seems to believe that he should be discharged
for the good of the service."

"What?" I asked, surprised.

"He claims to have discovered, quite recently, that—
well—we're both grown men, we don't have to beat
around the bush . . ." the captain said. "It's not the first
time we've heard about something like this. Particularly in
time of war, with men taken out of their normal life and
deprived of the companionship of women for years on
end. Bluntly," the captain said, "Lieutenant Biddell claims
that he finds himself attracted irresistibly to—uh—men."

"Oh," I said, thinking, Poor Ronny; the toilet water
and the handkerchief.

"The external evidence is all there, of course," the captain said, "the perfume, the manner of speech, et cetera. But he scarcely seems to be the type, although in my profession, of course, we are hardly surprised . . . You understand. At any rate, he says he's afraid that if he remains in the . . . uh . . . military atmosphere . . . he will be tempted into an overt act . . . which would, of course, have grave consequences. I've spoken to other of his fellow officers, and, as tactfully as possible, to his driver, and they all seem surprised. I hear that you've been very close and I wonder if you might be able to throw light on the situation."

"Well . . ." I hesitated. For a moment, I thought of telling the doctor the entire story. Then I decided against it. Maybe, I thought, it's really time for Ronny to get out. "I've noticed little indications here and there," I said. "He's had an exhausting war," I added loyally.

The captain nodded. "Who hasn't?" he said gloomily and got up and left, after shaking my hand.

The next day, without warning, our unit was ordered to move out of Paris. At the same time, Ronny was detached from us and assigned to a headquarters in Paris, where, I presumed, it would be easier for the doctor to conclude his examination. In the confusion of the move, I didn't see Ronny, and I didn't get back to Paris until the war was over and by that time he had departed. I heard that, whatever else had happened, he had not been given the discharge he had asked for. Somebody said that he thought Ronny had been sent back to England, but he wasn't sure, and it was impossible, without compromising Ronny, to make the only kind of inquiry that would enlighten me.

I was sent back to America without getting to England again, and over the years, from time to time, I wondered rather sadly about my friend and speculated, not without pity, on what paths he might have strayed into in peacetime London. I did not judge him harshly. It is not only twenty-four-hour barrages and being in the line without relief for months on end that destroys the will to continue in men, and in a war casualties are suffered in a variety of ways that have nothing to do with gunfire. But, occasionally, when I met a man who spoke with a little lilt or dressed in a certain, overfastidious way, I wondered if perhaps he would have been a different man at that moment if sometime in his past, at a moment of crisis, someone had arrived a half hour sooner or later.

Ronny kissed the bride before the altar, then they both turned and walked up the aisle, the music swelling behind them. As he came even with me, red-faced, triumphant, tender, bull-like, he winked. I winked back, thinking, Isn't this nice; not everything has turned out badly since 1944. As he went out of the church with his bride, I wondered if I could get the name and address of the psychiatrist from him for one or two of my other friends.

Voyage Out, Voyage Home

CONSTANCE SAT IMPATIENTLY IN THE LITTLE CHAIR IN the first-class cabin, taking occasional sips of the champagne that Mark had sent. Mark had been called out of town and hadn't been able to come, but he'd sent champagne. She didn't like champagne, but she didn't know what else to do with it, so she drank it. Her father stood in front of the porthole, drinking, too. From his expression, Constance could guess that he didn't like champagne either. Or perhaps he didn't like this particular vintage. Or he didn't like it because Mark had sent it. Or maybe it wasn't the champagne at all but just that he was embarrassed.

Constance knew that she was looking sullen, and she tried to change the set of her face, because she also knew that she looked younger, childish, sixteen, seventeen, when she was sullen. She was sure that everything she did with her face at that moment made her look more sullen than ever, and she wished the horn would blow and her father would get off the ship.

"You'll probably drink a lot of this," her father said. "In France."

"I don't expect to stay in France long," she said. "I'm going to look for someplace quiet." Her voice sounded to her as though it were coming out of the nursery, wailing and spiteful and spoiled. She tried to smile at her father. The last few weeks in the apartment, while the argument had been going on and the hostility had been so close to the surface, had been painful to her, and now, in the last ten minutes before the ship pulled away, she wanted to recapture an earlier, easier relationship as far as she could. So she smiled, but she had the impression that the smile was crafty and cold and coquettish. Her father turned around and looked vaguely out the port-hole at the covered wharf. It was rainy and there was a cold wind blowing and the men on the dock waiting to throw off the lines looked miserable.

"It's going to be a choppy night," her father said. "Have you got the Dramamine?"

The hostility returned, because he asked about the Dramamine. At a moment like that. "I won't need Dra-mamine," Constance said shortly. She took a long drink of the champagne. The label on the bottle was impeccable, like all Mark's gifts, but the wine was sourish and acidy.

Her father turned back toward her. He smiled at her, and she thought, bitterly, This is the last time he's going to get away with patronizing me. He stood there, a ro-bust, confident, healthy, youngish-seeming man, looking privately amused, and Constance thought, How would you like it if I just got out of here and walked off this precious boat—how would you ever like it?

"I envy you," her father said. "If someone had only sent me to Europe when I was twenty . . ."

Twenty, twenty, Constance thought. He's always harp-ing on twenty. "Please, Father, let's cut that out," she said. "I'm here and I'm going and it's all settled, but let's spare ourselves the envy."

"Every time I happen to remind you that you're twenty," her father said mildly, "you react as though I'd insulted you."

He smiled, pleased with himself that he was so damned perceptive, that he understood her so well, that he was not one of those fathers whose children slide irrevocably away from them into mysterious, modern depths.

"Let's not discuss it," Constance said, pitching her voice low. When she remembered, she always made a point of pitching her voice low. It sometimes made her sound forty years old on the telephone, or like a man.

"Have a great time," her father said. "Go to all the bright places. And if you decide you want to stay on, just let me know. Maybe I'll be able to come over and join you for a few weeks—"

"Three months from now," Constance said crisply, "to this day, I'll be coming up the harbor."

"Whatever you say, my dear."

When he said "my dear," Constance knew he was humoring her. She couldn't bear being humored there in the ugly little cabin, with the weather bad outside, and the ship ready to leave, and the sounds of people saying goodbye, laughing loudly, in the next room. If she had been on better terms with her father, she would have cried.

The horn blew for visitors to go ashore, and her father came and kissed her, holding her for an extra second, and she tried to be polite. But when he said, very seriously, "You'll see—three months from now you'll thank me for this," she pushed him back, furious with him for his obnoxious assurance, and mournful at the same time that they, who had been so close to each other, were no longer friends.

"Goodbye," she said, her voice choked and not pitched low. "The whistle's blowing. Goodbye."

He picked up his hat, patted her shoulder, hesitated a moment at the door, looking thoughtful but not disturbed, and went out into the corridor and disappeared among the other visitors who were streaming up toward the gangplank and the shore.

When she was sure her father was off, Constance went up to the boat deck and stood there, alone in the sharp, blowy rain, watching the tugs pull the ship into the stream. As the ship went slowly downriver into the harbor and then headed into open water, she shivered in the wintry air, and, approving of herself a little for the grandeur of the sentiment, thought, I am approaching a continent to which I have no connection.

Constance braced herself against the crossbar of the lift as she approached the mid-point of the hill. She made sure that her skis were firmly in the ruts as she came up onto the flat section of packed snow where there was a short line of skiers who had come down only halfway and were waiting to pick up empty hooks and go back to the top. She always felt a little uncertain here, because if you were alone on one side of the T bar, the first person in the line would swing into place alongside you and there would be an extra, sudden pull as the new weight caught that could throw you off balance. She saw that there was a man waiting for the place next to her, and she concentrated on keeping erect gracefully as he settled into place beside her. He did it smoothly, and they skidded easily past the waiting line. She was conscious that he was looking across at her, but she was too occupied for the moment with the terrain in front of her to turn her head.

"Oh, I know you," the man said as they started safely up the hill again, leaning against the pull of the bar, their skis bumping a little in the ruts. "You're the grave young American."

Constance looked at him for the first time. "And you," she said, because everybody talked to everybody else on the hills, "you're the gay young Englishman."

"Half right," he said. He smiled. His face was a skier's brown, with an almost girlish flush of blood along the cheekbones. "At least, one-third right." She knew his name was Pritchard, because she had heard people talking to him in the hotel. She remembered hearing one of the ski teachers say about him, "He is too reckless. He thinks he is better than he actually is. He does not have the technique for so much speed." She glanced across at him and decided he *did* look reckless. He had a long nose —the kind that doesn't photograph well but that looks all right just the same, especially in a long, thin face. Twenty-five, Constance thought, twenty-six. No more. He was leaning easily against the bar, not holding on with his hands. He took off his gloves and fished a package of cigarettes out of his pockets and offered them to Constance. "Players," he said. "I hope you won't hate me."

"No, thank you," Constance said. She was sure that if she tried to light a cigarette she would fall off the lift.

He lit his cigarette, bending over a little and squinting over his cupped hands as the smoke twisted up past his eyes. He had long, thin hands, and ordinarily you had the feeling that people with hands like that were nervous and easily upset. He was tall and slender, and his ski pants were very downhill, Constance noted, and he wore a red sweater and a checked scarf. He had the air of a dandy, but a dandy who was amused at himself. He moved easily on his skis, and you could tell he was one of the people who weren't afraid of falling.

"I never see you in the bar," he said, tossing the match into the snow and putting on his gloves.

"I don't drink," she said, not quite telling the truth.

"They have Coca-Cola," he said. "Switzerland, the forty-ninth state."

"I don't like Coca-Cola."

"Used to be one of the leading British colonies," he said, grinning. "Switzerland. But we lost it, along with India. Before the war, in this town, the English covered the hills like the edelweiss. If you wanted to find a Swiss between January 1st and March 13th, you had to hunt with dogs."

"Were you here before the war?" Constance asked, surprised.

"With my mother. She broke a leg a year."

"Is she here now?"

"No," he said. "She's dead."

I must be careful, Constance thought, avoiding looking at the man beside her, not to ask people in Europe about their relatives. So many of them turn out to be dead.

"It used to be very gay," he said, "the hotels swarming, and dances every night, and everybody dressing for dinner, and singing 'God Save the King' on New Year's. Did you know it was going to be this quiet?"

"Yes," Constance said. "I asked the man at the travel bureau in Paris."

"Oh. What did he say?"

"He said everybody was a serious skier here and went to bed by ten o'clock."

The Englishman glanced at her momentarily. "You're not a serious skier, are you?"

"No. I've only been two or three times before."

"You're not one of the delicate ones, are you?"

"Delicate?" Constance looked at him, puzzled. "What do you mean?"

"You know," he said, "the advertisements. Schools for delicate children. Swiss for t.b."

Constance laughed. "Do I look as though I have t.b.?"

He regarded her gravely, and she felt plump and unaustere and a little too bosomy in her tight clothes. "No," he said. "But you can never tell. Did you ever read *The Magic Mountain?*"

"Yes," she said, feeling proud that she could show she was not completely uncultured, although American and very young, and remembering that she had skipped the philosophic discussions and cried over the death of the cousin. "I read it. Why?"

"The sanitarium is was written about isn't far from

here," Pritchard said. "I'll show it to you someday when the snow's bad. Do you think this place is sad?"

"No," she said, surprised. "Why?"

"Some people do. The mixture. The pretty mountains and the healthy types walloping down the hills, risking their necks and feeling marvellous, and the people with the bad lungs hanging on, watching them and wondering if they're ever going to leave here alive."

"I guess I didn't think about it," Constance admitted honestly.

"It was worse right after the war," he said. "There was a boom here right after the war. All the people who hadn't eaten enough or had been living underground or in prison and who had been frightened so long—"

"Where're they now?"

Pritchard shrugged. "Dead, discharged, or destitute," he said. "Is it true that people refuse to die in America?"

"Yes," she said. "It would be an admission of failure."

He smiled and patted her gloved hand, which was clutching tightly onto the middle bar. "You mustn't be angry that we're jealous," he said. "It's the only way we can show our gratitude." Gently, he loosened her fingers from the wood. "And you mustn't be so tight when you ski. Not even with your fingers. You mustn't even frown until you go in for tea. The drill is—loose, desperate, and supremely confident."

"Is that how you are?"

"Mostly desperate," he said.

"What are you doing on this little beginners' slope, then?" Constance asked. "Why didn't you take the *téléphérique* up to the top?"

"I twisted my ankle yesterday," Pritchard said. "Overrated myself. The February disease. Out of control and into a gully, with a great deal of style. So today I can only do slow, majestic turns. But tomorrow we attack that one once more—" He gestured up toward the peak, half-closed in by fog, with the sun a wet, pale ball above it, making it look forbidding and dangerous. "Come along?" He looked at her inquiringly.

"I haven't been up there yet," Constance said, regarding the mountain respectfully. "I'm afraid it's a little too much for me so far."

"You must always do things that are a little too much for you," he said. "On skis. Otherwise, where's the fun?"

They were silent for several moments, moving slowly up the hill, feeling the wind cut across their faces, noticing the quiet and the queer, fogged mountain light. Twenty yards ahead of them, on the preceding bar, a girl in a yellow parka moved evenly upward like a bright, patient doll.

"Paris?" Pritchard said.

"What's that?" He jumps around entirely too much, Constance thought, feeling heavy.

"You said you came from Paris. Are you one of those nice people who come here to give us your government's money?"

"No," said Constance. "I just came over on a—well, on a vacation. I live in New York, really. And French food makes me break out."

He looked at her critically. "You look completely unbroken out now," he said. "You look like the girls who advertise soap and beer in American magazines." Then he added hastily. "If that's considered insulting in your country, I take it back."

"And the men in Paris," she said.

"Oh. Are there men in Paris?"

"Even in the museums. They follow you. With homburg hats. Looking at you as though they're weighing you by the pound. In front of religious pictures and everything."

"Girl I knew, English girl," Pritchard said, "was followed from Prestwick, Scotland, to the tip of Cornwall by an American gunner in 1944. Three months. No religious pictures, though, as far as I know."

"You know what I mean. It's an impolite atmosphere," she said primly, knowing he was making fun of her in that straight-faced English way but not knowing whether to be offended or not.

"Were you brought up in a convent?"

"No."

"It's amazing how many American girls sound as though they were brought up in a convent. Then it turns out they drink gin and roar in bars. What do you do at night?"

"Where? At home?"

"No. I know what people do at night in America. They look at television," he said. "I mean here."

"I—I wash my hair," she said defensively, feeling foolish. "And I write letters."

"How long are you staying up here?"

"Six weeks."

"Six weeks." He nodded, and swung his poles to his outside hand, because they were nearing the top. "Six weeks of shining hair and correspondence."

"I made a promise," she said, thinking, I might as well let him know now, just in case he's getting any ideas. "I promised someone I'd write him a letter a day while I was gone."

Pritchard nodded soberly, as though sympathizing with her. "Americans," he said as they came to the top and slid out from the T bar onto the flat place. "Americans baffle me."

Then he waved his poles at her and went straight down the hill, his red sweater a swift, diminishing gay speck against the blue-shadowed snow.

The sun slipped between the peaks, like a gold coin in a gigantic slot, and the light got flat and dangerous, making it almost impossible to see the bumps. Constance made her last descent, falling twice and feeling superstitious, because it was always when you said, "Well, this is the last one," that you got hurt.

Running out and coming to a stop on the packed snow between two farmhouses at the outskirts of the town, she kicked off her skis with a sense of accomplishment and relief. Her toes and fingers were frozen, but she was warm everywhere else and her cheeks were bright red and she breathed the thin, cold air with a mountain sense of tasting something delicious. She felt vigorous and friendly, and smiled at the other skiers clattering to a stop around her. She was brushing the snow of the last two falls off her clothes, so that she would look like a good skier as she walked through the town, when Pritchard came down over the last ridge and flicked to a stop beside her.

"I see you," he said, bending to unlock his bindings, "but I won't tell a soul."

Constance gave a final, self-conscious pat to the icy crystals on her parka. "I only fell four times all afternoon," she said.

"Up there, tomorrow"—he made a gesture of his head toward the mountain—"you'll crash all day."

"I didn't say I was going up there." Constance buckled her skis together and started to swing them up to her shoulder. Pritchard reached over and took them from her

"I can carry my own skis," she said.

"Don't be sturdy. American girls are always being sturdy about inessential points." He made a big V out of the two pairs of skis on his shoulders, and they started walking, their boots crunching on the stained, hard snow of the road. The lights came on in the town, pale in the fading light. The postman passed them, pulling his sled with his big dog yoked beside him. Six children in snow-suits on a linked whip of sleds came sliding down out of a steep side street and overturned in front of them in a fountain of laughter. A big brown horse with his belly clipped to keep the ice from forming there slowly pulled three huge logs toward the station. Old men in pale-blue parkas passed them and said *"Grüezi,"* and a maid from one of the houses up the hill shot out on a little sled, holding a milk can between her knees as she rock-eted around the turns. They were playing a French waltz over at the skating rink, and the music mingled with the laughter of the children and the bells on the horse's bridle and the distant, old-fashioned clanging of the gong at the railroad station, announcing a train's departure.

"Departure," the station bell said, insistent among the other sounds.

There was a booming noise far off in the hills, and Constance looked up, puzzled. "What's that?" she asked.

"Mortars," said Pritchard. "It snowed last night, and the patrols have been out all day firing at the overhangs. For the avalanches."

There was another shot, low and echoing, and they stopped and listened. "Like old times," Pritchard said as they started walking again. "Like the good old war."

"Oh," said Constance, feeling delicate, because she had never heard guns before. "The war. Were you in it?"

"A little." He grinned. "I had a little war."

"Doing what?"

"Night fighter," he said, shifting the yoke of the skis a little on his shoulders. "I flew an ugly black plane across an ugly black sky. That's that wonderful thing about the Swiss—the only thing they shoot is snow."

"Night fighter," Constance said vaguely. She had been only twelve years old when the war ended, and it was all jumbled and remote in her memory. It was like hear-ing about the graduating class two generations before you in school. People were always referring to names and dates and events that they expected you to recognize, but which you could never quite get straight. "Night fighter. What was that?"

"We flew interceptor missions over France," Pritchard said. "We'd fly on the deck to avoid the radar and flak, and hang around airfields making the Hun miserable, waiting for planes to come in slow, with their wheels down."

"Oh, I remember now," Constance said firmly. "You're the ones who ate carrots. For night vision."

Pritchard laughed. "For publication we ate carrots," he said. "Actually, we used radar. We'd locate them on the screen and fire when we saw the exhaust flares. Give me a radar screen over a carrot any day."

"Did you shoot down many planes?" Constance asked, wondering if she sounded morbid.

"*Grüezi,*" Pritchard said to the owner of a *pension* who was standing in front of his door looking up at the sky to see if it was going to snow that night. "Twenty centimetres by morning. Powder."

"You think?" the man said, looking doubtfully at the evening sky.

"I guarantee," Pritchard said.

"You're very polite," the man said, smiling. "You must come to Switzerland more often." He went into his *pension,* closing the door behind him.

"A couple," Pritchard said carelessly. "We shot down a couple. Should I tell you how brave I was?"

"You look so young," Constance said.

"I'm thirty," said Pritchard. "How old do you have to be to shoot down a plane? Especially poor, lumbering transports, running out of gas, full of clerks and rear-echelon types, wiping their glasses and being sorry the airplane was ever invented."

In the hills, there was the flat sound of the mortars again. Constance wished they'd stop. "You don't look thirty," she said to Pritchard.

"I've led a simple and salutary life. Here," he said. They were in front of one of the small hotels, and he put the skis in the rack and jammed the poles into the snow beside them. "Let's go in here and get a simple and salutary cup of tea."

"Well," said Constance, "I really—"

"Make the letter two pages shorter tonight, and more intense." He took her elbow gently, barely touching it, as he guided her toward the door. "And polish your hair some other night."

They went into the bar and sat down at a heavy, carefully carved wood table. There were no other skiers in the bar—just some village men sitting under the chamois antlers on the wall, quietly playing cards on felt cloths and drinking coffee out of small stemmed glasses.

"I told you," Pritchard said, taking off his scarf. "This country is being overrun by the Swiss."

The waitress came over, and Pritchard ordered, in German.

"What did you ask for?" Constance asked, because she could tell it wasn't only tea.

"Tea and lemon and black rum," said Pritchard.

"Do you think I ought to have rum?" she asked doubtfully.

"Everybody in the whole world should have rum," he said. "It will keep you from committing suicide in the twilight."

"You speak German, don't you?"

"I speak all the dead languages of Europe," he said. "German, French, Italian, and English. I was carefully educated for a world of interchangeable currency." He sat back, rubbing the knuckles of one hand against the palm of the other, to warm them. His head was leaning against the wood-panelled wall and he was smiling at her and she couldn't tell whether she was uncomfortable or not. "Let me hear you say 'Hi-ho, Silver.' "

"What?" she asked, puzzled.

"Isn't that what people say in America? I want to perfect my accent for the next invasion," he said.

"They stopped that," she said, thinking, My, he's a jumpy boy, I wonder what happened to him to make him that way. "They don't say it any more. It's out of date."

"All the best things go out of date so quickly in your country," he said regretfully. "Observe the Swiss." He gestured with his head toward where the men were playing. "That game has been going on since 1910," he said. "Living among the Swiss is so placid. It's like living alongside a lake. Many people can't stand it, of course. You remember that joke about the Swiss in that film about Vienna?"

"No," Constance said. "What film?" This is the first time, she thought, I've ever called a movie a film. I must be careful.

"One of the characters says, 'The Swiss haven't had a war in a hundred and fifty years and what have they pro-

duced? The cuckoo clock.' I don't know." Pritchard
shrugged. "Maybe it's better to live in a country that
invents the cuckoo clock than one that invents radar.
Time is nothing serious to a cuckoo clock. A little toy
that makes a silly, artificial sound every half hour. For
people who invent radar, time is ominous, because it's
the difference between the altitude of a plane and the location of the battery that's going to bring it down. It's an
invention for people who are suspicious and are thinking
of ambush. Here's your tea. As you see, I'm making a
serious effort to amuse you, because I've been watching
you for five days and you give the impression of a girl
who cries herself to sleep several times a week."

"How much of this stuff do I put in?" Constance asked,
confused by the flood of talk, holding up the glass of rum,
and carefully making sure not to look at Pritchard.

"Half," he said. "You have to have something in re-
serve for the second cup."

"It smells good," Constance said, sniffing the fragrance
that rose from the cup after she had measured out half
the glass of rum and squeezed the lemon into it.

"Perhaps"—Pritchard prepared his own cup—"perhaps I'd better talk only on impersonal subjects."

"Perhaps that would be better," Constance said.

"The chap who receives all those letters," Pritchard
said. "Why isn't he here?"

Constance hesitated for a moment. "He works," she
said.

"Oh. That vice." His sipped his tea, then put down his
cup and rubbed his nose with his handkerchief. "Hot tea
does that to you, too?"

"Yes."

"Are you going to marry him?"

"You said impersonal."

"So. The marriage is arranged."

"I didn't say that."

"No. But you would have said no if it wasn't."

Constance chuckled. "All right," she said. "Arranged.
Anyway, approximately arranged."

"When?"

"When the three months're up," she said, without
thinking.

"Is that a law in New York?" Pritchard asked. "That
you have to wait three months? Or is it a private family
taboo?"

Constance hesitated. Suddenly, she felt that she hadn't really talked to anyone in a long time. She had ordered meals and asked directions in railroad stations and said good morning to the people in shops, but everything else had been loneliness and silence, no less painful because she had imposed it on herself. Why not, she thought, selfishly and gratefully. Why not talk about it, for once?

"It's my father," she said, twisting her cup. "It's his idea. He's against it. He said wait three months and see. He thinks I'll forget Mark in three months in Europe."

"America," Pritchard said. "The only place left where people can afford to act in an old-fashioned manner. What's the matter with Mark? Is he a fright?"

"He's beautiful," Constance said. "Melancholy and beautiful."

Pritchard nodded, as though noting all this down. "No money, though," he said.

"Enough," said Constance. "At least, he has a good job."

"What's the matter with him, then?"

"My father thinks he's too old for me," Constance said. "He's forty."

"A grave complaint," Pritchard said. "Is that why he's melancholy?"

Constance smiled. "No. He was born that way. He's a thoughtful man."

"Do you only like forty-year-old men?" Pritchard asked.

"I only like Mark," said Constance. "Although it's true I never got along with the young men I knew. They—they're cruel. They make me feel shy—and angry with myself. When I go out with one of them, I come home feeling crooked."

"Crooked?" Pritchard looked puzzled.

"Yes. I feel I haven't behaved like me. I've behaved the way I think the other girls they've gone out with have behaved. Coquettish, cynical, amorous. Is this too complicated?"

"No."

"I hate the opinions other people have of me," Constance said, almost forgetting the young man at the table with her, and talking bitterly, and for herself. "I hate being used just for celebrations, when people come into town from college or from the Army. Somebody for parties, somebody to maul on the way home in the taxi. And

my father's opinion of me." She was getting it out for
the first time. "I used to think we were good friends, that
he thought I was a responsible, grown-up human being.
Then when I told him I wanted to marry Mark, I found
out it was all a fraud. What he really thinks of me is that
I'm a child. And a child is a form of idiot. My mother
left him when I was ten and we've been very close since
then, but we weren't as close as I thought we were. He
was just playing a game with me. Flattering me. When the
first real issue came up, the whole thing collapsed. He
wouldn't let me have my own opinion of me at all. That's
why I finally said all right to the three months. To prove
it to him once and for all." She looked suddenly, dis-
trustfully, at Pritchard, to see whether he was smiling.
"Are you being amused at me?"

"Of course not," he said. "I'm thinking of all the
people I've known who've had different opinions of me
than I've had of myself. What a frightening idea." He
looked at her speculatively, but it was hard for her to tell
how serious he was. "And what's your opinion of yourself?"

"It's not completely formed yet," she said slowly. "I
know what I want it to be. I want to be responsible and
I don't want to be a child and I don't want to be cruel—
and I want to move in a good direction." She shrugged,
embarrassed now. "That's pretty lame, isn't it?"

"Lame," Pritchard said, "but admirable."

"Oh, I'm not admirable yet," she said. "Maybe in ten
years. I haven't sorted myself out completely yet." She
laughed nervously. "Isn't it nice," she said, "you're going
away in a few days and I'll never see you again, so I can
talk like this to you."

"Yes," he said. "Very nice."

"I haven't talked to anyone for so long. Maybe it's the
rum."

Pritchard smiled. "Ready for your second cup?"

"Yes, thank you." She watched him pour the tea and
was surprised to notice that his hand shook. Perhaps, she
thought, he's one of those young men who came out of
the war drinking a bottle of whisky a day.

"So," he said. "Tomorrow we go up to the top of the
mountain."

She was grateful to him for realizing that she didn't
want to talk about herself any more and switching the
conversation without saying anything about it.

"How will you do it—with your ankle?" she asked.

"I'll get the doctor to put a shot of Novocain in it," he said. "And for a few hours my ankle will feel immortal."

"All right," she said, watching him pour his own tea, watching his hand shake. "In the morning?"

'I don't ski in the morning," he said. He added the rum to his tea and sniffed it appreciatively.

"What do you do in the morning?"

"I recover, and write poetry."

"Oh." She looked at him doubtfully. "Should I know your name?"

"No," he said. "I always tear it up the next morning."

She laughed, a little uncertainly, because the only other people she had ever known who wrote poetry had been fifteen-year-old boys in prep school. "My," she said, "you're a queer man."

"Queer?" He raised his eyebrows. "Doesn't that mean something a little obscene in America? Boys with boys, I mean."

"Only sometimes," Constance said, embarrassed. "Not now. What sort of poetry do you write?"

"Lyric, elegiac, and athletic," he said. "In praise of youth, death, and anarchy. Very good for tearing. Shall we have dinner together tonight?"

"Why?" she asked, unsettled by the way he jumped from one subject to another.

"That's a question that no European woman would ever ask," he said.

"I told the hotel that I was going to have dinner up in my room."

"I have great influence at the hotel," he said. "I think I may be able to prevent them from taking the tray up."

"Besides," Constance said, "what about the lady you've been having dinner with all week—the French lady?"

"Good." He smiled. "You've been watching me, too."

"There're only fifteen tables in the whole dining room," Constance said uncomfortably. "You can't help . . ." The French lady was at least thirty, with a short, fluffed haircut and a senselessly narrow waist. She wore black slacks and sweaters and very tight, shiny belts, and she and Pritchard always seemed to be laughing a great deal together over private jokes in the corner in which they sat every night. Whenever Constance was in the room with the French lady, she felt young and clumsy.

"The French lady is a good friend," Pritchard said, "but Anglo-Saxons are not *nuancé* enough for her, she says.

The French are patriots down to the last bedsheet. Besides, her husband is arriving tomorrow."

"I think I'd really rather stick to my plan," Constance said formally. She stood up. "Are we ready to go?"

He looked at her quietly for a moment. "You're beautiful," he said. "Sometimes it's impossible to keep from saying that."

"Please," she said. "Please, I do have to go now."

"Of course," he said. He stood up and left some money on the table. "Whatever you say."

They walked the hundred yards to their hotel in silence. It was completely dark now, and very cold, and their breath crystallized in little clouds before their mouths as they walked.

"I'll put your skis away," he said, at the door of the hotel.

"Thank you," she said in a low voice.

"Good night. And write a nice letter," he said.

"I'll try," she said. She turned and went into the hotel.

In her room, she took off her boots but didn't bother changing her clothes. She lay down on her bed, without putting on the lights, and stared at the dark ceiling, thinking, Nobody ever told me the English were like that.

"Dearest," she wrote. "Forgive me for not writing, but the weather has been glorious and for a little while I've just devoted myself to making turns and handling deep snow. . . . There's a young man here, an Englishman," she wrote conscientiously, "who's been very nice, who has been good enough to act as an instructor, and even if I say it myself, I'm really getting pretty good. He was in the R.A.F. and his father went down with the Hood and his mother was killed in a bombing—"

She stopped. No, she thought, it sounds tricky. As though I'm hiding something, and putting in the poor, dead, patriotic family as artful window dressing. She crumpled the letter and threw it in the wastebasket. She took out another sheet of paper. "Dearest," she wrote.

There was a knock on the door, and she called *"Ja."*

The door opened and Pritchard came in. She looked up in surprise. In all the three weeks, he'd never come to her room. She stood up, embarrassed. She was in her stocking feet, and the room was littered with the debris of the afternoon's skiing—boots standing near the window, sweaters thrown over a chair, gloves drying on the radiator, and her parka hanging near the bathroom door, with a little trickle of melting snow running down from the collar. The radio was on, and an American band was playing "Bali Ha'i" from an Armed Forces station in Germany.

Pritchard, standing in front of the open door, smiled at her. "Ah," he said, "some corner of a foreign room that is forever Vassar."

Constance turned the radio off. "I'm sorry," she said, waving vaguely and conscious that her hair was not combed. "Everything's such a mess."

Pritchard went over to the bureau and peered at Mark's picture, which was standing there in a leather frame. "The receiver of letters?" he asked.

"The receiver of letters." There was an open box of Kleenex on the bureau, and an eyelash curler, and a half-eaten bar of chocolate, and Constance felt guilty to be presenting Mark so frivolously.

"He's very handsome." Pritchard squinted at the photograph.

"Yes," Constance said. She found her moccasins and put them on, and felt a little less embarrassed.

"He looks serious." Pritchard moved the Kleenex to get a better view.

"He *is* serious," said Constance. In all the three weeks that she had been skiing with Pritchard, she had said hardly anything about Mark. They had talked about almost everything else, but somehow, by a tacit agreement, they had avoided Mark. They had skied together every afternoon and had talked a great deal about the necessity of leaning forward at all times, and about falling relaxed, and about Pritchard's time in public school in England, and about his father, and about the London theatre and American novelists, and they had talked gravely about what it was like to be twenty and what it was like to be thirty, and they had talked about Christmastime in New York and what football weekends were like at Princeton, and they had even had a rather sharp discussion on the nature of courage when Constance lost her nerve in the middle of a steep trail late one afternoon, with the sun going down and the mountain deserted. But they had never talked about Mark.

Pritchard turned away from the picture. "You didn't have to shoe yourself for me," he said, indicating her moccasins. "One of the nicest things about skiing is taking

those damned heavy boots off and walking around on a
warm floor in wool socks."

"I'm engaged in a constant struggle not to be sloppy,"
Constance said.

They stood there, facing each other in silence for a
moment. "Oh," Constance said. "Sit down."

"Thank you," Pritchard said formally. He seated
himself in the one easy chair. "I just came by for a minute. To say goodbye."

"Goodbye," Constance repeated stupidly. "Where're
you going?"

"Home. Or at least to England. I thought I'd like to
leave you my address," Pritchard said.

"Of course."

He reached over and picked up a piece of paper and
her pen and wrote for a moment. "It's just a hotel," he said.
"Until I find a place of my own." He put the paper down
on the desk but kept the pen in his hand, playing with it.
"Give you somebody else to write to," he said. "The English receiver of letters."

"Yes," she said.

"You can tell me what the snow's like," he said, "and
how many times you came down the mountain in one day
and who got drunk at the bar the night before."

"Isn't this sudden?" Constance asked. Somehow, after
the first few days, it had never occurred to her that Pritchard might leave. He had been there when she arrived and
he seemed to belong there so thoroughly, to be so much
a part of the furniture of the place, that it was hard to
conceive of being there without him.

"Not so sudden," Pritchard said. He stood up. "I wanted
to say goodbye in private," he said. She wondered if he
was going to kiss her. In all the three weeks, he hadn't as
much as held her hand, and the only times he had touched
her had been when he was helping her up after a particularly bad fall. But he made no move. He stood there,
smiling curiously, playing with the pen, unusually un-
talkative, as though waiting for her to say something.
"Well," he said, "will I see you later?"

"Yes," she said.

"We'll have a farewell dinner. They have veal on the
menu, but I'll see if we can't get something better, in
honor of the occasion." He put the pen down carefully
on the desk. "Until later," he said, and went out, closing
the door behind him.

Constance stared at the closed door. Everybody goes away, she thought. Unreasonably, she felt angry. She knew it was foolish, like a child protesting the end of a birthday party, but she couldn't help feeling that way. She looked around the room. It seemed cluttered and untidy to her, like the room of a silly and careless schoolgirl. She shook her head impatiently and began to put things in place. She put the boots out in the hall and hung the parka in the closet and carried the box of Kleenex into the bathroom and gave the half bar of chocolate to the chambermaid. She straightened the coverlet of the bed and cleaned the ashtray and, on a sudden impulse, dropped the eyelash curler into the wastebasket. It's too piddling, she thought, to worry about curling your eyelashes.

Pritchard ordered a bottle of Burgundy with dinner, because Swiss wine, he said, was too thin to say farewell on. They didn't talk much during dinner. It was as though he had already departed a little. Once or twice, Constance almost started to tell him how grateful she was for his patience with her on the hills, but somehow it never came out, and the dinner became more and more uncomfortable for both of them. Pritchard ordered brandy with the coffee, and she drank it, although it gave her heartburn. The three-piece band began to play for the evening's dancing while they were drinking their brandy, and then it was too noisy to talk.

"Do you want to dance?" he asked.

"No," she said.

"Good," he said. "I despise dancing."

"Let's get out of here," Constance said. "Let's take a walk."

They went to their rooms to get some warm clothes, and Pritchard was waiting for her outside the hotel door when she came down in her snow boots and the beaver coat her father had given her the year before. Pritchard was leaning against a pillar on the front porch and she stared at him for a moment before he turned around, and she was surprised to see how tired and suddenly old he seemed when he was unaware that he was being watched.

They walked down the main street, with the sounds of the band diminishing behind them. It was a clear night, and the stars shone above the moutains, electrically blue. At the top of the highest hill, at the end of the *télé-phérique,* a single light glittered from the hut there, where you could warm yourself before the descent, and buy spiced hot wine and biscuits.

They walked down to the bottom of the street and crossed over onto the path alongside the dark skating rink. The ice reflected the stars dimly and there was the noise of water from the brook that ran along one side of the rink and scarcely ever froze.

They stopped at a small, snow-covered bridge, and Pritchard lit a cigarette. The lights of the town were distant now and the trees stood around them in black silence. Pritchard put his head back, with the smoke escaping slowly from between his lips, and gestured up toward the light on top of the mountain.

"What a life," he said. "Those two people up there. Night after winter night alone on top of the hills, waiting for the world to arrive each morning." He took another puff of the cigarette. "They're not married, you know," he said. "Only the Swiss would think of putting two people who weren't married on top of a hill like that. He's an old man and she's a religious fanatic and they hate each other, but neither of them will give the other the satisfaction of taking another job." He chuckled as they both looked at the bright pinpoint above them. "Last year there was a blizzard and the *téléphérique* didn't run for a week and the power lines were down and they had to stay up there for six days and nights, breaking up chairs for firewood, living off chocolate and tins of soup, and not talking to each other." He stared reflectively at the faraway high light. "It will do as a symbol this year for this pretty continent," he said softly.

Suddenly Constance knew what she had to say. "Alan" —she moved squarely in front of him—"I don't want you to go."

Pritchard flicked at his cigarette. "Six days and six nights," he said. "For their hardness of heart."

"I don't want you to go."

"I've been here for a long time," he said. "I've had the best of the snow."

"I want you to marry me," Constance said.

Pritchard looked at her. She could see he was trying to smile. "That's the wonderful thing about being twenty years old," he said. "You can say things like that."

"I said I want you to marry me."

He tossed away his cigarette. It glowed on the snow. He took a step toward her and kissed her. She could taste the fumed grape of the brandy faint on his lips. He held her for a moment, then stepped back and buttoned her coat, like a nurse being careful with a little girl. "The things that can happen to a man," he said. He shook his head slowly.

"Alan," Constance said.

"I take it all back," Pritchard said. 'You're not at all like the girls who advertise soap and beer."

"Please," she said. "Don't make it hard."

"What do you know about me?" He knocked the snow off the bridge railing and leaned against it, brushing the snow off his hands with a dry sound. "Haven't you ever been warned about the young men you're liable to meet in Europe?"

"Don't confuse me," she said. "Please."

"What about the chap in the leather frame?"

Constance took a deep breath. She could feel the cold tingling in her lungs. "I don't know," she said. "He's not here."

Pritchard chuckled, but it sounded sad. "Lost," he said. "Lost by an ocean."

"It's not only the ocean," she said.

They walked in silence again, listening to the sound of their boots on the frozen path. The moon was coming up between the peaks and reflecting milkily off the snow.

"You ought to know one bit of information," Pritchard said in a low voice, looking down at the long shadow the moon cast on the path ahead of him. "I've been married."

"Oh," Constance said. She was very careful to walk in the footprints of the others who had tamped the path down before her.

"Not gravely married," Pritchard said, looking up. "We were divorced two years ago. Does that make a difference to you?"

"Your business," Constance said.

"I must visit America someday," Pritchard said, chuckling. "They are breeding a new type."

"What else?" Constance asked.

"The next thing is unattractive," Pritchard said. "I don't have a pound. I haven't worked since the war. I've been living off what was left of my mother's jewelry. There wasn't much and I sold the last brooch in Zurich last week. That's why I have to go back, even if there were no other reasons. You can see," he said, grinning painfully, "you've picked the prize of the litter."

"What else?" Constance asked.

"Do you still want to hear more?"

"Yes."

"I would never live in America," Pritchard said. "I'm a weary, poverty-stricken, grounded old R.A.F. type, and I'm committed to another place. Come on." He took her elbow brusquely, as though he didn't want to talk any more. "It's late. We'd better get to the hotel."

Constance hung back. "You're not telling me everything," she said.

"Isn't that enough?"

"No."

"All right," he said. "I couldn't go with you to America if I wanted to."

"Why not?"

"Because they wouldn't let me in."

"Why not?" Constance asked, puzzled.

"Because I am host to the worm," Pritchard said.

"What're you talking about?"

"Swiss for delicate," he said harshly. "They kicked D.H. Lawrence out of New Mexico and made him die along the Riviera for it. You can't blame them. They have enough diseases of their own. Now let's go back to the hotel."

"But you seem so healthy. You ski—"

"Everybody dies here in the best of health," Pritchard said. "It goes up and down with me. I almost get cured, then the next year"—he shrugged and chuckled soundlessly—"the next year I get almost uncured. The doctors hold their heads when they see me going up in the lift. Go home," he said. "I'm not for you. I'm oppressed. And you're not oppressed. It is the final miscegenation. Now shall we go back to the hotel?"

Constance nodded. They walked slowly. The town on the hill ahead of them was almost completely dark now, but they could hear the music of the dance band, thin and distant in the clear night air.

"I don't care," Constance said as they came to the first buildings. "I don't care about anything."

"When I was twenty—" Pritchard said. "When I was twenty I once said the same thing."

"First, we'll be practical," Constance said. "You'll need money to stay here. I'll give it to you tomorrow."

"I can't take your money."

"It's not mine," Constance said. "It's my father's."

"England is forever in your debt," Pritchard said. He was trying to smile. "Be careful of me."

"What do you mean?"

"I am beginning to feel as though I can be consoled."

"What's wrong with that?"

"It can prove to be mortal," Pritchard whispered, taking her clumsily and bulkily in his arms, "for those of us who are inconsolable.'

When they woke in the morning, they were solemn at first, and disconnectedly discussed the weather, which was revealed through the not quite closed curtains to be gray and uncertain. But then Pritchard asked, "How do you feel?" and Constance, taking her time and wrinkling her eyebrows in a deep attempt to be accurate, said, "I feel *enormously* grown up." Pritchard couldn't help roaring with laughter, and all solemnity was gone. They lay there comfortably discussing themselves, going over their future like misers, and Constance was worried, although not too seriously, about scandalizing the hotel people, and Pritchard said that there was nothing to worry about—nothing that foreigners could do could scandalize the Swiss—and Constance felt more comfortable than ever at being in such a civilized country.

They made plans about the wedding, and Pritchard said they'd go the French part of Switzerland to get married, because he didn't want to get married in German, and Constance said she was sorry she hadn't thought of it herself.

Then they decided to get dressed, because you could not spend the rest of your life in bed, and Constance had a sorrowful, stinging moment when she saw how thin he was, and thought, conspiratorially, Eggs, milk, butter, rest. They went out of the room together, bravely determined to brazen it out, but there was no one in the corridor or on the stairway to see them, so they had the double pleasure of being candid and being unobserved at the same time, which Constance regarded as an omen of good luck. They discovered that it was almost time for lunch, so they had some kirsch first, and then orange juice and bacon and eggs and wonderful, dark coffee in the scrubbed, wood-panelled dining room, and in the middle of it tears came into Constance's eyes and Pritchard asked why she was crying and she said, "I'm thinking of all the breakfasts we're going to eat together." Pritchard's eyes got a little wet then, too, as he stared across the table at her, and she said, "You must cry often, please."

"Why?" he asked.

"Because it's so un-English," she said, and they both laughed.

After breakfast, Pritchard said he was going up the hill to make a few runs and asked if she wanted to go with him, but she said she felt too melodious that day to ski, and he grinned at the "melodious."

She said she was going to write some letters, and he grew thoughtful. "If I were a gentleman, I'd write your father immediately and explain everything," he said.

"Don't you dare," she said, meaning it, because she knew her father would be over on the next plane if he got a letter like that.

"Don't worry," he said. "I'm not that much of a gentleman."

She watched him stride off between the snowbanks with his red sweater and his skis, looking boyish and jaunty, and then went to her room and wrote a letter to Mark, saying that she had thought it over and that she was sorry but she had decided it was a mistake. She wrote the letter calmly, without feeling anything, cozy in her warm room. She didn't mention Pritchard, because that was none of Mark's business.

Then she wrote a letter to her father and told him that she had broken off with Mark. She didn't mention Pritchard in the letter to her father, either, because she didn't want him over on the next plane, and she didn't say anything about coming home. All that could wait.

She sealed the letters, then lay down dreamily to nap, and slept without dreaming for more than an hour. She dressed for the snow and went to the post office to mail the letters and walked down to the skating rink to watch the children on the ice, and on her way back to the hotel she stopped at the ski shop and bought Pritchard a lightweight yellow sweater, because soon the sun would be very hot all day and the clothes of winter would all be too warm.

She was in the bar, waiting unhurriedly for Pritchard, when she heard that he was dead.

Nobody had come to tell her, because there was no particular reason for anybody to come to tell her.

There was an instructor with whom Pritchard had sometimes skied talking in the bar to some Americans, and he was saying, "He was out of control and he miscalculated and he went into a tree and he was dead in five minutes. He was a jolly fine fellow"—the ski teacher had learned his English from his British pupils before the war—"but he went too fast. He did not have the technique to handle the speed."

The ski teacher did not sound as though it were routine to die on skis, but he did not sound surprised. He himself had had many of his bones broken, as had all his friends, crashing into trees and stone walls and from falls in the summertime, when he was a guide for climbers, and he sounded as though it were inevitable, and even just, that from time to time people paid up to the mountain for faults of technique.

Constance stayed for the funeral, walking behind the black-draped sled to the churchyard and the hole in the snow and the unexpected dark color of the earth after the complete white of the winter. No one came from England, because there was no one to come, although the ex-wife telegraphed flowers. A good many of the villagers came, but merely as friends, and some of the other skiers, who had known Pritchard casually, and as far as anyone could tell, Constance was just one of them.

At the grave, the ski teacher, with the professional habit of repetition common to teachers, said, "He did not have the technique for that much speed."

Constance didn't know what to do with the yellow sweater, and she finally gave it to the chambermaid for her husband.

Eight days later, Constance was in New York. Her father was waiting for her on the pier and she waved to him and he waved back, and she could tell, even at that distance, how glad he was to see her again. They kissed when she walked off the gangplank, and he hugged her, very hard, then held her off at arm's length and stared at her delightedly, and said, "God, you look absolutely wonderful! See," he said, and she wished he hadn't said it, but she realized he couldn't help himself. "See—wasn't I right? Didn't I know what I was talking about?"

"Yes, Father," she said, thinking, How could I ever have been angry with him? He's not stupid or mean or selfish or uncomprehending—he is merely alone.

Holding her hand the way he used to do while they took walks together when she was a little girl, he led her into the customs shed, to wait for her trunk to come off the ship.